Dagmar's mouth dropped open. "You mean to see me married today?"

"Why wait?" Aedan said, capturing her hand. Despite his cold fury at her tricks, a warm thrill went up his arm. Dagmar would be his bride. She would be part of his life forever. "My people have been without a leader for long enough. I need to return to them. I see no reason to make two trips here."

Dagmar pulled away and her face became mutinous. He smiled inwardly. He'd guessed her game—stall and hope that something else turned up to prevent their marriage.

"Very well. I accept your offer when it is put like that."

"Swear it," Aedan demanded. "Give your solemn oath on your mother's shade."

Dagmar went pale and he knew that, despite everything, she'd truly had other plans than to go through with the wedding. No one played him for a fool, particularly not her.

Author Note

On my way to visit my youngest son, who was at the University of St. Andrews, I spotted a signpost for Dollar and wondered why a Scottish village would be named for a currency. When I returned home, I discovered that the village's name predated the currency by more than a thousand years! Dollar most likely comes from the Pictish word meaning "place of the *haugh*" or "low-lying meadow beside a river," and a pivotal battle in Scotland's formation happened near there in 875. At the time, I was struggling with this story. Nothing seemed to work and I had almost given up, but the battle between Vikings and the Picts was a perfect beginning. Procrastination research can pay dividends.

I do hope you enjoy Dagmar and Aedan's story as much as I did writing it once I finally knew how it had to be written.

I love getting comments from readers and can be reached at michelle@michellestyles.co.uk or through my publisher, Facebook or Twitter, @michellelstyles.

THE WARRIOR'S VIKING BRIDE

MICHELLE STYLES

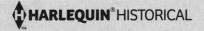

HARLEQUIN® HISTORICAL

Recycling programs
for this product may
not exist in your area.

ISBN-13: 978-1-335-46764-5

The Warrior's Viking Bride

Copyright © 2018 by Michelle Styles

Printed in U.S.A.

www.Harlequin.com

Michelle Styles was born and raised near San Francisco, California. She currently lives near Hadrian's Wall with her husband, a menagerie of pets and occasionally one of her three university-aged children. An avid reader, she became hooked on historical romance after discovering Georgette Heyer, Anya Seton and Victoria Holt. Her website is michellestyles.co.uk and she's on Twitter and Facebook.

Books by Michelle Styles

Harlequin Historical

A Question of Impropriety
Impoverished Miss, Convenient Wife
His Unsuitable Viscountess
Hattie Wilkinson Meets Her Match
An Ideal Husband?
Paying the Viking's Price
Return of the Viking Warrior
Saved by the Viking Warrior
Taming His Viking Woman
Summer of the Viking
Sold to the Viking Warrior
The Warrior's Viking Bride

Visit the Author Profile page
at Harlequin.com for more titles.

In memory of my father, Michael Phifer (1937–1990).

Prologue

865 A.D.—Bjorgvinfjord on the west coast of Viken, Norway. Modern-day Bergen, Norway

'You should allow me the honour of winning. It's my tenth name day,' Dagmar Kolbeinndottar argued with her father's best friend. 'It could be your present to me—telling my parents how accomplished I've suddenly become at swordplay. A good idea, yes?'

Dagmar gave a hopeful smile and batted her lashes. Not that she was very good at swords or warfare yet. Not that she'd ever be any good. She preferred playing with her dolls and weaving to practising in the dusty yard with a wooden sword. How her father, who was one of Viken's most-feared warriors, and her mother, who was a legendary shield maiden, had produced someone like her who kept making simple errors was one of life's mysteries, as her nurse would say. And she wanted to show her father how much she'd improved since he'd been away. She wanted to show him that she deserved the grown-up blue gown, the one he'd promised to buy her for her tenth birthday if she worked hard at her lessons.

'Your mother would use my guts for bowstrings if I said such things.' Old Alf rubbed his belly. 'To tell the truth, lass, I am quite fond of my innards. They are the only ones I've got.'

Dagmar screwed up her nose. 'My mother likes you too much to do that. She depends on you, now that my father is away so often. You're valuable to her. A precious jewel among men.'

Old Alf merely laughed and sent Dagmar's wooden sword flying from her hand for the fourth time that morning. 'You would be better if you actually practised, instead of finding excuses and using idle flattery. The gods seldom help a quitter.'

'I keep getting distracted.' Dagmar pursed her lips. 'I heard my mother crying again last night.'

Old Alf's face hardened. 'Kolbeinn should be here to dry Helga's tears.'

'Yes, everything will be much better when my father arrives.' Dagmar tilted her chin upwards. 'You will see. He will get here in time for my name day. He promised me a proper gown with an apron and brooches…provided I pay attention to my mother and do my lessons. He won't break his promise, will he?'

'I can't rightly say where his head is at, lass.'

'Attached to his body, I trust.' Dagmar gave a hiccupping laugh. Her father was alive. They knew that. Some of his men had returned, but for the first time in for ever, her father had not been the first one to step foot on the pier. He had not even been in the longboat. He was staying in Kaupang, dealing with important business, was what her mother had uncharacteristically snapped when Dagmar asked.

'Your mother has many troubles, but no one is born

clutching a sword, lass, not even your mother. You will get there, Dagmar, if you focus when you practise instead of gathering dreams. Try once more for your old friend?'

Dagmar nodded and picked up the sword. Old Alf had faith in her. If she could conquer this skill before her father came home, then maybe everything would be right once again.

'Jaarl Kolbeinn's ship is coming,' the cry went up before her sword connected with Old Alf's. Dagmar instantly dropped her weapon.

'My father does keep his promises.' Dagmar lifted her chin upwards. 'He will bring me my gown. My mother will smile again. My father will see to it.'

The wind whipped Old Alf's greying hair from his face. 'Aye, lass, we can but hope that he has seen sense.'

Her mother stalked past them, not even acknowledging Dagmar in her hurry to reach the waterfront. Dagmar considered her mother had never looked as lovely. The dark-red gown with its gold embroidery and the sleek fur cape she wore about her shoulders set off her colouring precisely. Her eyes appeared brighter than normal and her mouth held a determined cast, as though her mother was about to go into battle instead of greeting Dagmar's father.

Dagmar hurried to match her mother's stride. 'Old Alf says that I will be as good as you soon.'

A stretching of the truth, but she wanted her mother's intent expression to relax.

Her mother put a hand on Dagmar's shoulder. 'It is good that you want to be.'

'I want to please you. I want to be like you,' Dagmar whispered.

'Ah, Dagmar, you are such a good child. You are truly the light in my life.'

Dagmar basked in the sunshine of her mother's unaccustomed praise. 'It is my name day today.'

'We will do something special for it, but first your father must be welcomed.'

When her father came ashore, he greeted her mother very formally without his usual warmth. Her mother failed to throw her arms about his neck. Dagmar frowned. She'd never understand grown-ups. Everyone knew about their love story—the skalds sang about it and how her father had tamed the frost giants to win his bride. Dagmar never tired of hearing the tale. It was the principal reason why she wanted to linger at the feasts.

'You returned.' Her mother's voice resembled a frost giant's.

'I gave Dagmar a promise that I would be back for her birthday, Helga.' Her father's voice, if anything, was far colder than her mother's.

'Did you bring my blue gown?' Dagmar asked, giving into her impatience. 'I've worked ever so hard. Ask Old Alf. He'll tell you. Some day I will be as good a warrior as my mother.'

Her father bent down and put his hands on her shoulders. 'Something even better. I brought a woman who will teach you to be a true lady. You want that, don't you, Dagmar? To be someone to make your father proud?'

Beside her, her mother stiffened and drew in a sharp hiss of breath. Dagmar glanced up and saw a dark-haired woman with cat-like eyes and a large pregnant belly.

'You must be Dagmar. Your father has told me a lot about you. I am sure we will be great friends.'

'You brought her here? On such a day?' Her mother's screech hurt Dagmar's ears.

'Now, Helga, easy. She wanted to come.' He rubbed the back of his neck. 'It is like this—I need children.'

'You have a child, our daughter.'

'A daughter is not the same as sons.' The woman looped her arm through her father's and leant into him with an easy intimacy.

Dagmar wanted to scratch the woman's eyes out for being rude. The man she lolled over belonged to another woman—her mother. However, her father did not seem to mind; instead, he seemed to welcome her touch, placing a large hand on the woman's belly.

'You understand,' her father said, bestowing one of his special smiles on the woman.

'I see,' her mother proclaimed. 'You have made your choice. And I have made mine.'

Her mother stripped the gown from her back. Underneath she wore her trousers and tunic, her shield maiden clothes, the ones which were kept in a trunk and were supposed to be for Dagmar when she turned fourteen.

An ice-cold hand went around Dagmar's heart. Her mother had clearly known about her father and his new woman before they'd even arrived.

'Mother?' Dagmar whispered. 'What is happening?'

'We are leaving, Daughter.' Her mother placed a firm hand on Dagmar's shoulder. 'I refuse to stay where I am unwanted. I divorce you, Kolbeinn, here in front of everyone. I will take my warriors and my daughter and I will carve a new life.'

Her father's face became carved from ice as he stepped in front of her mother. 'Dagmar remains here. My daughter belongs to me.'

Her mother shoved her father and he stumbled backwards, nearly falling. 'Get out of my way, you miserable worm. Dagmar goes where I go.'

'You may take any man who will pledge allegiance to you, a second–rate warrior long past her prime, but you leave our daughter here.'

'Why?' Her mother put her hand on her hip. 'So she can become the fetch-and-carry handmaiden of your latest fancy? I know what that is like! I endured it!' Her mother's voice echoed over the fjord. 'My daughter is not and never will be second-best. She is worth ten of any sons you will ever have.'

Dagmar crossed her arms and stood next to her mother. Her mother wasn't going to abandon her. Her father wanted her. Maybe her parents could work something out. They had fought before.

Her father's cheeks became tinged with red. 'I have the law on my side. My daughter belongs to me to dispose of as I see fit.'

Her mother banged her sword on the ground. 'I challenge you. I will show you how second-rate I am, you puffed-up over-the-hill windbag!'

'You challenge me for what?'

'For the right to bring up our daughter as I see fit.'

Her father spat on his palm and held it out. 'Done! I can beat you with one hand tied behind my back.'

'No, Kolbeinn, no. You must not. The she-witch will trick you.' The woman clung to Dagmar's father's arm and rubbed her big belly against his side. 'Think of my dream. You will be the father of many kings. Our unborn son and I need our strong protector.'

Dagmar wanted to be sick. Surely her father would fight for her. She had seen her parents practise fighting before. At some point during that act, her parents would start laughing and they would realise that they still loved each other. This woman with her baby-swollen belly would be no match for her mother.

'Hush now.' Her father put an arm about the pregnant woman. 'I am a great jaarl now. I have responsibilities.'

Her mother made a disgusted noise in the back of her throat. 'Choose your champion then, Kolbeinn, pusillanimous coward that you are, and I will fight him. I will protect my daughter until all the breath has left my body. I will carve a new life for us.'

'You do this, Helga, and you will leave with only the clothes on your back rather than any ships. I need to be able to provide for my growing family.'

Dagmar clenched her fists. Her father wanted to steal her mother's life work. That woman had put him up to it. 'My mother brought fifteen ships to this marriage—all the skalds say so. My mother built this *felag* the same as you. Have you forgotten so quickly, Father?'

'You mustn't believe everything the skalds say,' the woman said, giving Dagmar a look of pure hatred. 'But I predict you will lead a miserable existence should you leave your father.'

Dagmar shrank back against her mother.

'Hush, Dagmar. You are the most precious thing in my life, worth far more than gold or even land,' her mother said in a low voice before holding out her hand to her father. 'Agreed. My daughter is worth that and much more besides. My daughter will have a brilliant life. My daughter will be the best warrior the world has ever encountered.'

Dagmar watched in horror as the fight began in earnest between her mother and the champion her father chose. All she had wanted was a blue gown for her name day and instead this had happened—she had lost her family and her home, the place where she knew she was safe. Somehow, she was going to have to find a way to make her mother proud of her as her father wanted nothing from her. She would find a way to give her mother a new home.

Chapter One

Ten years later—near Dollar, Pict-controlled Alba.
Modern-day Dollar, Clackmannanshire, Scotland

At daybreak, a major battle would commence. Aedan
mac Connall, King of Kintra on Ile in the Western Isles,
had no need of divine gifts to know this future; instead he used his eyes to see the two armies ranged no
more than a quarter of a mile apart. Each was as bad as
the other—the Northmen from the Black Pool or Dubh
Linn, and the Picts with King Constantine's rag-tag
army of hired Northmen from Jorvik and other sell-
swords intermingled with Pict warriors. But he had no
interest in the outcome beyond the thought that for once
they were fighting each other, rather than preying on
his people. His business was with a woman, a woman
who was somewhere in this melee.

His entire future and that of his people depended on
his returning her to her father where she belonged. He
didn't want to consider the fate of the hostages Kolbeinn
the Blood-Axe had required to ensure his co-operation
in fulfilling this quest. He had to retrieve Kolbeinn's
daughter now or he'd be damned for ever.

'Have you seen a woman, a shield maiden called Dagmar Kolbeinndottar?' he called to a warrior who was sitting gloomily by the dying embers of a fire.

The warrior raised his grizzled head. 'Dagmar Kolbeinndottar? She goes by Helgadottar and has done for several seasons.'

Aedan let out a breath. Success at last. Tracking down Dagmar, the daughter of the north warlord Kolbeinn the Blood-Axe, was far worse than tracking a will-o'-the-wisp. He had travelled the entire length of Alba and well into Bernicia searching for her. Kolbeinn the Blood-Axe's vague description of his daughter as a meek and mild slip of a thing with golden hair, kidnapped by her mother ten years before, had been deliberately misleading. In Bernicia, Aedan had learned that she like her mother before her had pledged her sword to King Constantine.

'Dagmar Helgadottar, then,' he said, inclining his head. 'I have a great desire to speak with her.'

The warrior sucked his teeth. 'More than my life is worth.'

'But she is here, in this place?'

'Oh, aye. That she is.' The warrior gave a conspiratorial tap against his nose. 'The King sets a mighty store by her and her men, but can they do more than rattle their shields and look fierce?'

Aedan held out the ring Kolbeinn the Blood-Axe had given him as well as a gold piece. 'I have important information for her from her father.'

The grizzled warrior nodded and took the piece. 'I hope you fare better than the others.'

Aedan blinked. 'Others?'

'Oh, aye, she cut off their heads and sent them back

to her father.' He scratched his nose. 'Mind she hasn't done that since afore her mother died.'

'She will listen to me.'

'You must have the skill of Loki to have got this far.'

'I prefer to think it is the saints who have kept me safe this far.'

The man spat on his palm and made a cross in the air. 'Them, too.'

Aedan whistled and his wolfhound, Mor, bounded up from where she had been lurking in the undergrowth. 'Further up the line you said.'

The warrior took a step back. 'Aye, you can't miss her. She's the one with her face covered in blue swirls. And she wears hissing snakes in her hair.'

Dagmar concentrated on putting the final flourishes of paint on her face. She had done them for so long, they had become second nature to her. First the black and then the blue.

She had acceded to her mother's wishes and used paint every morning, rather than getting a permanent tattoo. Even now when her mother had been gone for five months she could not bring herself to go against her wishes. It was the design which was important, rather than the medium. One day, her mother had remarked as she'd applied Dagmar's paint in the early days, it might be necessary to change course and design. But it served her purpose for now to let everyone think them tattoos. A new whorl for each battle she had won.

'He means to kill you.' Old Alf sidled up just as Dagmar finished the final whorl. He was the only one besides her mother who knew of the slight deception about the paint. Lately he made simple errors and struggled to lift his shield and sword at the same time. 'Did you hear me, Dagmar? He means to kill you for real this time.'

Dagmar wiped her fingers on a spare bit of cloth. There was no need to ask who 'he' was—Olafr Rolfson, her mother's last lover. She'd seen how Olafr undermined her, damning her with faint praise, whilst being outspoken about what he considered was the correct course of action. 'I can handle him.'

The embers of her mother's funeral pyre had still been glowing when Olafr had started making noises about sharing a marriage bed with Dagmar. She knew his sudden declaration of overwhelming desire for her had nothing to do with her figure or the curve of her mouth. The whispers of how truly hideous she was had followed her since she was fourteen. Snakes for hair. An overlong nose and pointed chin. A face like a misshapen pile of rocks. A woman no real man could truly desire.

When Olafr persisted with his lies about her beauty, she threatened to forcibly unman any man who tried to warm her bed, including him. He had gone green and had never repeated the request.

'I need every warrior who is willing to pick up a sword for me.'

'*Pah*, you don't need him that bad.'

'I gave my word to my mother. Would you have me break my promise with the final season nearly done?' Dagmar's throat closed. Her mother had ignored a minor injury until it was too late and the infection raged throughout her body. As she lay dying, she had made Dagmar promise to fulfil her pledge to support Constantine, to get the title to those lands. Land for the men who had shown loyalty to her mother during the lean years and a proper home for her daughter, as she'd vowed when Dagmar was ten. She would hang her sword over the hearth and only bring it down to defend what was hers, instead of using it to further someone else's ambition. 'Constantine must honour his pledge.'

'Your mother knew when a king was not worthy of support. She would not want her only child to be out here, facing these odds. She valued your life above all.'

'It will be as the gods will.' Dagmar took her sword, and began the next part of the ritual she always did before going into battle—plaiting her hair so it hung about her face like snakes. 'Perhaps the Dubh Linn raiders will render this conversation unnecessary. Olafr often leaves his left side exposed.'

'Make an old man happy—keep an eye on him. You may face more than one enemy today.'

'I've taken care since my tenth name day,' she said standing up. After her stepmother's son had been born, the first attack on Dagmar's life had happened— poison in her stew which her dog had eaten instead of her. A servant had confessed to the entire plot. Her mother had sent the man's tongue and ears back to her father, but there had been other attempts from men desperate enough to believe her stepmother's promises of gold if only they'd rid her of her son's rival.

'Perhaps you should consider an alliance, marriage to a warrior you can trust, someone who can counter Olafr.'

Dagmar took a practice swing with her sword. It made a satisfactory slicing noise. 'I don't need any warrior to counter Olafr. My sword arm remains strong.'

'Dagmar!' Olafr called out. 'Someone asks after you.'

Dagmar swallowed the quick retort when she spied a tall man with dark auburn hair and piercing blue-green eyes, the sort of man who made women go weak at the knees and more than likely knew it. The sort of man who enjoyed a buxom woman in his bed and who would curl his lip at her meagre assets even if they were not bound tightly to her chest.

His clothes immediately proclaimed that he was not from the North. A wolfhound stood by his side. A Gael. Dagmar frowned as she spied the sword stuck in his belt—the hilt resembled one of her father's, one she remembered from her childhood.

'Who requires me?' she said in a snarl, annoyed that she had noticed the breadth of his shoulders.

'Ah, there you are, Dagmar,' Olafr said with a smirk. 'I had wondered if you in your eagerness had already departed for battle.'

Dagmar ignored the jibe. Before her first battle, she had set off early as her mother had been delayed with a split shield. Dagmar's actions had ensured they surprised the raiders and carried the day. Olafr had not even been part of the *felag* then. Her mother had found it amusing and the tale had grown with each telling.

Whenever Olafr repeated the tale, he made it seem as though she was some sort of spoilt and naive girl, rather than a shield maiden who had taken a wise course of action and turned the tide of the battle.

'A visitor before battle?' Dagmar tapped her sword against her hand.

'Sweetling...' Olafr began with another smirk.

Dagmar cut him off with an imperious gesture. 'My mother bequeathed her men to me. I should've been informed immediately when a stranger came into the camp.'

'Always leaping to the wrong conclusion.' Olafr's

smile grew broader. 'I brought him to you. Is it my fault that he encountered me first? If so, I beg your pardon and will turn my back on any other messenger. No, no, I will tell them, I'm but a humble servant who can give no counsel.'

'Humble is the last thing you are, Olafr.'

'I know my worth.' He gave a little swagger. 'Your mother saw it. Others see it, Dagmar the Blind Shield Maiden.'

Dagmar belatedly wondered if she had fallen into a trap. For all his bluster, Olafr was a capable warrior. Her mother had relied on his counsel during her final few months. On her deathbed, she'd urged Dagmar to do the same. However, there was something about the man which made her flesh crawl.

'Go on. Why do you seek me out rather than readying your men for battle as I instructed?'

'This man, Aedan mac Connall, seeks Dagmar Kolbeinndottar. Urgently.' He bowed. 'Are you acquainted with such a person? Or shall I send him away to seek her elsewhere?'

Dagmar pressed her lips together. Her stepmother would not send a Gael if her father had died, she would send an assassin to ensure that her son inherited all her father's holdings, rather than sharing it out equally between his children like the law in the North demanded. Her mother had drummed this into her since the night they fled into the forest with only Old Alf for protection—to be prepared for the knife in the night.

'I've no time for riddles or to slit his throat. More's the pity. The men need to be ready to march when the trumpet sounds.' She turned towards the warrior and said very slowly in his tongue. 'I will lead my men to victory and then we will speak, Gael.'

Olafr raised a brow in that irritatingly smug way of his. 'It might be worth your while to hear the man out before cutting his throat. No harm, unless you wish to continue with a battle that you must surely lose. You get more impulsive by the day, Dagmar.'

Dagmar ground her teeth. He made it sound as though she was unblooded, rather than being a veteran of five summers' fighting. She'd stopped being so eager years ago. There was a sort of nervous anticipation, a wanting to get the waiting finished. But after her first experience, she had never been eager for a battle. People she loved died or were injured. Battles were ugly messy things and had to be endured. If today went as she planned, this would be her final one.

'I gave my word to my mother and she gave hers to the King.' She crossed her arms over her bound breasts and glared at Olafr. 'Would you have me break my promise? Would you have me lose my mother's lands? Would you have me branded an untrustworthy traitor?'

'What I have to say can wait until you have time.' Aedan mac Connall made a smooth bow. 'But it will be in your interest to hear me out before you slit my throat, Dagmar, daughter of both the great Helga and Kolbeinn the Blood-Axe.'

'If you wish to stay, you must be prepared to fight,' Dagmar said, her look scathing. 'We require warriors who are capable of lifting a shield.'

'My skill with sword and shield has never been in question.' He raised an arrogant brow. 'If I fight for you, will you hear me out? Will you listen to your father's message right to the end? Will you allow me to keep my head attached to my shoulders and breathing?'

Dagmar hated the small shiver of anticipation that ran down her spine. Her father must have heard about her mother's death. Perhaps he would be open to an alliance now... But then she dismissed the thought as wishful thinking. Her father cared little for her hopes and dreams and everything for his legacy, the one which would go to his son. 'After the battle, much can happen including listening to my father's emissary.'

His blue-green eyes assessed her as if he could see the woman beyond the snake-plaited hair and the paint. 'Very well, my dog and I will fight for you in the coming battle.'

She noted that Olafr appeared to be nonplussed. Perhaps Old Alf was correct—he did intend mischief during the battle. 'Problem, Olafr?'

He smoothed his face. His smile was far too quick and assured to be genuine. 'Not in the slightest, Lady. After the battle, you say...'

'I will fulfil my promise to my mother before I entertain anything else.' Dagmar grabbed her shield. She felt more in control with it in her hand. Her father's messenger could wait. What he wanted from her was the least of her concerns. If he died in battle, then the fates will have decided her path. 'Go to the westernmost edge of the line, Olafr, and fill the gap caused by the loss of Gunnar.'

Olafr's eyes flashed. 'I thought I would go more to the right.'

'Do you wish to challenge me for the leadership of this *felag*, Olafr?' she asked, putting a hand on her hip. 'If so, I would suggest making that challenge before the battle begins. Otherwise allow me to deploy the men as I see fit.'

A tick developed under his right eye. 'I will go where my lady desires.'

'What happened to your missing warrior?' the Gael asked.

'He ate something which disagreed with him and lurks in his tent with watery bowels,' she replied, rubbing the back of her neck and trying to get rid of the sudden tightness. 'As you don't appear to have a working shield, you may use his, if you are sincere about wishing to assist me. Or return to my father and inform him that I have little time for him. You're lucky. I'm in a good mood. Did my father inform you of his other messengers' fate?'

'I appreciate the shield, Lady.' The Gael made another bow, perfectly correct, but there was a hint of arrogance in it as if he could make her change her mind about not having anything to do with her father.

'After the battle, we will talk.' Silently she prayed to Odin that it would not be necessary to kill this Gael, but anyone sent from her father's house usually brought trouble.

Aedan ground his teeth as he waited for the signal that the attack could begin. How Kolbeinn must have chortled when he waved Aedan goodbye. Kolbeinn stood to win whatever the outcome—either the man got his daughter returned or a troublesome enemy was eliminated and his lands acquired. Aedan had gone into this quest blind and naive. A Northman never offered a fair deal. He had little hope in winning this wager without divine intervention.

'He means to kill her.' An old man sidled up to Aedan while keeping a wary eye on Aedan's dog.

'Who? Olafr Rolfson?' Aedan asked the grizzled warrior.

The man gave the briefest of nods towards the warrior who had greeted him. 'Now he has to wait until you have said your piece, to see if it brings him some advantage. He is greedy, that one, make no mistake.'

'Why are you telling me this?'

'You're from her father rather than that witch of a stepmother. You mean to take her back. There is no point denying it or causing your dog to growl at me. I'm far too long in the tooth, but I know the meaning of the sword you carry. Now that her mother has died, I am the only one left who does. You are to be treated like a friend, not an enemy. After all this time, he remembered the signal.'

'That surprises you?'

The warrior gave a lopsided smile. 'I know what he is like. His daughter takes after him in many ways, except she wants her way, not his.'

Aedan narrowed his eyes, wondering how much he should confide. 'My honour and my people depend on me fulfilling this quest.'

The man nodded. 'I always knew he would send someone honourable one day. Where is the she-witch of a second wife? Quickly now.'

Aedan cocked his head to one side. 'His wife died. It is why he has sent for his daughter. He wants her near.'

'A hard woman, that one, but Kolbeinn was obsessed with her. He destroyed his marriage and his daughter's life to be with her.' He gestured towards where Dagmar stood, waiting with her sword raised. 'Her mother bargained her entire life's work away to keep her daughter safe.'

'And this is what she considered safe?' Aedan regarded the woman with the strange blue markings on her face and plaited hair which quivered like snakes when she spoke. From what he could tell she was slender to the point of being mannish under the armour she wore. But she waved her hand with absolute authority.

'We advance,' she cried. 'As long as our shields hold, Constantine holds the field. Thorsten and his Northmen have overreached. We will carry the day and with it, our lands, the lands Constantine has promised. Our servitude is at an end. One more battle. One more victory.'

The men cheered and gave their battle cry and beat their swords against their shields.

'Can she fight?' Aedan asked in an undertone.

'Her mother saw to that. Few men can compete with her. Kolbeinn in his prime, maybe.' The man shrugged. 'I do not worry about the enemies in front of her. I worry about the ones behind her. Gunnar drank the goblet Olafr intended for her this morning and now his bowels suffer.'

'How do you know this?'

'I switched them.' The old man gave a chuckle. 'Serves Gunnar right for throwing his lot in with Olafr.'

'You are her protector.'

'Helga was far from an easy woman, but I gave her my oath to protect her daughter and I do.' His eyes narrowed. 'What does her father require from her now that the witch is dead?'

'He wishes to speak with her. I am to return with her.'

'Where precisely is Kolbeinn these days?'

'Out to the west, in command of Colbhasa,' Aedan said, naming the Hebridean island where most of the Northmen from the Western fleet were based. 'He requires his daughter by All Hallows or my people will die.'

'I see your difficulty.' The old man nodded gravely. 'She will not go willingly to see her father. But you must first guard against that snake Olafr.'

'Would Olafr shift his allegiance on the battlefield?'

The man was silent for a long heartbeat. 'I believe in my heart he is capable of that.'

Aedan nodded. His mission had suddenly become more complicated. Not only did he have to convince Dagmar to meet with her father, he might also have to save her life first.

A horn sounded and the lines moved forward. Out of the corner of his eye Aedan kept a watch on Olafr. He hung back slightly, never quite being part of the action while there was no doubting Dagmar's courage. She shouted orders, rushed to reinforce the shield wall and encouraged her men to keep going forward.

Slowly, against the odds, it appeared that she was gaining the upper hand in the battle. She was keeping her vow, delivering the victory for Constantine.

When the battle was at its height, Olafr raised his sword and lifted his shield, shouting for Thorsten over and over again. A sudden hush fell over the battlefield. Aedan froze in mid-swipe of his sword. Immediately several of Dagmar's men stopped fighting, allowing the shield wall to collapse and the Northmen from the Black Pool to stream through.

'Treachery!' someone yelled.

Aedan hacked his way to where Dagmar fought against several warriors. In a matter of heartbeats, she would be dead along with his hopes for his people and their freedom. The sword he carried shattered as he reached her.

He brought the hilt of his broken sword down on the back of her head. She crumpled.

He scooped her unconscious body up. She was slender, but all sinewy muscle, rather than soft womanly curves.

'You go to her father?' the old warrior cried.

'God and the saints willing.'

The man smiled and tossed him a brooch. 'Look after her. I will distract them. Give her that when she goes to rip out your throat. Tell her that Old Alf kept the faith.'

He gave a shout and went forward, drawing the opposing warriors to him, giving Aedan a corridor to escape.

'Good.' Aedan whistled to his wolfhound who bounded forward, snarling. 'Time to fulfil our vow and return to the West.'

Behind him, he heard the old man's dying agonies, but he honoured his sacrifice and did not slacken his pace.

Chapter Two

Dagmar slowly struggled from an all-engulfing black pit and tried to make sense of the world. Positively, she lived. She knew that from the faint drizzle which landed on her face and the prickle of pine needles in her back. However, instead of the sounds of battle raging about her, there was a low hum of crickets and the faint chirp of some bird.

She flexed her fingers and toes, relieved everything seemed to work. Her right arm was a bit stiff and her thighs screamed like they always did after a battle.

Her mouth was drier than the sand on the beach below Constantine's court at St Andrew's. But mostly, it was the back of her head which pained her, a great searing ache which made her nauseous and threatened to cause the enveloping blackness to return.

She tried to piece together how she'd arrived here but could only remember in snatches—the sword thrust towards her chest that she'd been certain would end her life, the sudden searing pain in the back of her head, the bumpy movement of a galloping horse and the strong arms about her as a low voice told her she would live if she obeyed. She pinched the bridge of her nose, trying to rid the buzzing noise from her ears.

She cautiously raised herself up on one elbow. A wave of pain rocked her, causing the world to spin and blur, but she fought against it, refusing to return to that black nothingness. Gradually it cleared and her eyes focused.

She lay on a bed of dry leaves and pine needles. From the sky, she reckoned it was nearing owl-light, then she immediately revised her opinion. The world was becoming lighter by the breath. She'd lost at least one day and night. A large multi-coloured wolfhound stood guard over her. Nearby she saw a dark auburn-haired figure sitting on a log, watching her intently. But her men had vanished. Neither were there any horses. She put a hand to her head, trying to remember where she'd seen her captor before.

At her small movement, the man straightened, his hand going to his sword and recognition crashed through her. The Gael! The man who claimed to have a message from her father. The man had kidnapped her! She'd been ten thousand times a fool not to consider such a possibility.

'Aedan mac Connall!' she spluttered, but it came out weaker than a kitten's mewl.

She ground her teeth. Olafr had not required a confrontation; he'd simply arranged for her removal. She had been fooled by the oldest trick in the book. Her father would never have sent a Gael. He despised them. The only mistake Olafr had made was that she still lived. Silently she swore revenge for everything he and this Gael had done.

'Aedan mac Connall, you'll pay for what you've

done!' she said again, this time with greater force. 'My men will be massing! Release me at once and you may yet live!'

'You're awake and in good voice,' Aedan mac Connall said, lifting a brow but seemingly unimpressed and unperturbed by her threat. 'Good. It makes things easier.'

Dagmar's next snarled threat died in her throat. 'Easier for whom?'

'Everyone concerned, but mainly for me.' He leant forward. 'I require you to be alive, Dagmar Kolbeinndottar.'

Her hand instinctively searched for a sword, but found none. She cursed under her breath. Someone, probably the Gael, had divested her of her armour. She was simply clad in her trousers and tunic. Nearly defenceless, but her boots with their hidden gold remained on her feet and she possessed a mind if she cared to use it, instead of panicking and behaving like a feeble-minded female.

'Helgadottar, not Kolbeinndottar,' she said, curling her hands into impotent fists.

'Yet your father remains Kolbeinn the Blood-Axe. Changing your parents is a privilege given only to a few.'

Dagmar screwed up her eyes and refused to allow tears to fall. Tears were what other women did, not the daughter of Helga the Red. She concentrated on breathing until she felt in control of her body once again.

The Gael had removed her sword. It was what happened when a person was kidnapped. The kidnappers took steps to secure their prisoner. She needed to stop acting like a thick-headed panic-stricken mouse and formulate a plan for escape.

The Gael wanted her alive and he claimed to be from her father. If her stepmother had sent him, she would be lying in a pool of blood with her life slowly ebbing from her. Small comfort, but a chance for escape would present itself.

'Where are my men? Where is the High King?' she asked, fixing him with one of her harder stares. 'Take me to Constantine immediately. There are things which need to be said before we depart. My father wouldn't want to anger the High King of the Picts.'

She breathed easier. The Gael would have to see the logic and yield. Once she was back in Constantine's camp, she would not be going anywhere near her father.

'Constantine was last seen on a horse headed towards the coast. He lost. A comprehensive defeat. No longer High King of the Picts. Perhaps he remains King of a very small slice of Alba's eastern shore.' The Gael rose and dusted down his trousers. 'Thorsten and his Northmen from the Black Pool now control the Northern Alba, from the isles of Orkney to the Firth of Forth and beyond.'

She winced. Constantine had lost. Badly. The day was getting worse and worse. Her mother's lands would also be gone. Overrun and parcelled out to some Northern jaarl. 'And my men? Did any survive?'

'Those who lived switched sides. Celebrating Thorsten's historic victory for the north.'

She cursed Olafr under her breath. Old Alf had been correct in his mutterings about betrayal. 'Who are you?'

'Your saviour. You were supposed to die on the battlefield. I saved your life.' His lips curved upwards. 'You may thank me appropriately later.'

Dagmar balled her fists and struggled to breathe slowly. Saviour? Thank him? How—by sharing his bed? Not likely. Even if he did have shoulders which blocked out the light and long legs that went on for ever. She pressed her hand to her head. The blow was affecting her reason. Men had no interest in her in that way. Her chin was too pointed and her nose too long.

She had no business noticing the Gael as a man. She was dedicated to the arts of war, rather than the pleasures of bed sport.

Her finger drew a line in the dirt. He'd taken away her world. She might as well be dead. She'd lost everything that her mother had worked so hard to achieve. She'd betrayed her final vow to her mother. But she had someone to blame—Aedan mac Connall with that self-satisfied smile on his face, proclaiming he had saved her from certain death by snatching her while the battle still raged.

'Saved my life?' The words exploded from deep within her. 'You kidnapped me in the heat of the battle! I could have fought my way to Thorsten and bested him.'

'Forgive me, but I was on the battlefield. An axe was aimed at your back as well as a sword at your neck. Your man—that elderly warrior—leapt in front of the sword while I handled the axe. He perished to assist our escape, so you could live.'

The angry words dried in her throat. The man had unerringly found the flaw—why leave her alive if he only meant to kill her at a time of his choosing? 'Old Alf died?'

'No man could have survived that scene.'

She silently whispered a prayer for the grizzled warrior who had served her mother and her so faithfully. He'd taught her how to handle a sword and had dried her tears when her mother had become too exacting.

'Then he is fighting for Odin now as he always wanted to,' she said around the lump in her throat. Old Alf would be the first to scoff at tears, acting like a fragile female he'd call it, instead of behaving like a warrior. She wiped an eye. 'A fitting end for him. Good. Old Alf trusted you. Why?'

The Gael shrugged. 'He understood what I had to do. He urged me to do it. He knew the sword I wore came from your father, the sword which shattered saving your life. Your friend died so that you could live.'

'My men...' Dagmar whispered as the lump in her throat had begun to choke her. 'My men are loyal.'

He lifted a brow. 'Obviously not as loyal as you might have thought. Some of them betrayed you, led by Olafr. As we were leaving, they shouted for Thorsten while beating their swords against their shields. They turned the tide against Constantine.'

The buzzing in her ears increased. Her men, her mother's men had betrayed her and broke the fellowship when she needed them the most. How was that even possible? Her mouth tasted bitter. The Gael had to be lying, hoping she'd go quietly to wherever he intended for her to be ransomed.

'They wanted the land the King promised my mother,' she said as her gut hollowed out. 'One more victorious battle and it would have been theirs.'

'Your mother is dead. Why would Constantine honour that promise even if he could? Or perhaps you know more than I, *Shield Maiden*.'

Dagmar's fingers itched for a knife, for anything to wipe the knowing look off his face. He mocked her. She didn't need telling that competing with her mother was an impossibility. Her mother had been more than an equal to men, a legend in her own time and Dagmar was merely the daughter.

She forced her hand to relax. She had to start behaving like her mother's daughter, rather than giving in to her desires and curling up in a pathetic ball.

'How do I know you tell the truth? I take it you conveniently disposed of this shattered sword.'

'Old Alf gave me this brooch. It apparently belonged to your mother. He entrusted me to get you to safety and that means going to your father.'

He held out her mother's favourite brooch, the one she had used to fasten her cloak, the one she had handed to Old Alf as she'd breathed her last. Dagmar's heart twisted. The Gael was telling the truth. Why else would Old Alf have entrusted his most beloved possession to him?

With great difficulty, she rose. The world swirled about her, making her stomach swoop, but she forced her spine to stay erect. 'I will go to see the High King. I will not allow this insult to go unavenged. Constantine will see sense once I explain the situation. If not for Olafr's double-dealing, I would have given him victory. I can still do it. Once the land is confirmed, the men will see they made a mistake in betraying me and return to my *felag*. Without them, Thorsten will find it impossible to hold Northern Alba.'

'You will go nowhere except where I say you go.' The Gael snapped his fingers and his giant dog instantly blocked her way. It bared its teeth and gave a low growl. Dagmar retreated several steps.

'I need to go there and confront the King. Please, call off your dog.' She hated how her voice trembled on the words. 'There are women and children's lives who depend on me making this right. I gave my word to my mother. My first duty is to them.'

'Your name will be the byword for treachery in Constantine's camp,' he said in a low voice. 'You will not be allowed within ten paces of him. Your life expectancy would be a few breaths at most. I regret I cannot allow you to go there to your death. My people and I need you alive. Afterwards...you may go where you will, but my people come first.'

She swayed slightly. Her name a word for treachery. She rapidly sat down before she fell. 'I had nothing to do with it. I'm innocent.'

'Do you think Constantine cares?' The Gael's eyes burned fiercely. 'He needs a scapegoat to blame for his failure and you are a pagan woman warrior, an abomination in the eyes of his priests and counsellors. A woman who lives for blood, rather than her brood. You are no peace-weaver, Dagmar Kolbeinndottar, but a peace-destroyer in his eyes.'

'And the people who work the lands promised to my mother?'

'They will do what people always do—work the land for the new overlord, one whom Thorsten appoints.'

'Or they will depart, hoping to find refuge.' She held out her arms and willed him to understand. 'I must be able to offer them that refuge.'

'You can do little for them if you are dead.'

She hugged her arms about her waist, hating that

Aedan mac Connall's words made sense. She had heard the whispers from Constantine's priests about her and her mother, but always Constantine had refused to listen. She and her mother were his favourite weapon, the unbeatable combination who kept the Northmen from Dubh Linn from gaining sway over his lands. She had almost achieved her goal—her own estate with plenty of land for her men. But that was before. Before she had lost this battle. Before Constantine had been badly humiliated.

'You appear to know a great deal about what that future holds.'

'I know what Constantine and the Picts are like,' the Gael said with a faint smile. 'I know their prejudices. How little they think of the Northmen. I heard the mutterings as we escaped. Thankfully they were too busy trying to save their hides to worry about a single man leading a pack horse with a dog trotting alongside.'

'We were winning. I sensed the shield wall beginning to break. A few feet more…' She put her hand to her head as the blackness threatened to overwhelm her again. She had nearly tasted victory, victory which was hers alone, rather than sharing part of her mother's triumph. 'Or at least I think it was like that. My recollections are hazy.'

'It doesn't matter what you think or sensed.' He banged his fists. 'My task is to take you alive to your father by All Hallows. Therefore, we will not be journeying to Constantine or your lands or anywhere else you might think will serve your purpose first. We go to Colbhasa and your father.'

'My father cares nothing for me. He turned his back on me a long time ago. He requires sons, not daughters.' Dagmar crossed her arms. There, she had said the words out loud, words which had been written on her soul on her tenth name day.

'Your mother hid you from him. She actively kept the two of you apart. She made sure you received no word from him. The old warrior who perished asked me to tell you that. Said it would calm you down.'

The stark words were hammer blows to her heart. Trust the Gael? Old Alf might have, but she saw no reason to. She could never trust her father—not after how he'd treated her mother and her, after he chose her stepmother and her swollen belly over them. And despite her stepmother's prophetic dreams about bearing her father many warriors, the woman had produced only one sickly son.

Gunnar's mysterious illness should have warned her that Old Alf had spoken true about Olafr's attempts to betray her, but she'd ignored his warnings. All she had needed was one good victory to cement her position, gain the land she required—what she had achieved, instead, was a resounding defeat. Everything had slipped through her fingers. Her life had become the dregs of the pond as her stepmother had predicted it would—the only words the witch had ever spoken directly to her. 'I'll listen to what you say, Gael, before I decide.'

'Will you behave yourself?' he asked. 'Or does my dog have to keep you in check?'

'Do I have any choice?'

'Not really.' He gave a smile which was like the sun breaking through the mist on an autumn morning. 'Be content with breathing, Dagmar.'

'I would like to carve Olafr Rolfson's heart out. I would like to slit his throat and leave him to die slowly and in great pain.' She shook her head and tried to control her temper. 'But I have to approach it sensibly. However, I, Dagmar Helgadottar, promise you that one day those men will pay for what they have done. I will honour my fallen friends. They may have seemed like men who failed to you, but they were my friends and comrades. Some of them I had known since I was a little girl. I'll not forget them. Nor will I let their sacrifice be in vain.'

'A good and worthy sentiment provided you can bend the future to your will.'

She could hear the scepticism in his voice.

'It will happen.' She leant forward. 'Tell me why my father suddenly requires me? Why he sent a Gael to do his dirty work?'

'Maybe he expects you to save him the trouble of killing me.'

Dagmar screwed up her nose, considering the words. The Gael had a point. Her father was capable of such treachery. 'I am not inclined to do anything my father wants. I'm pleased I spared your life earlier.'

'That makes two of us.'

'My father hasn't wanted anything to do with me for over ten years.' She lifted her chin proudly. 'He only thinks of his other family, his son that he had with that woman.'

'Nevertheless, he sent me.' Aedan held out a gold ring with a double-axe motif engraved in it and struggled to keep his temper. The woman should be on her knees in gratitude to him. He had saved her life. She owed him a life debt.

He knew her type. He had encountered Northern women over the years. Invariably they were proud and stubborn, inclined to argue rather than accepting his word. And this one was the worst—the most stubborn and pig-headed. She rivalled her father in that.

'His token. Kolbeinn said it would be enough. You would understand that I came from him.'

She looked at it warily as if it was a snake which might bite her. 'My father sent you. Truly? Not my stepmother?'

'I've never encountered your stepmother,' Aedan said truthfully. There would be time enough to explain about the death of Kolbeinn's second wife and, more importantly, her son's. It amazed him that she remained in ignorance of these events, but if she kept slitting messengers' throats, what could she expect?

She was silent for a long while. The tattooed whorls on her cheeks trembled. 'That is my father's ring. He did indeed send you, but that doesn't mean I'm going with you like a lamb to the slaughter.'

Aedan clung on to his temper with the barest of threads. If he could have rid himself of this burden, he would have. 'What other options do you have?'

She lifted her chin. 'Plenty. Give me time and I will detail them to you.'

Mor stiffened, gave a low growl and began backing into the undergrowth. Every muscle in Aedan's body stiffened.

'Is there a problem with your dog? I haven't moved,' she asked, cocking her head to one side.

Without giving her a chance to react, Aedan clamped his hand over her mouth and pulled her into the undergrowth, next to where his dog crouched. His body hit hers and somewhere in his mind he registered that Dagmar Kolbeinndottar was made up of far more curves than he had originally thought.

Her furious blue eyes stared back at him. Without the facial decoration, she would be pretty.

'Listen with your ears. Stop struggling,' he muttered. 'My dog has heard something. I trust her instincts far more than your prattling.'

She pressed her mouth shut and lay still, her skin pale against the blue whorls.

'Can't believe we are searching for the Gael,' came one voice, far closer than Aedan would have liked.

'Olafr wants to make sure the Shield Maiden is dead. He didn't find her body,' another said. 'Just her armour.'

'I'm sure I heard a woman's voice coming from around here.'

'You hear women's voices all the time. Why should this be any different?'

Five Northmen barged into the clearing. Aedan's other hand inched towards his sword.

'If she is around, she'll be dead easy to spot.' The man gave a guffaw. 'How many women do you know who sport blue whorls and snakes in their hair? Nah, she'll be dead.'

'What do you think that was all about anyway?' asked the voice.

'Her mother had the whorls as well. Maybe she was born with them.'

'Tattoos more like. After her first battle. I was there. I smelt the stench of burning flesh. And they ain't no snakes, just plaits. By Loki, some people are gullible.'

'All I know is that it is beginning to rain again. They didn't go this way. Let's get back to camp. At least we found a horse and if they have gone into the marshes they're goners. It ain't no one who can survive that.'

'Wee Davy...'

'Wee Davy has a big mouth for tall tales, but the Gael went north, I know that for a fact.'

'Why?'

'He came from the north. There ain't no way man nor beast can get through what lies due west—those marshes are full of spirits who sup on the souls of the living.'

'Aye. If the Shield Maiden has gone in there, it'll be the last we see of her. She will have left the horse here as a diversion and taken the road north. It is the only way.'

'We will catch her and claim the reward. She can't hide those tattoos.'

Aedan breathed a sigh of relief as the group disappeared back the way they came. He waited, holding his body and hers completely still until the footsteps had faded.

He slowly took his hand away from Dagmar's mouth and rolled away. 'Believe me now?'

'About Olafr's treachery?' Her mouth twisted. 'Can there be any doubt? Your words hold merit, Gael. To stay in the lands Thorsten controls is to court death.'

Aedan released a breath. One hurdle overcome. Now for the rest. 'I've spent long enough chasing after you. Time slips through my fingers. We go now.'

'How close are we to the battle?' she asked in a low voice.

'I thought we were far enough away. You were beginning to stir when I stopped. I didn't know how hard I hit you.'

'And the horse?'

'One I stole. I let it go free. Obviously someone rec-ognised it.'

She nodded. 'You did well there, Gael.'

Aedan rubbed the back of his neck, unable to decide if she was serious or being ironic. 'We go across the marshes from here. The horse would only have slowed us down.'

'Those men said that it would be certain suicide. Spirits inhabit those marshes.'

'They're wrong. There is a way through and we will take it.'

'Are you touched in the head?' She slapped her hands together. 'Don't answer that. Of course you are, why else brave a battle with only a dog? Gods help me.'

'A large portion of my family might agree with you, but I like to think that I take calculated risks. The marsh is a calculated risk.' Aedan shifted the pack on to his other shoulder. 'Are you ready?'

Dagmar remained where she stood, fingering her cheek with a thoughtful expression.

He sighed. 'What else does my lady fair require afore we depart?'

'I require clean water, and I'm not some fragile spoilt flower of a lady. I'm a shield maiden. Remember that.'

'If you're thirsty, I've the dregs of small beer re-maining.'

'To wash the paint off my face, of course. Once I no longer sport blue whorls on my face and snakes in my hair, then we can travel on the road right under Olafr's nose.' She gave a self-satisfied smile. 'I do have ears. They search for a woman with blue and black circles tattooed on her face and tightly plaited hair. Both things are easy to change.'

He started. 'Your whorls are not tattoos? In Bernicia I was told—'

She gave her first real smile. 'Amazing what people will believe without questioning. How could anyone have venomous snakes for hair?'

Aedan frowned. He'd believed it simply because it was a rumour. He should have thought to question. Or when she was unconscious, to check for himself. Fundamental mistake. 'It is what I was told.'

'My mother refused to permit the tattoos as one day I might have cause to change my mind. I railed against her, but to no avail. I was going to make them permanent after I'd fulfilled my vow and won my lands,' she said with a sigh. 'Once again I see her wisdom and foresight.' She picked up a handful of moss and made an imperious gesture. 'The water, Gael. The sooner my face is clean, the sooner we can depart on the road north.'

Aedan stared at her. 'I'm not your servant.'

'No, but you're my father's. Why else wouldn't you have a horse?'

It was on the tip of his tongue to her inform her of the truth that he owned estates and many horses on Ile, but then he decided that it was not worth it. Their acquaintance wouldn't be longer than strictly necessary. The less she knew of him and his true reasons for the quest to find her and return her to her father, the better.

'Why indeed?' he murmured instead. Leaving Mor to guard his reluctant companion, he fetched water from the edge of the mist-shrouded marsh.

She poured it on the moss and began to rub her face. Rivulets of blue and black trickled down her cheeks and neck. He shook his head, disgusted with his blindness. 'Paint. Such a simple, obvious trick.'

'But highly effective.' She concentrated on removing the paint. 'It gave my face a fierceness that men respected.'

She dried her face on the corner of her tunic. Then, with quick fingers, she undid the tight plaits in her hair so that it hung about her face like a golden wavy cloud.

'Do I look like the same woman?'

Aedan tried not to gape in surprise. The woman who regarded him had a certain vulnerability to her mouth. Her other features were a bit angular, but her skin was no longer stretched tight from the plaits. Before he'd only noticed the strange whorls of the tattoos; now he noticed her—and very delectable she was, too. Aedan struggled to remember when he had last seen a woman with skin that translucent. It was little wonder that her mother had kept Dagmar's beauty hidden, surrounded as she was by so many men.

'It will make it easier to travel unnoticed,' he said, busying himself with checking the pack. His body's intense reaction to her was because he'd been without a woman for far too long, that was all. 'The marsh awaits, my lady fair.'

Her jaw dropped. 'But there is no need. I have disguised myself.'

'We must still go through the marshes. The mist is lifting. We need to make the most of the daylight.'

'Those men spoke the truth. They are treacherous. People have perished. Several of my mother's men lost their way last spring and only one body was ever found.' She gave her imperious nod as if she expected him to obey her without question.

Aedan gritted his teeth. She would soon learn he was

no brainless servant who would fawn over her every utterance.

'We go around,' she proclaimed, tilting her chin arrogantly upwards. 'To the south, rather than to the north if we must.'

'My dog has an excellent nose. She got me through them before. She will get us through again.' He forced his tone to be gentle as though he was soothing a frightened horse. 'If Olafr believes you survived, he will check all the roads. He will know that you will make for your father.'

She was silent for a long time. 'Olafr knows that would be my last resort. He might consider the south and Halfdan at Eoforwic. My mother had dealings with him six warring seasons ago. The road south will be difficult, but he won't be looking for me when I look like this.'

'Who do you resemble?'

She lowered her brow. 'What does that have to do with anything?'

'Your mother may have confided the paint trick to him. You can't discount it.'

'I look like my father's mother except for my hair.' Her eyes flashed. 'I get that from my mother's mother.' She tapped her finger against the dusky pink of her mouth. 'But you've a point. He has obviously been planning this for some time. My mother may have been foolish and confided our secret to him. She was besotted. I underestimated him before, but I won't make that mistake again.'

'He knows your father sent me,' he reminded her. 'He is searching for the both of us.'

'What does that have to do with anything?'

'We go through the marshes, even if I have to carry you every step of the way.'

'I can walk.'

'I carried you before.'

'Across the back of a horse, a horse which is presently elsewhere. I can make it difficult for you, Gael. Give in to my sensible request. I tend to win.'

That he did not doubt. Her strong jawline told of an inner strength and stubbornness.

'It is best that we are gone before they work out their mistake. Before the mist comes down. Unless you wish to throw yourself on Olafr's mercy, you will join me.'

He whistled for Mor and started off. His heart thumped in his ears. She had to believe the bluff. He couldn't afford to leave her, but going through the marshes would save precious time and the one commodity he lacked was time if he was to beat Kolbeinn at his game.

'Are you abandoning me?' Her voice held a plaintive note.

'I'm going the way which leads to safety, the only way open to us. Decide—do you want to live to enact your revenge against Olafr or do you wish to die, slowly and painfully?'

'Wait! I'll brave the marshes,' she called.

Chapter Three

Dagmar carefully picked her way through the bog with its squelching mud and hidden pools of bad water, following in the Gael's footsteps, trying not to think about all the tales and legends she had heard about this place.

Old Alf had delighted in reciting them when they skirted around it earlier in the season—tales of unquiet ghosts and elves who lured men into the deep where they drowned. A king's army had once ridden in and had never been seen again. However, on the days when the mist rolled out, then the sound of their dying cries echoed across the land.

She concentrated on the Gael's broad shoulders and the way his cloak swung instead. The man moved far too arrogantly as if the entire world should bow to him. Women probably melted under his gaze and populated his bed. She'd encountered the type before. Her body's earlier reaction to the Gael was definitely a result of the blow to her head. She'd be immune to him from now on.

'Does your dog have a name?' she called out when the Gael halted beside a particularly malodorous bog.

She was certain he'd chosen to stop there simply to be awkward. The Gael was like that.

The mist had started to rise, obscuring even the limited view. The small wisps of cold resembled humans with outstretched hands. A few loons called out over the marsh, sounding precisely like men begging for help.

'Mor,' he answered without bothering to glance back. 'My dog is called Mor. She is a wolfhound and dislikes imperious people from the north.'

'I'm not imperious!'

He raised a brow. 'That is for my dog to decide.'

Since they had entered the marshes, he had not bothered really to see if she was keeping up. It was only because his dog Mor kept stopping, turning to look at her every so often and occasionally returning to her to nudge her hand and prevent her from stepping in thick oozing mud, that she remained alive and not lost for ever in the growing mist. Something else to hold against him. Soon he'd have to admit that this trek was impossible and they'd have to retrace their steps and go the way she'd suggested in the first place. She wasn't imperious, she simply had better ideas and wasn't afraid to say so.

'Mor as in big or Mor as in Sarah?' she asked to keep her mind away from the way the mist had shrouded the few scrubby trees which suddenly punctuated the landscape.

He stopped so suddenly that she nearly bumped into him. 'Of course, you know Gaelic. I forgot that you spoke to me in Gaelic when we first met. How did you learn it?'

'My nurse when I was little was a Gael.' Dagmar looped a strand of damp hair about her ear. 'It was her name. Mor like Sarah.'

His brows drew together in a fierce frown. He cursed loud and long. 'One of the captured women, forced to work for the Northmen, but all the while longing to be free.'

She concentrated on a tuft of dead grass. He made it seem as though it was somehow wrong to have had a nurse. 'Thralls exist. Even the Picts and the Gaels have them. Estates could not function without workers. If you know of a better way, do tell me. My mother had other duties and both her mother and my father's mother were dead, long before I was born. Someone had to look after me when I was little.'

She waited with a thumping heart. She did not doubt that if he could, the Gael would abandon her here. She had to be grateful that his desire for payment from her father was greater than his loathing of the people from the north.

'Even so, the Northmen have captured too many of our women. My aunt disappeared before I was born. She never returned. There were rumours about my grandfather selling her, but I know the truth.'

'Just as you supposedly knew the truth about my hair and tattoos?'

'That is different.'

Dagmar regarded the ground and wished she had never said anything. The Gael obviously despised her and her kind. At least her mother had never sunk so low as to become a snatcher of women. 'And you're certain it was Northmen.'

'From Dubh Linn, from the Black Pool, according to my mother. They came in their ships and took her.'

'We have been at war with the Northmen from the Black Pool for as long as I can remember. My mother despised them and what they did to women,' Dagmar said fiercely.

'What happened to your nurse?'

'My nurse was a second mother to me. Mor in the north tongue means *mother* and she truly was kind and loving. I revere her memory.' Dagmar hated how her voice caught. Mor had been one of the few people to show tenderness to her, drying her eyes when she failed at her lessons.

'How convenient.'

Ignoring the Gael and his ill humour, she went and knelt beside the dog, holding out her hand and softly called her name. Mor the dog sniffed her outstretched palm and then gave it a tentative lick with a rough tongue. 'Mor, I mean you no harm. I'm grateful for your nose which has led us thus far and I pray to Thor and Freyja that you lead us to safety.'

Mor cocked her head to one side and gave a small woof with a wag of her tail.

'She approves of you,' the Gael said with a frown.

'As someone from the north, I'm honoured not to be considered imperious.'

'It takes time for her to fully trust someone.'

Dagmar attempted a smile. 'Like her master.'

He gestured towards the thickening mist. The bog in front of them looked particularly treacherous. The gesture revealed the breadth of his shoulders and the power in his arms. 'Shall we get going?'

Dagmar gave the dog one last pat. 'You'll get us through, won't you? You won't allow the elves who lurk in such places to capture me.'

'There are no such things as elves.'

'Says the man who believed a woman could have snakes for hair.'

Mor woofed in response and started off, picking her way through the oozing mud and pools with complete assurance.

Dagmar concentrated on following the dog and ignoring the Gael. He was a temporary irritation. She would get rid of him as soon as she no longer required his dog.

He stopped abruptly and she banged into him.

'What happened to your nurse after you finished with her?' the Gael asked, breaking the uneasy silence that had sprung up between them.

'Do you truly want to know?'

'Yes. I've no idea what happened to my aunt. I made enquiries, but discovered only silence. I've accepted that I will never know. Maybe your nurse's fate is hers. Maybe she did find some measure of happiness.'

Dagmar gave a careful shrug. How much to tell? She had learned that lesson long ago that no one needed her life story, particularly about things which had happened before the divorce, the bloody battle between her mother and her father's chosen champion and then their terrifying flight off her father's lands through the dark forest.

Her mother hated her talking about it and had once slapped her face when she discovered Dagmar clinging on to the small carved doll Mor had slipped her as they'd parted. The slap had startled her mother and she was instantly sorry, hugging Dagmar and weeping in a dreadful way that she'd never heard before or since. But Dagmar had learned her lesson—she never mentioned her nurse after that and she threw the doll away before her mother spied it again.

'I've no idea,' she confessed. 'My Mor was one of the people I left behind when my mother and I departed my father's lands. I presume she looked after my half-brother. She was a good woman who loved babies. For years, I used to recite her stories in order to get to sleep at night.'

Her throat closed. She could hardly explain how much that woman had meant to her, not to this man. He would only laugh at her. He wouldn't understand that until the divorce, her mother had been so distracted with the demands of the running the estates and settling disputes, she'd had little time for wiping Dagmar's tears when she skinned her knee or when her threads tangled or when she woke from bad dreams.

'No, I've no idea what happened to my nurse,' she reiterated instead. 'If my mother knew, she kept it to herself.'

'You'll soon find out, if you are bothered. Perhaps she will have remained with your father's family. Perhaps you can do the decent thing and prevail on your father to return her to her kin. She may have a home with my people if her kin have vanished.'

'I am bothered and it is always best to see what a person desires before making decisions for them,' she said. 'You have given me a good reason to look forward to getting to Colbhasa. I thank you for that kindness.'

The Gael grunted.

'My father must have given you a reason for bringing me back. You must have some idea,' she said to keep her mind away from the potential reunion with Mor and the fact that she desperately wanted to see her again. She wanted to believe that Mor had been well treated and rewarded for staying with her father. Her mother had forbidden any talk of her previous life when they left the compound on Bjorgvinfjord.

Your life before must be as nothing, keep your face turned to the future.

'You must ask him when we arrive on Colbhasa. He failed to inform me of the specific reasons, but he is eager to see you and the sort of woman you have become. It was part of the message he sent.'

'May I hear the precise message?' She pulled her cloak tighter about her shoulders. 'I was rude earlier and I apologise. My only excuse was that the battle was about to begin.'

'It has been overtaken by subsequent events, but here goes.' The Gael stared out at the marshes, rather than looking at her. 'Your father requires that you attend him on Colbhasa immediately. He has much to say to you and is eager to see you again after all these years. He wants to see the sort of woman you have become. Do as he requires without delay and all will be well.'

Her mind buzzed. That part of her which had remained a little girl who adored her father wanted desperately for it to be true, that her father had belatedly remembered her and the way they used to be. Just as quickly she remembered the bitter parting—at her stepmother's urging, he had given them until nightfall to leave his lands or be hunted like wolf's heads—people who could be slaughtered without having to pay a blood price to their next of kin because they were vermin and not fit to live. Then he'd turned his back on them.

He would want to dictate her future and who she'd marry, but he would soon learn that she was the one who would choose what happened to her. She had earned that right. The Gael would also discover that her fate ran along a different path from the one her father plotted for her, and she looked forward to seeing his face when he realised it irrevocably.

She caught the Gael's arm. 'Why does my father want to see the sort of woman I have become? He has another child, a son.'

His eyes blazed and he pulled away from her as if her touch burnt him. 'His son has died. A snake bite. None could save him. Kolbeinn's wife claimed it was your mother's curse. After your half-brother was born, all her other children were either stillborn or died shortly after birth.'

'Was my brother a robust child?'

'It doesn't matter if he was. He is no longer alive.'

Her half-brother, the boy she had never met. The one whose existence had changed hers irrevocably. And now his death was about to change it again, if she allowed it. Her father wanted to secure his legacy. He would certainly have a warrior in mind for her to marry.

She glanced at the Gael and rejected the idea. After what had happened, her father would never risk his chosen bridegroom on retrieving her. This Gael was simply the messenger, the one whose throat she had been supposed to slit. She'd acted like his unwitting executioner.

'I won't pretend sorrow.' Dagmar lifted her chin up. 'I never knew him. I'm sorry that my father is upset. Tell him that. Tell him that I've become a fine and honourable warrior, but I am required elsewhere.'

He inclined his head. 'You will have the opportunity to tell him that yourself when we reach his hall.'

'I won't be seeing him. You may take me back, but it'll be my stepmother who deals with me. I know who runs that household. Similar sorts of messages have arrived in the past. They were all designed to lure me and my mother into a false sense of security before they attempted to end my life. The messengers all came from my stepmother, rather than my father. Old Alf knew, but how he knew, I couldn't say.'

Dagmar swallowed hard, remembering how her mother had dispatched one of the messengers and sent the head back—the one who demanded Dagmar make a marriage alliance with a man old enough to be her grandfather, but who had also concealed a knife in his boot.

Her mother had believed that Dagmar should be able to follow her destiny of being a great warrior, rather than being trapped into any sort of marriage.

'I carried your father's sword, a parting gift from your father's current mistress. Old Alf understood its intended meaning.' A dimple flashed his cheek. 'He said that he was the only one left who remembered the signal your father had agreed with him.'

'And how would his mistress know such a thing?'

'Who knows? She is an older woman.' The Gael shrugged. 'I didn't realise its import myself until I met Old Alf.'

Dagmar clenched her fists. Just when she was starting to feel charitable towards the Gael, he said something so arrogant and short-sighted that it took her breath away. 'What is it about that particular sword? What is its meaning?'

The tone she used would have her men running for cover, but the Gael dusted an imaginary speck from his cloak as he shook his head as if her antics had no more significance than Mor chasing her tail round and round.

'Kolbeinn's wife has died. She lost the will to live when her son died and faded away. I believe the sword signifies that you are no longer in danger.'

Dagmar's jaw dropped and she staggered back a step, only avoiding falling into a puddle because the Gael's hand shot out and hauled her back. She shook him off. 'Dead? My stepmother has perished?'

'You could see her funeral pyre blazing away across the seas.'

Her stepmother and her son were both dead. The words hammered against her brain. The witch who had featured in her nightmares, the woman who had vowed that she would ensure that Dagmar would not take anything from her children was dead. She no longer had to fear the killers in the night.

'Forgive me. My head pains me.' She sank down heavily on a rock and stared at the vast marsh which stretched out in front of her. A faint mist rose off the many pools of water. 'I can't pretend anything but joy at the news. She wanted me dead. For the past ten years, I've expected an assassin, not a saviour.'

'Your father wants you alive and with him. Now. I can't answer for the past.' He put his hand on her shoulder. To prevent her from running away or to give comfort? Dagmar found that she didn't care. She drew comfort from it. The last person to touch her like that had been her mother before she'd faced her first battle. 'Will you come quietly now? Meet him with an open mind?'

'Does he know about my mother's death?' she asked, standing up and moving away from him and the dangerous comfort he offered.

'He made no mention of it. Kolbeinn kept certain information close to his chest.'

'Why would he do that?'

'He has his reasons. Mayhap he wanted rid of a thorn in his side and I was foolish enough to take him up on the offer. I arrogantly considered I could win the wager without too much trouble.'

'Wagering with my father is unwise.'

Dagmar tapped a finger against her mouth. She could see her father's reasoning for the wager. He won either way—if she eliminated Aedan mac Connall, he got rid of someone troublesome, but if Aedan returned with her, he gained control of his daughter and his legacy, but it still added up to the end of her dream of independence. He would not understand her desire to stay a shield maiden. He would marry her off to his chosen warrior and increase his own power and prestige. She simply had to figure out a way to get what she desired.

A sudden suspicion made her miss her step. Mor instantly stopped and looked back at her, giving a low woof. The Gael instantly stopped. 'Why did he choose you, a Gael, and not one of his men? What reason did he give you?'

His eyes grew shadowed. 'I failed to enquire closely enough it would seem. I was simply grateful of the opportunity.'

'Why?' She pressed her hands against her eyes. 'Surely you have to know the fate of the other messengers. Why risk your life for the promise of gold? You had best tell me all the terms. My father can be trickier than Loki.'

He gave a half-smile. 'The fate of those other men was hidden from me. We wagered about a debt I owe him. I fulfil the wager and the debt is forgiven. Additionally I get an amount in gold equal to what I owe him if I return with you in the allotted time. He has kept hostages to ensure that I do as he commands. Time marches ever closer to All Hallows.'

Dagmar winced. All Hallows was in a little over a week. She could begin to understand now why this Gael was willing to brave the marshes. 'What happens if you return with me outside the time?'

'I lose and become his personal slave and everything I own will belong to him.'

'How came you to owe him the debt?'

'It was my brother's doing. I inherited it when he died.'

'And you pay your debts.'

'Being beholden to anyone causes difficulties particularly when they appear with longships, ready to raid.' His face became grimly set. Dagmar silently cursed her father. Typical of the man. He used others to enforce his will. 'I will not allow Mhairi or her brothers to remain enslaved.'

'Who is this Mhairi?'

'A woman I know.'

'Your wife?'

'I'm unmarried, but she volunteered to be a hostage rather than allowing Kolbeinn to make his choice from the women. Her brothers went along to protect her honour. You must admire her courage.'

Dagmar nodded. This Mhairi had sacrificed herself for the Gael with the broad shoulders and the eyes to drown in, even if he refused to admit it. 'I'd have done that for my mother. This woman has feelings for you.'

He gave a harsh laugh. 'Mhairi did it for her people,

for Kintra, our home, and not for me. She has a deep abiding love for the place and wishes to keep it free from the north. It is what she proclaimed in front of everyone and I've no reason to doubt her.'

She nodded again, seeing the sense of it but also knowing there was something that the Gael kept back. Once she had found that out, she'd use it. Right now, without a weapon to defend herself and an army searching for her, she required a protector. One man and his dog. The odds were less than brilliant, but she needed someone on her side and that someone had to be the Gael Aedan mac Connall.

'My father wants me alive?' she asked, hardly daring to believe it after so many years. It was only down to her stepmother's death, but it was more than she had expected. She silently vowed that she would make him see that she would lead the life she had chosen, rather than following whichever path he had chosen.

'Yes, he does. Very much so. Remember he arranged that sword signal with your friend to keep you safe.'

'Good to know.' Dagmar held out her hand. 'I accept your protection. We travel together once the marshes finish. I will not allow others to be enslaved while I go free.'

He put his fingers about hers—sure and strong. She felt safe as if someone had thrown a warm blanket over her. Dagmar rapidly withdrew her hand.

'How fares your head?' he asked. 'It must hurt like the devil.'

'It aches as though someone hit me with a very hard object, but I can keep going. I learned a long time ago that the world does not wait for my aches. There are far more important considerations than my discomfort.'

The Gael...no...Aedan mac Connall grunted. It would be easy to start liking him. 'Good.'

'We have miles to go before we can sleep,' she said quickly before she made a fool of herself and confessed how hard trudging through this ghost land was for her. She had to trust this Gael and his dog would find a way out and trust came hard for her as well.

Aedan glanced back at Dagmar. Her face was pale and intense. Against all expectation, she had trudged through the marsh with barely a murmur. She was far tougher than any other woman he'd ever encountered, and he included Mhairi and his former sister-in-law, Liddy, in that group.

Liddy possessed a different sort of courage, one which he had not fully appreciated until after his brother fell in battle as he single-handedly charged the enemy line and the truth about the boating accident where his niece and nephew were drowned had been revealed. And he'd never thought much of Mhairi until she'd volunteered to be a hostage. But she had done so without shedding a tear or hesitation, declaring that her faith would keep her safe until he had completed his quest. To his eternal regret, he hadn't appreciated the depth of her feeling for Kintra until that moment.

'We will stop at the hut. I passed it when I travelled to the east. We still have a long way to go.'

She shaded her eyes and squinted. 'Are you sure it is there?'

'I can make out the outlines. We can stop and beg some food.'

'Steal it, you mean.'

Aedan shook his head in mock despair. 'Typical Northern response.'

'You were the one who stole the horse.'

'That was different.'

She gave a pointed cough. 'Different how?'

'There wasn't time to seek the owner and ask permission,' Aedan said between gritted teeth. This infuriating woman had a way of twisting things and getting under his skin.

She gave a brilliant smile which transformed her features. His breath caught in his throat. There was something about the hazy light, the damp cloud of golden curls and her smile which did strange things to his insides. His body, which had seemed encased in ice since his former fiancée Brigid's betrayal, was starting to thaw rapidly. 'I am very glad you did.'

A strand of her hair touched his fingers. He cleared his throat. 'The hut. It is where we stop tonight.'

'I'll race you.'

'Mind the oozing mud.'

He caught her arm and prevented her from slipping and falling. A jolt of awareness coursed through him. He released her abruptly.

'Having come this far, I've no wish to lose you to a sink hole.'

She put her hand over where he had held her. Her eyes grew wide. 'I didn't see it. I guess I need a protector in more ways than one.'

'Next time look before you race off.'

Her laugh rang out over the marshes. 'Now you sound like my old nurse. She used to be always hauling me back from one thing or another.'

'It has been a long day.' A long day was reason

enough for his unexpected reaction to her. Kolbeinn wanted his daughter back. More than likely to marry her off and secure his legacy. He would want his daughter untouched. Aedan gritted his teeth. There would be more repercussions for his people if he gave in to this attraction for her and he had already caused them enough sorrow. He had to focus on the important things. Mhairi had sacrificed herself without hesitation or expectation. He should be thinking about her and making her his wife, instead of desiring this infuriating witch of a woman. But Mhairi had never sent his blood racing like this shield maiden did.

'You have done well.'

'High praise indeed,' she said drily.

Dagmar's stomach gave a loud rumble when they reached the hut, reminding her that it had been some time since she had last eaten. Dead grasses and leaves were blown against the door and the roof exhibited a gaping hole. Closer inspection revealed that the far wall had tumbled down.

'Shelter for the night,' Aedan said. 'Better than sleeping completely out in the open with the rain and midges for company.'

She hated that her dismay must have shown on her face and that he was being kind. Aedan mac Connall was a far easier proposition to hate when he was being officious. 'It makes it easier that no one is here. No awkward questions. No half-truths to remember.'

'Sit with Mor by the hut. I will fetch supper.'

'Oh, you can magic it up out of thin air, can you?'

'I'm a man of many talents.' He gave a bow and set off.

Mor flopped down at Dagmar's feet. When Dagmar made a move to go into the hut, she gave a low growl and shook her head.

'Shall we be friends? I could use a friend.' Dagmar held out her hand again. 'Without you, I'd have been lost.'

The dog gave a cautious sniff before settling her head on her paws.

'Your master is right,' Dagmar said, leaning back against the wall and allowing the pale sun which cautiously peeped through the mist to warm her face. She had forgotten what it was like simply to sit. Ever since her mother had died, she had not had a moment to spare. 'Going through the marshes saves us time. Olafr will suspect that we are making for my father's, though. The question is—does he realise that I am my father's sole heir now? Had my mother confided in him about the sword signal? Could it be something he hid from me? Thinking that I'd marry him? He certainly seemed perturbed by your master's appearance.'

Mor exhaled a loud breath of air which Dagmar took for a 'yes, you idiotic human' noise.

She had made the mistake of underestimating Olafr before. She could not afford to make that mistake again. Olafr remained her most potent enemy now that her stepmother was dead.

There was a possibility that Olafr would show up on Colbhasa and spin a convincing tale, something her father would believe and put her in danger, but that was a problem for the future.

Reaching her father was her best hope of long-term survival. Once there, she could make him see that she was equal to any of his warriors, that she could fight for his *felag*. Marriage to some unknown warrior with more muscles than brains was not inevitable. She could demonstrate to her father that her mother had kept her promise and had ensured her child could compete with the best warriors. Then she could wreak revenge on Olafr. And after that was done, she'd find the peace she'd sought. Some day she would sit with the sun warming her face and nothing more pressing to worry about than harvesting the crops.

'You needn't fear, you know. I'll go to Colbhasa, but I'll find a way to make the sort of life I want.'

'Talking to yourself or the dog?' Aedan reappeared carrying several trout.

Her stomach rumbled. She hated to think how long it had been since she'd had a proper meal.

'That was fast.'

'It is easy when you know how to fish. A line and hook is all I require. Simple.'

'A man of many hidden talents.'

'An old family secret.' He turned his back and busied himself with the fire.

'Have you passed it on to your children?'

'I don't have children.' The tone of his voice had become chipped from ice.

Dagmar frowned. Aedan definitely didn't like talking about himself. She should leave it, but it was like a sore that she could not stop prodding. 'Am I keeping you from your bride? Your intended? Is that who Mhairi truly is? It would be like my father to do that as he likes to get his own way.'

'No. There is no bride. Mhairi lives on Kintra. It surprised me that she even volunteered to be a hostage. I'd not have thought she had it in her, but she obviously did. I'd never considered her as wife material.'

'Why not?'

Aedan concentrated on building the fire. Why not?

It was a question his people and his priest kept asking. His excuses were wearing thin—first Brigid, his betrothed, the woman he'd loved as a young man, had died, ostensibly while she visited relations. To the world he had grieved, but he and his brother had been the only ones to understand the full extent of her betrayal. Then there was no hurry because his brother had married and had two children. And that marriage had proved little better than his parents'.

Then there was the mess his brother had left behind after he perished in battle which had had to be sorted, but lately the murmurings had grown, particularly his need to provide an heir. Without an heir, Kintra would go to his distant cousin and many doubted if Sean would manage to hold out against the Northmen in the same way as Aedan had, but Aedan wanted something more than a duty-bound marriage doomed to failure.

'I've my reasons,' he said as he felt Dagmar's eyes boring into him. 'Are you married? Before the battle, I had wondered about Olafr and you. He has the sort of looks women usually find irresistible. My brother was the same with women forever buzzing about him.'

'I'd have sooner married a viper than him.' Dagmar's brows lowered and her mouth became a thin white line. She used a pointed stick to draw a line in the dirt. 'Olafr was my mother's lover, not mine. Old Alf told me that I should have banished him after he asked for my hand in marriage before the ashes on my mother's pyre had even gone cold. But I thought he could be useful with his ability to charm Constantine's court. What a fool I was!'

Deep within him, something rejoiced. Aedan suppressed it. Who she married was none of his business. His business was getting her back to her father so the hostages would be released and his people could prosper. Dagmar was forbidden to him. Aedan inclined his head. 'I beg your pardon. He simply made it seem as though you two were as one.'

'Apology accepted. Olafr could charm the birds out of the trees. The ladies certainly twittered about him. He was better at dealing with Constantine and his advisors. I can be too abrupt at times. I dislike fools and see little reason to hide my thoughts.'

'I hadn't noticed.'

Her answering laugh rang out, before her face became full of serious intent. 'My father must accept that I will follow my own chosen path and have no intention of marrying to please him or anyone else.'

'Indeed.' Aedan hid his smile. There was little point in explaining that her father would be seeking a son-in-law to rule his lands and command his ships. Dagmar would have little choice but to obey. He would be interested to hear of the clash between father and daughter when it occurred, but please God, make it after he returned to Kintra.

She leant forward. 'Being a warrior is what my mother trained me for. She believed a woman could and should be a man's equal. She distrusted marriage and considered that it sapped a woman's strength.'

'Did she train you well?'

'Warfare has been my way of life ever since we left my father's compound in the north country. I inherited my mother's *felag* because she considered me a worthy successor, not because I was her daughter. I've an eye for strategy and forward planning. Why should a woman be treated differently than a man?'

'My former sister-in-law would agree with you.'

'Former?'

'My late brother's wife. She is now married to a Northman—Sigurd Sigmundson.'

'Sigurd Sigmundson shot an arrow that killed his mother.'

'You've heard of him.'

'I thought it right and proper—they'd put her alive on the fire after her master died. Being raped and burnt alive is a barbaric practice whatever a soothsayer says. Soothsayers can be bribed.'

'You know the story?'

'I've encountered him. We fought together in Ireland a few seasons ago, right before my mother pledged her *felag* to Constantine's service. He chose to ally with Ketil.' She gave a small laugh. 'I'd quite forgotten about him. Perchance...'

'Sigurd will do nothing to jeopardise his relationship with Kolbeinn. We may have our differences, but I believe he prefers me to be the laird at Kintra. I'm a known quantity.'

Dagmar stared at the small fire, watching the sparks fly up. 'I've given you my word that I will see my father. I will, but if he forces me to do anything I disapprove of, I shall become a sell-sword. Sigurd prospered that way. I can as well.'

Dagmar as a sell-sword. He doubted Kolbeinn would agree to that. Or allow her out of his sight. She would be married off to one of his most trusted warriors as soon as it could be arranged. Kolbeinn wanted to secure his legacy. Her desires would count for nothing.

Kolbeinn would triumph one way or another. But her future was not his problem or concern as his mother would have said.

'A hard way to survive,' he said mildly. He'd allow Kolbeinn to break the news to her and deal with his daughter's fiery temper. Aedan had a kingdom to save.

'My mother did it.'

'Your mother must have been an exceptional woman.'

Her eyes lit with undisguised pleasure and her entire being sparkled. 'She was. One of the bravest people I ever met. If I can be one-tenth the warrior she was, I will die happy. She had terrible taste in men. Olafr was a mistake from start to finish. And my father. I have to wonder where her brain was then.'

'Wait until you see what your father offers you.'

'Or who.' She stifled a yawn. 'I know what my father will want of me, Aedan. He'll have handpicked a blockhead of a warrior for me, one he didn't want to risk on this journey. But I'll find a way to teach my father a lesson and then we negotiate.' Her eyes narrowed. 'Did my father—'

'I have no idea of Kolbeinn's intentions, but it won't be me.' Aedan watched the sparks circling in the sky. 'Kolbeinn wants me destroyed. He expected you to kill me, remember? Throat slit by an unknowing executioner.'

'You had the sword.'

'Only because his mistress ran down to the water and tossed it to me as I was shoving the boat off.'

She gave a soft laugh, one which sent pleasurable shivers down his spine. 'I suspect he reckoned any bridegroom will be far less eager after they encounter me and it was best accomplished where he had control over the situation.'

He inclined his head and kept his expression neutral. The firelight had highlighted the planes of her face. 'Whatever you are planning, do it after I leave with my people. Your father's temper is uncertain at the best of times.'

'I know my father's temper.' The bleakness in her voice surprised him.

'Do you fear him?'

She tilted her head to one side. 'Surprisingly, no, now that my stepmother is dead. He was good to me when I was little. I used to wait by the jetty for him when he returned. Once he brought me a wooden horse. Another time, a bow and arrow. When he came back the final time it was for my tenth name day. He had promised me a beautiful blue gown to match my eyes, but he brought my stepmother instead. She was supposed to teach me to be a fine lady as that was why I had desired the gown. So, her arrival was all my fault.'

'There will be more to it than a little girl desiring a pretty dress. You said that your mother told you that her marriage had sapped her strength. Perhaps they were both deeply unhappy.'

She stifled a large yawn. Her eyes blinked shut and her chin dropped. When she looked like that, he had a hard time believing this woman could lift a sword, let alone lead an army. Without her blue whorls and plaits in her hair, she seemed vulnerable. He, however, knew that it was a mere illusion. Suddenly she sat bolt upright. 'My childhood! I try never to speak of my childhood. It doesn't do any good to remember. We won't speak of it again. Promise.'

He leant over and took the remains of her meal from her. Their fingers brushed, sending an unexpected charge up his arm.

He silently sighed. Why her? Why not one of the women who had been touted as his bride after his brother died? Why not one of the Northwomen who lived with Sigurd Sigmundson and his wife? Why not Mhairi who had offered her freedom for his people?

Starting anything with Dagmar would be a bad idea. It was troubling that the thought of facing her father had failed to dampen his body's response to the inadvertent touch.

'Get some sleep. No protests. You will give in gracefully, instead of being contrary and protesting.'

She laughed her tinkling brook laugh and he found that he had been waiting for it. He watched her mouth and wondered what it would taste like. He quickly concentrated on the fire.

'I'll give in only because you ask so politely. Besides, I can't risk you leaving me alone in the marsh.' She wiped her fingers on her trousers. 'Where should I sleep?'

'In the hut. The roof will give at least some shelter from the rain.'

'Where will you sleep?'

'Not in the rain.'

'We can share the hut without a problem. I trust you are not a noisy sleeper.'

'You've no weapons to stop me snoring.'

Her smile lit up her eyes. With any other woman, he'd have taken it as an invitation to flirtation, but with Dagmar, he knew it was because she enjoyed a challenge. 'I find a quick sharp kick to the shins with my boots works wonders.'

'I'll bear that in mind and take the first watch.'

'Wake me when you tire and I'll take over the watch. I rarely sleep long.'

She went into the hut with her backside slightly swaying. Her trousers revealed her curves far more neatly than a gown ever could. He wondered why he had ever considered trousers mannish. On Dagmar with her hair falling softly about her shoulders, they were positively indecent.

He rapidly tried to conjure Mhairi's face, but the image singularly failed.

Chapter Four

Aedan stamped out the remains of the dying fire as the yellow harvest moon rose. The faint drizzle had stopped and the sky had cleared. A touch of frost on the grass in the morning was a real possibility. The grain would be being brought into the storehouses at Kintra now.

He gave one last look about the clearing where the hut was situated. All was at peace. Given the blackness of the night, none would risk the marshes now. They were safe here. The ashes of a burnt-out fire were from some fellow traveller days before and the hut had been abandoned long ago.

A great weariness settled over his bones. He hated to think how long he'd been awake, risking no more than a doze as he'd waited for Dagmar to come around after the battle. Several times he'd checked her breathing, fearful that he might have hit her too hard.

A small plea for help made his blood freeze. It came again. Aedan drew his sword and looked about him, trying to figure out where the noise was coming from. Mor merely opened one eye and nudged her head towards the hut. He peeped in.

In her sleep, Dagmar was crying for her mother to stop, that she couldn't go further, that she couldn't take another step, that she didn't want to be abandoned in the forest, that she hadn't meant for everything to be lost. Her body thrashed about on the hut's earthen floor.

Aedan put his hand on Dagmar's shoulder and shook her slightly. 'Hush now. You're safe. You're no longer a little girl. You're a capable woman. No one is going to leave you behind.'

Her screams increased. Mor lifted her head from her paws and gave him a look which said that he needed to solve this quickly or none of them would get any sleep.

He stretched out beside her, put his arm across her and stroked her hair. Her hair was like silk against his fingers. The invincible warrior was a shield which hid this frightened woman. He hated to think what she must have faced as a young girl. 'It'll be fine, Dagmar,' he said. 'You're safe. I'll protect you. You've done enough.'

She gave an indistinct murmur and snuggled closer, laid her head against his chest and pinned him down. Every time he attempted to move, she followed.

Keeping one arm about her, he took off his cloak and spread it over them both. She instantly smiled in her sleep. The hut descended into a peaceful silence. Mor gave a soft woof of approval and settled her head back on her paws.

'We shall both have to sleep here then. Mor has decreed it necessary and you know how I hate to go against my dog.'

Her old dream returned, the one which had plagued her since her tenth name day. In it, she became separated from her mother and had to continue alone in the dark wood where the owls hooted and the bats swooped as they raced to reach the edge of her father's lands before daybreak. Even Old Alf had disappeared, despite her calling. She screamed, knowing what was to come next and being unable to prevent it—a big berserker looming out of the darkness with murder in his eyes and her mother weakened from the fight, struggling to hold him off. Then suddenly, unexpectedly a heavy weight went over her and the dream changed. A warrior appeared to protect her, but a light shone, hiding his face. The berserker vanished and she knew all would be well.

Dagmar woke to realise that her ear rested on Aedan's chest. The comforting sound of his steady heartbeat echoed the sound of the brook from her dream. Her hand had twisted about his tunic as if she was afraid to let him go. Was this the warrior of her dream? She knew that if she turned her head slightly, her lips would encounter his bare flesh. Her mouth tingled in anticipation of the possibility.

She stopped breathing and eased her fingers away. She had difficulty remembering if she had lain next to him or had moved there in the night. It counted for nothing. What mattered was getting away from his encircling arms before he woke. The last thing she needed was developing an attraction for this man. She knew how such things ended.

When she was fourteen, she'd thought one of the warriors might be sweet on her. He had a pretty face and legs which went on for ever, but his swordsmanship lacked precision. However, she still liked to watch him move. Arriving early and hoping to catch him alone, she'd overheard him boasting to his friends that he would soon get that pig-ugly creature Dagmar in his bed and the rest could pay him the gold they owed him for doing it. Then he'd find a pretty girl to warm his bed and banish the memory.

Later that day, she demolished him on the training ground, giving no mercy and leaving him with blood on his pretty face. Then one by one she had defeated his friends in combat. The sniggering and the wagering had stopped and they simply praised her skill with weapons. But she never forgot the lesson—her overly long nose, sharp chin and strong jaw repulsed men rather than attracted them.

She started to ease her way to safer ground, but his arms tightened about her, pulling her closer.

'Imagine finding you here. Curled up like this.'

His breath tickled her ear, doing strange things to her insides. She suddenly discovered that the last thing she wanted to do was escape.

'Morning,' she said, tucking her chin into her neck and inwardly winced. Her voice was far too breathless. She had wanted deceptively casual as if she woke up in a man's arms all the time, rather than this being the first time. She wriggled slightly, but only succeeded in pressing her body closer to his. She put a hand against his chest. 'You should've woken me. I'd have taken the second watch so you could sleep.'

'You had bad dreams last night and were beyond waking. Sounds echo over the marsh. I'd no wish to alert anyone who might be searching for us.'

She gave an involuntary shudder, hating that he was right. She should have considered the potential for the dream returning and found a way to remain alert. 'Some nights are worse than others. I regret disturbing you. Next time, shake me harder.'

'I tried to wake you, but you called out even louder. Cradling you in my arms was the only thing which quietened you. Mor needs her beauty sleep if she is to find our way out of the marshes.'

'I must've been exhausted.' She put her elbow against his chest and pushed. His arms immediately fell away. 'I'm rested now. I do apologise.'

'Don't, it isn't often I get to sleep with a beautiful woman in my arms.'

'I'm far from beautiful. My nose is too long, my ears stick out at odd angles and my mouth is far too big. Ask anyone.'

He gave a crooked smile. 'I'm the one who can see your face in the morning dawn. I am the one who makes the judgement about your beauty, not you.'

Every particle of her was aware of him. A great ache filled her insides. Aedan is this mood was dangerous in a way that he hadn't been before. She forced a laugh. 'You walked into an army with just a dog for protection. Your judgement is suspect.'

'But it remains mine.' He gave a soft laugh which made her insides melt. 'Mor is more than simply a dog. She is a wolfhound of renowned parentage.'

Her mouth ached, longing to feel his against it. There was a piece of her which wanted to believe his words about her beauty and that frightened her. 'We need to get going.'

Mor gave a low growl and the hairs stood up on the back of the dog's neck. Aedan's body instantly tensed.

'Get under the cloak and keep very still if you value your life.'

'Why?' She hated that her voice sounded as though she had been running. She cleared her throat. 'What's going on?'

'Mor always does that when she catches the scent of unknown people. I might be able to get us out of this peacefully.'

'I've no fear of men as long as my sword arm has strength.'

'Please. I'm keeping you in reserve if it comes to a fight, but they may be searching for a couple.'

The request tugged at her heart. He was asking rather than telling her. She gave a small nod and curled herself into a small ball and pulled the cloak firmly over her. 'Very well. If they overwhelm you, call out my name.'

'Your name might produce unexpected results.' His voice shook with barely suppressed laughter.

'You know what I mean,' she retorted through gritted teeth. 'I will come to your aid.'

'I wish to avoid blood, rather than starting a war. No point in antagonising people until you know the odds. It sounds like a crowd. They may be looking for a stray sheep or cow.'

'I will wait quietly, I promise.'

'I'm counting on it.' Was it her imagination or did his hand brush her hair as he adjusted the cloak about her? Her hand curled about the short dagger, hidden within its depths that had not been there a breath before. A mistake or deliberate? She burrowed deeper into the cloak, but kept a peephole.

A group of three men and a boy burst into the hut, talking in loud voices. Their clothes were reasonably well kept but there was a hardness about the eyes that she distrusted. The heavy-set one carried a large satchel.

Too lightly armed for warriors, but neither were they simple farmers. They moved with unexpected familiarity about the hut.

All conversation died when they caught sight of Aedan standing in the centre of the hut. They exchanged glances before the lead man gave an evil leer. Dagmar's stomach tensed as it always did before battle.

She curled her fingers tighter about the knife, getting ready to throw it when Aedan called for assistance. He'd seen her safely through the marshes thus far, so she'd wait rather than following her instincts. But if he faltered, she reserved the right to take steps of her own.

Aedan tightened his grip on his sword while motioning for Mor to stay down. Against expectation, Dagmar had obeyed his instructions and kept hidden.

'Gentlemen. What brings you here on this fair morning? Chasing sheep?'

'We are searching for a missing horse,' the tallest one said, putting a restraining arm on one of the men and giving a falsely jovial smile. 'One with a white blaze on its forehead. Went missing in the night.'

Aedan released a breath. They were not searching for Dagmar, but they remained a potential threat. An air of desperation hung like a bad smell about them. He massaged the back of his neck and willed his muscles to relax. He watched, and waited, rather than seeking trouble.

'No horse here. Just my woman and me, sheltering from last night's storm.' He smiled. 'The sun has risen. We will be on our way and leave you in peace.'

The tall man scratched his scar. 'Most give this place a wide berth. Only a few know their way through the marshes.'

'Obviously I am one of the few,' Aedan said mildly, trying to work out who precisely these men were and what their true purpose was—they did not have northern accents, more the lilt of a Pict. These men could be what they said they were—labourers in search of a horse, rather than thieves returning to their lair, but... he hoped Dagmar had discovered the dagger that he had hidden in the folds of his cloak when he'd adjusted it over her. Given the numbers, he would welcome help if it came to it.

Their leader eyed him suspiciously. 'Full of yourself, aren't you?'

'I merely state the obvious. I'm here and alive. Therefore, I know the way.'

The man drew his upper lip over his teeth. 'How long have you been here? Just the night? Where is your woman?'

'We need to move on. My woman's father requires her.' He gave them a hard look. 'Give my woman a moment to compose herself and then we will go, leaving this place in peace.'

He held out his hands to show that he meant no harm.

The man did not move. 'And you have come from where?'

'From the east. There looked to be a battle brewing. Great armies on the move. It is why we braved the marshes.'

'And found your way from the east. Just like that.'

Aedan shrugged. 'Why would I lie?'

The spokesman glanced at his companions. One gave an almost imperceptible nod and moved at lightning speed. He drew his sword and placed it against Aedan's neck while the other one pounced on the cloak, grabbed

Dagmar's arm and hauled her up against him and held her with a dagger against her throat. Aedan gave a low curse under his breath to be caught by such a basic trick.

'It is my regret that on a sunny morning like this, we must take your valuables and enjoy your woman before we kill you because you are lying through your back teeth. A way through the marshes indeed.'

'You might want to put that away and release my woman before anyone gets hurt. She objects to being manhandled. Go before it gets worse for you.'

'Why? Give me one good reason.' The man pressed the dagger harder against Dagmar's neck.

'My dog does not take kindly to my woman enduring a stranger's touch. Release her before my dog rips out your throat. She has quite a taste for man flesh when provoked.' Aedan made a small motion towards where Mor lurked in the shadows. Her loud growl echoed through the hut.

As Mor's growl increased, Dagmar shoved an elbow into her captor's gut while she grabbed his arm and pulled downwards.

Forget about letting Aedan handle it in a peaceful manner. Time these men learned that women were not to be used in that fashion.

Her captor's brief catch of breath gave her a chance to spin away from the dagger and wrench the man's arm from its socket. He gave an agonising scream and released the knife. Dagmar kicked it away and crouched low as she assessed the scene.

Unfortunately, the leader had had the presence of mind to keep his sword against Aedan's neck. Dagmar silently cursed.

'First man who tries anything with me will be wearing a new sort of smile and singing much higher when I am finished,' Dagmar said. 'Release my man and maybe you will live. Otherwise, you will die.'

'A wee lass like you? What can you do?' One of the men laughed. He signalled to someone outside and Dagmar knew that there were more than these pieces of scum.

'I just broke his arm. Be thankful I did not kill him.'

'Be a good woman and shut your mouth. We will attend to you later. Your man needs to be taught his manners. You don't stay in people's huts without first asking permission.'

A distinct chill went down her back. Not just thieves, but rapists and murderers. Men who took without asking. They deserved what was coming to them. 'Do you actively desire death?'

He wiped his hand across his face. 'By God, I like them feisty. Makes the surrender much more enjoyable.'

'Don't do anything rash!' Aedan shouted to her.

She gave a brief nod to show she understood the implied command and contented herself with tossing the knife back and forth between her hands while she waited for Aedan's signal. There was no telling how many others might be outside. They had to work as a pair.

'I asked you politely to let us go. You have abused me and my woman.' Aedan stood with a slightly bored expression on his face. 'Even now I will give you a chance. Go, leaving my sword, and live, or face the consequences.'

'You bargaining? With us? With a sword against your neck? Don't you know who we are?' the first of the gang said.

'Return my sword and we shall forget all about this. We are unlikely to be passing this way again. We can part in peace.'

Dagmar silently vowed that she would return and clear out this nest of murderers and thieves, once she had dealt with her father.

'A pretty tale you weave,' the man ground out. 'But I must decline your offer. I hold all the advantage here.'

'Pity.' Aedan clicked his fingers.

With a snarl Mor leapt. Her mouth closed about the leader's wrist, causing him to drop the sword. Aedan caught it before it fell to the ground and thrusted it upwards. 'Dagmar, do your worst!'

At Aedan's movement, Dagmar rushed forward, giving her battle roar. The men started to run, but Dagmar caught the leader.

'I despise men who threaten women,' she said, plunging the knife between his ribs. The man fell with a surprised expression on his face. She pivoted and caught the man who held her captive. 'That goes double for you.'

That man, too, fell.

The boy fled, abandoning the sack.

Mor chased them out the door and they saw the others running, too, but at Aedan's low whistle, she returned and flopped down at his feet.

'We won!' Dagmar called out. Giving into an impulse she threw her arms about Aedan. 'We beat them. They are on the run!'

He lifted her up, so that her feet did not touch the ground. Then he swung her round and round like her father had done when she was a little girl.

'That we did.' His mouth was only a breath away. Up close, she could see the vividness of his eyes. Her lips tingled. He was going to kiss her. She wanted him to, desperately.

Instead she stepped away from him, crossed her arms over her suddenly aching breasts and forced a scowl.

'You are a good warrior, Gael. Your timing is impeccable,' she said, awkwardly holding out her hand. 'I'm honoured to be part of your *felag*.'

His laugh rang out over the marshes. 'You're not so bad yourself, Shield Maiden. Your moves were a joy to watch.'

He took her hand and enclosed it in his warm embrace. She drew away sharply as a heated pulse travelled up her arm.

'I begin to see why you and Mor are such a formidable team.' Dagmar quickly cleaned the dagger and stuck it in her belt before he had a chance to ask for it to be returned. She crossed to where she'd kicked the dagger belonging to one of the men she'd killed and put that next to the first knife.

The simple action helped restore her equilibrium. She had fought in battles, but she had never wanted to kiss a man before. Not in that deep-down spine-tingling way as though there could be something more for her than endless campaigns to be fought.

He continued to watch her with speculative eyes. 'Mor is the best dog I have had.'

At the sound of her name, Mor trotted back and lolled against Aedan, breaking the tension that had sprung up between them. His long fingers fondled the dog's ears as she stuck her nose into his palm.

Mor then trotted over to Dagmar, rising up to put her paws on her shoulders and proceeded to give her a big lick on the side of her face. Mor's tongue was rough against her cheek. Dagmar gave a little laugh. She'd missed having a dog. After her dog died from poisoning, her mother had declared that no space existed for one on a campaign as they could never contribute to the fellowship. Her mother had been wrong about that as well as Olafr. Dagmar bit her lip. How many other things had her mother been wrong about?

'Mor has decided you belong, Shield Maiden. You are now officially part of this fellowship, this *felag* as you call it.'

Dagmar blinked hard. Aedan said that she belonged. It felt good to belong and not to be fighting for her place and trying to keep her mother's band from disintegrating, something she had done ever since her mother had died. At times the feelings of loneliness had threatened to overwhelm her. When they arrived at her father's, this *felag* would end and she'd be alone again. But for right now, she was part of something. It was an improvement from yesterday.

Dagmar made a careful bow. 'I'm delighted to play my part for as long as the fellowship lasts.'

He appeared about to say something else, but simply regarded her with his deep blue-green eyes. Her mouth started aching again. She wiped her hand across it and willed the feeling to go.

'We should see if they have left anything of value behind,' she said to fill the awkward silence that had sprung up. 'Anything we can use on our journey.'

'Excellent thinking.' Aedan went quickly through the pack the boy had abandoned in his haste to leave. 'Some food, a few gold coins, a necklace and a woman's gown, far finer than I would have expected. That is fortunate.'

He held out a gown of dark-blue wool. She hated to

think of what must have happened to that unknown woman. Hopefully what had just transpired in the hut provided some justice for her.

The fabric held a slight shimmer and rippled in his hands. It was the sort of gown that Dagmar had seen the fine Pict ladies wear at Constantine's court, rather than a peasant's dress. She'd occasionally envied them their beauty and grace, but not enough to ever wish to wear one of their gowns or pluck her eyebrows as they had done or wear their elaborate headgear. 'A lady's gown. You want to take it?'

'Then you are agreed we take the items.'

'The gold, jewels and food, yes.' Dagmar wrinkled her nose. 'I doubt we will need a gown.'

A dimple fluttered at the corner of his mouth. 'Might come in useful when you meet your father. The ladies of his court are always finely decked out.'

Dagmar pursed her lips. There was no point in telling him that she would greet her father naked rather than wear a gown. Her father was going to have to understand that she came as a shield maiden, rather than a peace-weaver, and her attire was the best way to do it.

Her mother had always striven to make her point visually. Her face might not be painted any longer or her hair elaborately plaited, but she would wear these clothes, her clothes, the clothes which proclaimed to the world that she was a shield maiden who only ever considered the arts of war.

'My father shall see me as I am. I will never wear a gown in front of him. Leave it here. The mice can use it for their nests.'

Aedan calmly folded the gown and stuffed it into his

pack. 'I will keep the gown if only to keep it out of the gang's grubby paws.'

'I hope it fits you then,' Dagmar muttered.

His eyes flared and she knew the barb had struck home. She winced. Aedan was the one person she didn't want to risk offending. Her and her quick tongue. At this rate, their fellowship would be over before it had begun.

'We shall see who wears it when the time comes.' He shouldered his pack. 'If you are quite ready…if you think we haven't forgotten to do anything of importance, we go.'

Dagmar put her hand over the daggers in her belt. Strictly speaking, she should mention them, but he hadn't asked for them back. She hated being unarmed. 'Nothing at all. Why?'

He gave her a hard stare. 'No reason.'

He strode off without a backward glance and she had to run to keep up. They marched along for a little while without Aedan saying anything. Every now and then, he gave her a glower. Dagmar winced as she missed the easy camaraderie that had sprung up between them last night and early this morning.

'What are you angry about now?' she asked before he had the opportunity to make good his implied threat and made her try the gown on. 'I haven't worn a gown in a very long time. Not for years. Not since I was blooded as a shield maiden. I see no reason to start now. It might give my father ideas.'

Aedan's mouth became a thin white line. 'Who says I'm angry about your refusal to wear the gown?'

'I do. I thought we belonged as a team.' She tapped her foot on the ground. 'How can we be one if you go storming off without an explanation? Why do you consider it imperative for me to wear it? I can travel much faster if I'm not tripping over the hem all the time.'

He stopped and put the pack down. 'You want to be a team? Truly?'

'I said I did.' She lifted her chin. 'I can see how you'd be a handy warrior to have around after the marshes. And Mor's value is beyond question. I've no wish to lose either of you. We're going to my father's so that you can win your wager and free your people. After that, we part.'

'If you seek to bargain with me, simply come out with it.'

'What are you talking about? What have I done besides refusing to wear the gown in front of my father!' She crossed her arms. 'It is really none of your business what I wear when I greet him. The important thing from your perspective is that I am there.'

'The blasted gown has nothing to do with it! Stop going on about it or I will personally shove it over your head!'

'Out with it. How have I upset you this time? What little thing besides killing two men who threatened us.'

'I can see where you secured that dagger, Dagmar. You have made no attempt to return it to me. Nor did you seek to hand me the knife you retrieved from your captor. You never discussed if I felt comfortable travelling with you, fully armed.'

'You never asked for them! Two knives is not fully armed, not in the slightest.'

'But you killed two men with only one.'

'I had assumed you would see the sense in me having them. We've no idea what other creatures we're going to meet along the way.'

'I asked you if you had forgotten to do anything. You knew the dagger was mine and that I might have cause to need it.'

Dagmar lifted her chin. When he put it that way, she could understand why he was upset. 'You marched off without a backward glance. How could I know you wanted it back? I assumed that you would prefer me to be armed if we encountered the robbers again. Their gang may even now be massing. You need me armed. I simply gave you the benefit of the doubt.'

An edited version of the truth, but Dagmar knew she couldn't confess about how vulnerable she felt back in the hut being unarmed, and how much safer she felt with a weapon. Being armed was as natural as breathing.

The hardness of his face increased. 'A simple request would have done. I'd have said yes. Like you, I am aware of the possibility for further attack. Either we work together or we don't. A fellowship cannot hold if there are two leaders.'

She scuffed the toe of her boot in the mud. 'I'm asking now since it obviously means so much to you. Please, Aedan mac Connall, sir, please may I have these two daggers? Satisfied?'

He continued to glare at her with lowered brows as if she were a spoilt child.

'Can I help it if you were careless with your dagger?' she added. 'I've learned to take advantage of the opportunities life presents.'

'Careless? You wrong me.' He made a disgusted noise. 'I left it for you to find, deliberately. When I adjusted the cloak, I dropped it for you. There was no time for explanations. I assumed you were intelligent, but that you were no thief.'

Dagmar winced. He had not been stroking her hair or giving her any type of caress. And from his perspective, she had stolen something from him. She held out his dagger. 'I'm sorry I mistook the situation. I made a grave error in not returning this to you immediately. Forgive me? Please?'

He tilted his head to one side. 'Why should I trust you?'

'You're in no danger from me. Once I've given my word, particularly when I've sworn on my mother's shade, I keep it. We're allies.' She took the other dagger out of her belt. 'But if me being armed bothers you that much, you may have them both. Your trust is more important to me than my safety. I will cope somehow if we encounter the robbers. I always do. My mother taught me well.'

'As long as no one attacks you from behind.'

'Well, there is that.'

Her heart thumped so loudly that she thought he must hear it. The knot in her stomach had eased when she had the daggers. She hated feeling powerless and alone as she did in her nightmares and as she actually had in the forest when they had departed from her father's compound and she'd encountered the berserker. And she had the uncomfortable feeling that the unknown warrior in her dream bore a distinct resemblance to Aedan.

He made no move to take the knives from her. 'If we are allies, then we put more distance between us and that hut, before that boy returns with the remainder of the gang. Before they meet someone who starts asking awkward questions about an escaped shield maiden.'

He started to walk away, but she put a hand on his arm.

'And the daggers?'

'Keep them. You are little use to me unarmed. And you are right—I, too, find it hard to trust.'

Dagmar made a disgusted noise in the back of her throat. 'I swear I will never understand you Gaels!'

'I wanted to see what you would do. Did you actually value our alliance or were you merely mouthing words?' He gave a sudden smile, transforming his face and it was like the clouds parting. 'Your apology was unexpected, but very welcome.'

Dagmar roughly put the daggers back in her belt and mentally scolded her body for noticing him. There would be so many women panting after him that he would never be interested in anyone like her. 'Glad to see you have an iota of sense in your head, Gael.'

'Besides, Mor likes you.' He shrugged. 'And I trust her judgement. You are part of this *felag* but you also must realise that I am in charge. You do as I say.'

Dagmar waggled her fingers at Mor who came and gave them a lick. She gave a quiet smile. There was no *must* about anything, but he would learn—she only obeyed as long as it suited her purpose.

'A *felag* works better with one leader. You appear to know where we are going. I will follow your orders as long as you do not force me to wear a dress.'

Aedan knelt down and spoke to Mor. 'What do you say, Mor? Shall we give Dagmar a second chance? Do we agree to her terms?'

Mor gave a sharp bark of assent and did a few spins, running between Aedan and Dagmar.

'You see your dog agrees. Stop testing me. The sooner we arrive at my father's, the sooner we can both get back to our lives.'

'Mor likes you. For some reason.' He gave a smile that warmed her down to her toes. 'I promise I won't force you to wear the gown. But I'm sure you will come to the correct decision about that on your own.'

'You have a slim grasp on reality. I begin to understand why my father decided to wager with you,' she said loudly. 'He believes he will gain your land no matter what.'

'Yet here you are heading towards your father's within the allotted time.' A glint appeared in his eyes. 'Would you care for a wager?'

'I've agreed to help because it suits my purpose.'

The dimple appeared in his cheek. 'About something else.'

'I won't be wearing that gown ever.' Dagmar crossed her arms over her suddenly tingling breasts. 'You can forget wagering about that!'

The dimple deepened. 'You do like to make pronouncements about what you will and won't do. When will you learn that I do enjoy a challenge?'

Dagmar ground her teeth. He was treating her with amused contempt as though she was a young child, instead of a fully grown warrior who had weathered five years of campaigning. 'I state facts.'

His eyes began to dance. 'Here I thought you enjoyed issuing challenges. I stand corrected. But for the future, be aware I seldom back away from a challenge, particularly when it's issued by a beautiful woman.'

Dagmar glared at him. 'Your eyesight needs improvement.'

His face grew serious. 'I know enough about you.'

'Like what?'

'I know you have led a hard life, harder than most

women of your rank could comprehend or endure, that you idolised your mother and that you were right— Thorsten's shield wall was breaking when Olafr and his allies switched sides. It was your determined leadership that did that. You dispatched those robbers without hesitation or hysterics. You are the sort of warrior I'd be proud to have in my fellowship.'

Dagmar stared at him. Aedan was praising her. He appreciated her skills. And he could have left her in ignorance about why the battle had been lost. She struggled to think when her mother had last praised her beyond a quiet well done.

'As long as I obey you. As long as I acknowledge your leadership and don't keep weapons without asking first.'

'My *felag*. My rules.' He gave another smile, this one lighting his entire face.

Dagmar hated that his smile turned her insides to liquid. She had to stop feeling attracted to him before the ultimate humiliation happened, before she started believing he might be the one man who could see into the depths of her soul and understand her inner desires.

She found it impossible to dismiss the notion that Aedan wanted something more than simply winning his wager with her father. Until she figured out Aedan's game, she'd keep her attraction to him under control. Even though she'd dreamt of being more than just a sell-sword, she could see now her mother was right—she could not afford to be beholden to any man.

Chapter Five

The dangerous oozing mud and squelching moss of the marsh rapidly gave way to scrubland and then strips of cultivated fields, punctuated with small stands of trees and the occasional dwelling. Once they reached a well-travelled road which led vaguely west, Aedan picked up the pace. Dagmar matched him stride for stride, never complaining. He struggled to think of any woman he knew who would do that.

The heavy rain from last night left puddles to be skirted around, but it had become a fine autumn day where the sun held more than a hint of warmth, the sort of day that always gave Aedan hope. Things would work out. Finally he would be able to prove that he was worthy of being King, and he would be able to save the hostages by returning this woman to her father. Once he had done that, she would become someone else's problem.

Aedan watched Dagmar from under his lashes. Today, she had done her hair in a simple braid which, when she looped it over her shoulder, revealed the slender column of her neck. Aedan returned his eyes firmly to the road ahead and tried to think of Mhairi patiently waiting for her rescue and how grateful she'd be to him. But it was no good, Mhairi held no physical attraction for him. Her dark beauty was the sort his brother had admired. However, for Aedan, it reminded him far too much of Brigid and the mistakes he'd made.

Mor gave a low whine. Aedan glanced over and saw that Dagmar had gone white about her mouth. He gave a soft curse. The woman needed to rest, but stubbornly refused to admit it to anyone, let alone herself. He doubted if he had ever met someone that determinedly stubborn before.

'We will rest and eat here.' He gestured towards a flat rock that overlooked a small pond just to one side of the path they had been following. 'We've put enough distance between us and that gang of murdering thieves. We missed breakfast.'

Her bottom lip jutted out. 'I can go further. No need to stop on my account.'

He recalled her screams in the night, begging someone to wait for her. How many times had her mother refused to stop until Dagmar ceased to listen to the demands of her body? She might idolise her mother, but Aedan wanted to shake the woman.

'Stop flattering yourself. This has nothing to do with you and everything to do with my empty stomach. We stop when I say—my *felag*, remember?'

Dagmar gave one of her smiles which lit her eyes and took his breath away. 'I'm in no mood to fight you for the leadership. We can stop and eat.'

'There has been enough fighting for today.'

'I so agree.' She sank down on to a dry rock and gathered her knees to her chest. Her plait looped over one shoulder and pointed to the shadowy vee where her skin met her tunic. Unable to stop, he watched how her chest rose and fell. Her breasts seemed more curved than he remembered. Did she have to bind them?

Aedan scratched his nose and tried to ignore the way his body tightened in response to his thoughts.

'What a perfect spot,' she said arching her back and causing her chest to jut out more. He'd be willing to wager that she did bind them.

'It is rather beautiful.'

'No, it is the perfect spot to rest without fear of being attacked.' She leant forward. 'Getting the best ground possible is the first requirement to winning a battle. Although sometimes you have to make the best of what you have.'

'Do you ever think of things beyond warfare?'

'Is there something wrong with that? It is how I have lived my life.' She tilted her chin. 'It saves me having to think about the past or the future.'

'Life is more than such things. Life is about enjoying sunsets over crystal-clear bays, finding the first buds of spring after a hard winter, and a good meal with fresh clothes on your back with a solid roof over your head and a roaring fire in the hearth. It is about being with the ones you love and knowing that they love you back.'

'You are a man of simple tastes.'

'Try it. Try talking about something which isn't war or strategy.'

Dagmar was silent for a long heartbeat. 'My belly aches from hunger. We neglected breakfast.'

Aedan burst out laughing.

'What? What is wrong with that? That is something different than war and battle.'

Aedan cast his eyes heavenward. 'I can't promise how fresh the cheese and hard bread are.'

'It will fill a hole. Simple pleasures, yes?'

She bent her head and he could see the long sweep of her neck. She was daintily boned. It seemed almost impossible that someone who was so exquisite would be a deadly killing machine whose sole interest appeared to be the art of warfare. He blamed her mother who had trained her that there was no other way to survive except as a sell-sword. She had kept Dagmar as a tightly closed bud rather than allowing her to flower and develop as a woman and Aedan loathed her for it.

Someone else would ensure the full flowering happened. When she arrived at her father's, there would be many warriors waiting for the favour of her hand, even if she'd had a face like a rocky cliff and was the size of a small hut. The fact that she possessed a smile which could light up the darkest of days, translucent skin and hair like a golden cloud, would mean even more warriors eager to vie for her hand. A stab of jealousy shot through him.

Kolbeinn had made it very clear—he wanted an excellent marriage for his daughter. He would use her as a counter in his quest to gain ever more power. When he'd departed, his ears rang with the warning from Kolbeinn's latest mistress—Kolbeinn would not take kindly to a Gaelic warrior with a minor kingdom worming his way into the daughter's affections; Kolbeinn had big plans for her.

He'd have to find another way to keep her bad dreams at bay. This morning could not be repeated for the sake of his people and kingdom. They'd suffered enough because of his failings. He'd nearly brushed her dawn-kissed mouth with his.

Even now as she thoughtfully chewed the last of the hardened bread, she only had to give him a sideways look and his body which, since he had learned of Brigid's betrayal and subsequent death had felt encased in ice, responded. He was worse than a youth who'd just discovered that girls were a very different proposition.

Once they reached a village, he'd use some of the gold he'd liberated earlier to get swift horses for them both. The sooner she was safely installed in her father's household, the sooner he could get the hostages released. Redemption was within his grasp if he could only control his desire.

'Are you going to tell me what is troubling you? You appear very serious suddenly,' Dagmar said, dusting her fingers on her trousers and inadvertently tightening her tunic across her chest again.

'Is something troubling me?' he said pushing the image of freeing her breasts from his mind.

Her little laugh sent a ripple of warmth down his spine. 'You wear your fierce expression. It always seems to be a sign of trouble. Has Mor heard more travellers?'

'I'm trying to figure out how long it will take us to get to where I left my boat,' Aedan said, opting for a half-truth. 'Your father will enforce the exact terms of the wager and I don't want to be even a heartbeat too late. You take after him in some ways.'

'Take that back!' Dagmar clenched her fists. 'I'm nothing like my father. I am entirely like my mother.'

'Two people made you, Dagmar.'

She ducked her head. 'Two people may have made me, but only one cared for me.'

'Now that your mother is dead, your father requires you.'

'His beloved son and second wife are dead, that is all. My father has exhausted his options. He has always been overly concerned with his legacy.'

The bleakness of her tone clawed at his chest. He wanted to gather her into his arms and hold her tight. Aedan forced his hands to throw a stick for Mor instead.

'He was willing to risk his fleet to force my hand. There are easier ways to kill a man then sending him to his estranged daughter. Does that sound like someone who doesn't care? Would Old Alf have assisted me if he truly believed that your father meant you harm? Is it possible he charged Old Alf with keeping you safe because your mother had won the right to look after you?'

She turned away from him so that he could not see her face. 'Do you think he actually cares about me as a person and not just as a way to increase his own power?'

The tremor of hope in her voice tugged at his heart and he wanted to take her somewhere where no one could hurt her like that ever again but that was impossible. His people came first, always.

'Maybe he wants to make amends for what happened. Maybe his recent losses have taught him that all his children matter.'

Dagmar sat for a long while. Her cheek resting against her knees.

'You're a good man,' she said finally. 'But you've no idea what my father is capable of. He has serious designs on your Kintra. He sent you to your probable death. It is mere luck that I decided not to slit your throat. And he will never have anticipated that I would return so swiftly with you.'

'I simply want to save Kintra and the people who live there. I am their King and I can't fail them again.'

She tapped a finger against her mouth. 'I know how he cheated my mother. There are measures you will have to take to prevent it.'

Aedan sat up. 'You intrigue me. What should I be doing? How can I keep my people safe?'

She waved an airy hand. 'Leave that to me. I will get you the full terms of the wager and will keep your people safe from his immediate attention. We're in a fellowship together. It is the least I can do. He was wrong to place such a burden on you without explaining the perils.'

'Why does that not fill me with confidence? What are you planning, Dagmar?'

'Do you see that knot in the tree?'

Aedan gave a nod.

'Imagine that is my father's head if he fails to honour your wager completely after I ask him to, in a way only I can.'

He shook his head. Dagmar was trying to bolster his confidence in her. 'It is a bit far away.'

'Keep still.' She reached down, grabbed her dagger and sent it flying, narrowly missing his head before becoming embedded in the tree's knot. She then threw the second one, hitting the tree squarely where Kolbeinn's heart would be.

Aedan whistled softly. Unless he'd seen the demonstration, he wouldn't have believed it.

'People often underestimate me. Leave my father and his men to me. Trust works both ways.'

Aedan marched over and retrieved the knives out of the tree. She was on his side. 'Should I be concerned for my life?'

'No, it was purely a demonstration of what I am capable of. It is my father who should fear for his life if he plays you false.'

'Will you teach me to throw them?'

'It takes years to learn to throw that accurately.'

'Well then, will you teach me how you managed to flip that robber so swiftly?'

Dagmar gave a soft laugh. 'I'm rather proud of that move, but, yes, I can do that. It is all about working with your opponent's weight rather than against it.' Dagmar held out her hand. 'My daggers, if you please.'

He handed them back to her. 'Let us hope it does not come to that.'

'Violence is always a last resort. I thought you knew that.'

Dagmar spent the remainder of the afternoon trying to digest the news that, rather than being a sellsword whom she could potentially bribe, Aedan was a king who had undertaken this quest to save his people. A noble sentiment, but she was certain that her father would try to wriggle out of paying the promised gold, just as he'd wriggled out of returning her mother's ships or the gold her mother had brought to the marriage, gold she'd earned with the sweat of her brow and the strength of her sword arm. He'd even kept the jewellery which had belong to Dagmar's grandmother.

This time her father was going to pay the full amount or he would pay for the consequences of his actions rather than behaving like he had towards her mother.

* * *

They had made steady progress during the day and reached the outskirts of a hamlet as the sun began to sink lower. A small church stood slightly isolated from the rest of the houses. There was a certain peace to the place as if nothing bad could ever happen there. It was on the tip of her tongue to ask Aedan if this was what Kintra was like. She'd heard the longing in his voice when he spoke about the sunsets over crystal-clear bays and a solid roof over his head. He'd been speaking of home.

One day, she promised her heart, she, too, would have a home where she was loved and valued, where she could sit at the end of the day and watch the sunset without worrying about the next battle she needed to fight to prove her worth.

If she couldn't enjoy sitting with her face in the sun, watching the waves crash on a beach, what had been the point of all the years of dreary marches, the wearisome practices and the ache of watching good men die before they should for some petty king's ambition? Her mother might not have approved of the sentiment but at the end, all her mother had wanted was to feel the sun on her face one more time, too.

Aedan halted. 'The rain clouds have gathered and owl-light approaches.'

'I'd rather take my chances under a tree than in an abandoned hut again.'

'I've something better in mind.'

His smile was slow and sure, melting something deep within her core. She pinched her fingers against her nose. Those few heartbeats in his arms this morning had been an aberration. If men made eyes at her it was because they were being devious and required something from her, thinking her a fool. Right now, she suspected that the something he wanted was her in a gown to prove his superiority, and he wasn't getting that. Ever!

She adopted her fiercest scowl, the one which had sent Constantine's advisers cowering. 'What? What is better than a tree?'

His eyes fairly danced, a myriad of shifting colours. A woman could lose herself in those eyes. Dagmar increased the depth of her scowl.

'Change into the gown and I will explain. Think about a having a hot meal and a roof over your head. They have to be worth changing clothes for.'

Dagmar carefully arched a brow. Aedan needed to alter his approach if he wanted her to do anything that drastic. 'I believe we discussed this before. No gowns for me. Ever.'

'No, you announced what you were going to do then. The circumstances have changed.' The dimple was there again in his cheek. 'Remember, I find challenges hard to resist. There is another storm coming, a big one with rain and wind. I can feel it in my bones.'

'Your bones are suspect.'

'Mor agrees with me so it is two against one. A definite storm. Do you want to be cold and wet or warm as toast?'

His voice flowed over her like a hot tide. Something deep within her stirred and answered it.

'Changed how?' she said, crossing her arms over her suddenly aching breasts. 'Everything looks pretty much the same from where I stand.'

'We finished the last of the bread and cheese. There is a possibility of warmth and food here. Mor likes her comforts, but she won't get them unless you are in a gown.'

At the sound of her name, Mor gave a sharp bark and ran about Dagmar twice before flopping down at her feet with a hopeful expression.

'How I dress will not make a difference to obtaining shelter here.'

'All doors will be barred to us if you remain as you are.'

'What is wrong with how I am dressed? I have been able to match you stride for stride.'

'It proclaims you are a north warrior.' His smile increased. 'We've no idea if news of the battle has spread. News can pass from village to village very quickly when something momentous happens. Olafr and Thorsten may have offered a reward for you.'

Dagmar frowned. Aedan had a point about news travelling quickly. She'd seen it before. The last thing she wanted was to fall into Olafr's clutches. Mor's big-eyed expression was hard to resist. Wearing a gown once would not alter things. It would not turn her suddenly into the sort of prancing female who had populated Constantine's court, the ones who had sighed and batted their eyes at the warriors they admired.

'Can I wear it over my clothes?'

Aedan retrieved the gown and held it out. 'We have no idea of the sort of woman who originally wore this gown. Slip it on over your clothes if you can. I doubt anyone will ask you to disrobe while wearing this.'

Dagmar scowled. Proof if she needed it that this attraction was one-sided. Wearing the gown over her clothes was not the same as wearing it properly in any case. She'd remain a shield maiden underneath.

'Hand it over then. It goes over my clothes or I don't wear it at all.'

Aedan adopted an expression of outraged innocence which she immediately distrusted. 'Did I say any differently?'

Dagmar regarded the garment, really looking at it for the first time. It was a beautiful deep blue which would match her eyes, the sort of gown she'd clamoured for when she was a little girl. She banished the memory.

She put it over her head and pulled. It was far tighter than she anticipated. She squirmed slightly, but the cloth began to tear on her right side.

'You appear a bit larger than I had first considered, but I am sure we can force it over your body.' Aedan's words flowed over her.

She froze as her mind considered his hands running down her body, helping. She did not want to think about his hands touching her body as he adjusted the tight bodice. The image was enough to take her breath away and make her knees go weak but for him, it would be impersonal and meaningless. She'd stopped making those sorts of mistakes long ago.

'When I need your help, I will ask for it.' Dagmar eased the garment back over her head, aware that her cheeks were flaming. 'Turn your back.'

'Why?'

'Because I am giving into the inevitable before you have a chance to say that you suspected as much. The design is like the gowns the ladies were wearing at Constantine's court—very fitted. My stomach would like a hot meal.'

He widened his eyes. 'I know enough about women

and their ways to know sometimes it is best to keep quiet.'

She made one last attempt but the cloth only seemed to tear more. 'I shall have to properly change. I never like knowingly missing supper.'

He duly turned. Dagmar quickly changed. The gown was cut in the Pict fashion with long narrow sleeves, a tight bodice and a gently gathered skirt which fell softly about her hips, rather than being straight like Northern women wore. Equally, there was no apron to fasten over it with brooches.

She did an experimental twirl. The gown flowed when she moved. In it, she could almost believe that she was beautiful, rather than the lump she knew she was.

'You may turn around now.'

Something appreciative flared in his face, but was quickly masked. 'You are far more efficient than I considered. I thought you would be asking for help.'

'When you grow up around men, you learn to change quickly. There is an art to it.'

'Didn't your mother keep any ladies?'

'She had me, but she insisted that I learn to cope. In the summers we travelled together, fighting for whomever she pledged her services to. She refused to be parted from me, particularly as she had fought so hard for me, especially after we left the compound.'

'In your dream, you kept calling out for your mother to wait.'

'After the fight, my father gave us until sundown to be off his lands or he would hunt us down as wolf's heads.' Dagmar did not bother to disguise the bitterness in her voice. 'Then he sent berserkers after us. Old Alf rescued me when I became separated from them. My mother bore a scar from that battle on her upper thigh. I still dream of it sometimes. Silly really.' She attempted a shrug to show it no longer mattered, but she knew the terror still lingered.

'Less than commendable behaviour from your father.'

'My mother had humiliated him in front of his men and in front of the woman he desired,' Dagmar admitted with a sigh as she fastened her own clothes into a bundle. Even now her stomach ached when she thought of that day and how it had started with her innocently asking if her father would return with the gift he'd promised for her tenth name day. She'd ruined her mother's life and her mother never complained, but every so often her mother would remind her of the request and its consequences. 'She was my hero. I have tried to live up to her ideal and have failed. With her final breaths, she only requested land for her followers, the land Constantine promised in exchange for her service for five summers. She wanted to give her followers and their kin a better life. I swore I would get it for them and I failed.' Dagmar pressed her hand into her eyes. 'I'm pleased my mother was spared that disappointment and this latest failure of mine.'

He tilted his head to one side and assessed her. 'You see wearing the gown as a failure?'

'My mother would have marched into the town and demanded accommodation as her right, but then she had warriors and I only have you and Mor.' Dagmar wrinkled her nose, grateful that he did not mention her true failure back on the battlefield. 'However, I shall do as you suggest. It is best to keep a low profile until we reach my father's. I gave you a solemn oath. You need to win your wager for the sake of your people. This is one wager my father will have to pay up on.'

'It sounds as though your mother wanted you to survive more than she wanted a great warrior for a daughter. And she must not have wanted to play the warrior all the time, because she had you. And she chose you over all the material riches she could have possessed.'

'Perhaps.' Dagmar frowned. To hear her mother describe it, her failed marriage had been one of the unhappiest times of her life—full of anger and growing resentment. But Dagmar remembered a golden time when she had felt secure in the love she'd received from both her father and mother. It was only when her stepmother with her great belly had appeared that everything had changed. And that had only happened because she had asked her father for a grown-up gown. Whatever Aedan said, she had destroyed her mother's life.

'Can you walk in that?'

She did a little twirl. The skirt flared out gracefully from her legs. 'The woman was slightly shorter than me so there is no need to gather the skirt about my waist.'

'You've kept your boots on.'

'No one will see them and they are moulded to my feet.' Dagmar clamped her mouth shut. There was no need for Aedan to know about the gold she kept secreted in her boots in case everything went wrong.

She used to resent carrying the extra weight, but now she could see the wisdom in it. If her father would not listen to reason and forced her to marry, she'd steal a boat and offer her services to any warlord who would have her. South to Wessex remained a possibility. 'But will I pass for a subservient maiden?'

'Fishing for compliments? How like a woman!' The dimple appeared again. 'But you will never pass for a subservient woman and nor should you.'

'Damning me with faint praise.' She tilted her chin upwards to show that his words had meant little rather than paining her. Against all her expectations, she did want to feel beautiful. 'I used my ears at Constantine's court. I know what they said about my lack of beauty.'

'If you must know, you will do, more than do.' A low husky note in his voice made her breath hitch in her throat. 'The gown fits you as if it was made for you. It is nearly the precise shade of your eyes.'

She scowled, hating how much his words meant to her. 'There, that wasn't so hard. I do respond well to kindness. But I dislike this colour.'

'It certainly likes you.' He rubbed the back of his neck. 'Shall we go find supper? Or are you going to challenge for the leadership?'

'The priest will turn us away. Even when my mother pledged her service to Constantine, the priests refused to have anything to do with us.' She bit her lip. 'It was because my mother was very vocal about following Odin, Thor and Freyja. Sometimes, though, I used to sneak in and watch them chanting and waving their smoke about.'

Her words felt vaguely disloyal as she was criticising her mother, but he deserved the truth.

'I am a Gael, rather than a Northman. If you can hold your tongue instead of blurting out who you are, he will not guess whose daughter you are. Or which gods you follow. Sometimes it is better to allow people to assume rather than rubbing their noses in it.'

Dagmar swallowed a furious retort. As if she didn't

know the slightest bit about manipulating people and how to be charming. 'Not actually lying, then. Just keeping quiet.'

'Totally silent. I'm not responsible for other people's conclusions. Nor are you.'

'A very wise suggestion. Thank you.' She allowed her voice to drip with a hint of sarcasm.

'And thank you. Compliments run both ways, my lady fair. It is not weak to be kind.'

She blinked twice. Aedan was perfectly serious. 'I... I'll try to remember that.'

Dagmar allowed Aedan to lead the way to the church. He spoke quietly to the middle-aged priest who listened to Aedan's highly edited story of how they came to be there. His kindly face immediately creased. He invited them in to share his evening meal, refusing any of Aedan's protestations that all they required were scraps.

'What did you say to him?' Dagmar murmured while the priest's back was turned.

'The truth. We're refugees from a great battle and are travelling to your relations on the west coast.'

She hid a smile. 'A fair approximation.'

'It served its purpose. He'll provide us with a hot meal of pottage. If our luck holds, he will insist we stay the night.'

'And you trust this priest not to betray us?'

'Priests care about people. They assist those in need.'

He went over to the priest and spoke to him in a low tone. She caught the general drift that she was shy and had seen things that no woman should. The priest's face became shadowed with concern.

'You will be safe from now on, my dear daughter,'

he said, holding out his hands. 'I will pray you discover perfect peace in your new home.'

Dagmar found that she wanted to believe him, but remembered just in time to swallow the words. Instead she gave a meaningful glance to Aedan.

'My wife thanks you.'

'Hopefully she will rediscover her tongue. She will see that she has nothing to fear here.' The priest made the sign of the cross in the air. 'May the love which passes all understanding heal you, my daughter.'

The priest's house was spartanly furnished with a simple wooden table and a few benches, but it exuded warmth. A pot of stew stood bubbling on the hearth. Two dogs looked up from their place at the fire, but neither bothered with Mor who sniffed about, turned around three times and then lay down next to them.

'You see,' the priest said, beaming from ear to ear. 'We are all at peace here.'

'We're grateful for the hospitality,' Aedan said, sitting down. 'You will allow us to pay for the meal.'

The priest shook his head. 'You've suffered greatly. Now shall we bow our heads and give thanks for your deliverance?'

Dagmar kept her eyes on Aedan and followed his movements. This priest was certainly different from others she had encountered at Constantine's court or indeed her own priests. There was a simple goodness about him.

'Drink deep from the mead.' The priest produced two tankards. 'My brothers at the abbey make it. They say that King Constantine enjoyed it when he stopped once on his way to fight with the evil Northmen. It has many curative properties, or so they say.'

'Have you heard that the King fled from the battle? Thorsten and his men now control the north,' Aedan said.

'That is very bad,' the priest said. 'I must trust in God's plan. He won't allow the Heathen Horde to keep hold of this blessed country for long.'

Dagmar tentatively tried a sample. The taste of fizzy honey filled her mouth as she listened to Aedan and the priest talk about the harvest and various political developments. She noticed how the firelight played over Aedan's features, highlighting the planes of his cheeks and the way his upper lip curved.

When she discovered her tankard was empty, Aedan started to pass her his, but the priest immediately poured more.

'It will do your lady good to drink the mead after what she has seen. Sleep will come easier.'

'Thank you,' Dagmar said before she thought.

'It helps you recover your tongue.' The priest clapped his hands in delight. 'Its curative effects are truly marvellous.'

'I'm grateful to you.' Aedan gave her a warning look.

Dagmar tightened her hands about the tankard and resolved to be silent. The last thing she wanted to do was to give this kind man a fright. Or to expose Aedan's skating over of the truth.

It felt good to just sit and allow the conversation to flow over her, instead of worrying about what battle she should be fighting next, or how she could influence the outcome.

She didn't dare ask how many more days she had until they reached her father's. There was every likelihood her father would force her to marry someone horrible, despite her protestations to Aedan. She had no doubt the joining would be rough. She'd seen enough women in tears after their first time. She took another drink of the mead.

The firelight turned Aedan's hair to a deep red and highlighted the breadth of his shoulders. A shiver ran through her as she remembered this morning in the hut before the men had arrived. At the time she'd been glad of the intervention and the humiliation she'd been saved from, but what if she'd been wrong? What if he had been interested in her as a woman, instead of just what she could bring? His eyes had flared when he saw her in the gown…

She tried to concentrate on the flames, but they seemed to depict men and women coupling. She rubbed her eyes, trying to banish the image.

'I've bored your wife with all this talk of politics and war,' the priest said, moving away from the table. 'When will I remember that women prefer talk of gowns, flowers and babies? Forgive me, my dear. No more talk of bloodshed.'

'My wife has had a long day.'

Dagmar gestured with her hands that she wanted to stay and wasn't tired.

'It is why your eyes were half-shut,' Aedan said with a small smile. 'We've another long journey tomorrow. Come. We'll be on our way. I'm sure we can find a place to rest our heads. Perhaps the storm will pass over us without breaking.'

He held out his hand. She curled her fingers about his and again that jolt of awareness which turned her insides to liquid fire coursed through her.

From the brief flaring of his eyes, she wondered if

he felt it as well. How could he? She knew what men thought of her. She had heard them joking. She knew she was not her mother, who only had to smile for men to go weak at the knees.

'You must stay. The roads will be full of rogues and thieves.'

'May we sleep in front of the fire?'

'Somewhere far more comfortable. Allow me to show you where you may sleep. You were truly meant to stop here tonight.' The priest led the way to a small alcove at the back of the church. 'It is where my helper normally resides with his wife, but they are away visiting her mother as her sister has just had a new baby. Your dog may stay with you or sleep next to mine.'

'It will be perfect,' Aedan said.

She smiled. 'Yes, it will be.'

'May God's blessing be on you both.' The priest left a small tallow candle and went off to his own room.

'Shall I stay?' Aedan asked, watching Dagmar as she stood in the middle of the alcove, a far better place than he had originally anticipated, a place which seemed designed for sleep or bed sport… Aedan dragged his mind away from the mound of covered dry straw. 'Or shall I sleep by the fire with Mor?'

Dagmar gave him one of her sideways looks, a look that made her eyes appear bigger than ever. 'The priest will discover you. And before you say you'll sleep outside, I can hear the rain drumming down on the roof.'

'The church, then.'

'And if the priest comes in for one of his masses, how will you explain that we are sleeping apart? We are supposed to be married.'

Aedan gritted his teeth. Nothing had happened between them. Nothing would happen. He'd return her to her father and then he and his people would be free to go. She would go to her new life and he would return to his old one. Having proved his worth, he would seriously see about the business of marrying the correct woman for Kintra. Maybe not Mhairi, but a woman who could help run Kintra. Each time he repeated the words in his mind, they appeared more unattractive. If he wasn't careful, they would soon become meaningless compared to the temptation Dagmar presented.

He would simply have to spend tonight awake. When he found a lake in the morning, he'd take a cold plunge. That, exercise and making sure Dagmar changed back into her ordinary clothes would keep his now-rampant desire for her in check.

'The offer is there,' he said, inclining his head. 'I wanted you to know.'

His voice sounded hoarse and unfamiliar to his ears. He knew he should turn around and walk out no matter what she said, but his legs refused to move.

'I will be going then. The porch will be comfortable.'

'Stay. Please. I... I fear my bad dream will return. The berserker comes when I'm troubled.'

'You are no longer a little girl, but a capable woman.'

'If I don't sleep tonight, our progress will be slower tomorrow. We need to make Colbhasa by All Hallows.'

She made a show of plumping up the straw before spreading out his cloak. Her back was to him and in that dress, the gentle curve of her backside was clearly visible. His suggestion she change out of her trousers had been short-sighted.

Aedan sighed. He should have foreseen this eventuality. Tomorrow morning, however, he was not going to wake up with her in his arms. 'I should attend to Mor.'

'Mor will be asleep beside the hearth.'

'Even so...'

Dagmar turned and, before he had a chance to react, she brushed her lips against his. 'For luck. To keep the nightmares at bay as my mother used to say.'

Her lips were softer than a butterfly's wing, tentatively moving against his. There was something artless to her kiss, but deeply appealing. He tried to tell himself that she had kissed a hundred men and knew precisely what she was doing, that it was a cynical ploy, but his body was having none of it.

The smouldering fire deep within him which had been ignited earlier burst into flames. He lowered his head and pressed his body closer. She gave a small groan and clung to his neck. Her slender curves fitted easily into his body as if she had been made for him. The thought acted like ice water and brought him back from the brink.

With a great effort, he put her away from him. She stood slim and sure in the flickering candlelight.

'Say something.' Her voice wobbled.

'It is the mead acting. You will have a bad head in the morning.'

'Is it?' She stepped back into his arms and pressed her breasts against his chest. 'How much did I have?'

'More than enough.'

She looped her arm about his neck. Her face was very close to his. It took all his willpower not to crush her to him. 'I grew up with warriors. I know how to hold my alcohol.'

He gently put her from him again. 'You are playing with fire and fire burns.'

Her mouth remained a breath away from his. The woman could tempt a saint. Her lips turned up into a sensual smile. 'Am I? I thought I was keeping the nightmares away.'

'There are other ways.'

'Are there?' Her eyes searched his. 'Do they help you?'

He thought of the nightmares which had plagued his existence—the parade of warriors he'd killed in battle and, worse, the horror of watching his men drown, powerless to stop it and all the while knowing if he had believed his sister-in-law after the boating accident which killed her children, rather than his brother's self-serving lies, those men would still be alive. 'No, they don't.'

'But I've discovered the perfect cure.'

Aedan groaned and dipped his head. Her lips parted under his and he tasted the honey scent of the mead and something else that sent his senses reeling, something that was pure Dagmar. He knew he wanted more, much more, and that his duty to his people has ceased to have any meaning.

Chapter Six

A heady triumph filled Dagmar, competing with the glow from the mead. She was kissing a man and he was kissing her back for no other reason than he wanted to, not because he had been dared to do it by his companions.

Aedan was kissing her thoroughly and completely.

Her blood raced through her body in a way it had rarely done before. It was as though it was on fire and singing, as though she had won a great battle, as though she was actually beautiful.

Dagmar gave in to the pressure from Aedan's lips and opened her mouth. The world spun. Her tongue touched his. The jolt made her knees tremble. She put her palms on his chest, clung on and opened her mouth further.

Their tongues touched, tangled and intertwined, warring with each other and he pulled her against the hard planes of his body as he moved his mouth along the sensitive line of her jaw until he reached her earlobe where he gently tugged.

She held on to his neck because otherwise she'd fall. She laid her head against his chest. 'Is that your heart thundering or mine?'

'Both.'

'Good,' she said and drew a shuddering breath. 'It is very good.'

He moved his mouth lower. She arched her neck and allow him access to her throat. His mouth travelled further and at her neckline he halted. Her breasts felt heavy and tight, constricted against the material.

'Help me get this off,' Dagmar said struggling with her gown. She'd gone about it wrong and the hole under the sleeve from earlier had greatly increased. 'Oh, Freyja, what have I done?'

The words seemed to shock Aedan back to his senses. He caught her hands. 'I should go. Or otherwise in the morning, you'll blame me.'

She stilled. Go? What was he talking about? She wanted to explore these feelings further, see if she could finally begin to understand the soft whispering in the dark after feasts, or why her mother had become obsessed with Olafr. Until this moment, she'd been at a loss to understand why women might welcome the act, as it seemed like a lot of grunting and sweating for little reward. Except no one had told her about how Aedan's mouth could feel as it moved against hers.

'For tearing the gown?' she asked, pretending she had no idea what he was speaking about. 'Unlikely. It is just that you are likely to make me wear it again and the priest might object to it being torn. They can be quite peculiar about such things.'

He put her further away from him and the cold air rushed around her.

'You appear to know a great deal about priests.'

'Constantine's court. One burst in on Constantine the first time I was at his council and began to berate

him on the inappropriateness of his wife's clothing.'
She looped her hands about his neck and nestled herself against his body. 'My gown is a problem for the
future. I won't shame you.'

'I wasn't speaking about your clothes,' he growled
against her ear. 'I was speaking about what we are about
to do, what I hope we will do, but you need a choice. I'm
offering one while I still can. You're drunk, Dagmar.'

'It takes far more than a tankard or two of mead to
get me drunk.'

She reached up a hand and stroked his cheek. Aedan
seemed uncertain that she would know about coupling,
about where this would lead. She understood the me-
chanics of coupling. She had seen the furtive fumbling
after feasts and had heard men boasting about their
prowess. She simply had never wanted to experience it
for herself. Now she did. She wanted to dream that she
was his woman for one night. And she hadn't lied—he
did keep the nightmares at bay.

She put her mouth next to his, making one final attempt. 'Stay. We've already agreed. You stay. You must
think me a green girl, not a warrior who has served for
five summers. I take full responsibility for my actions
and I want you in my bed.' A small hiccup escaped her
throat. 'I want you under me, over me and in me. Is that
explicit enough?'

He simply stood there not moving a muscle.

'Say something,' she whispered. 'I beg you.'

'That is definitely the mead talking. I smell its honey
sweetness on you. In the morning, you will have a bad
head and I hope no more regrets than normal.'

'You wrong me greatly. Yes, the mead may have

loosened my tongue but I haven't said anything that I wasn't already thinking. Why must we keep silent?'

Dagmar clasped her hands together. Her stomach roiled. Had she made a fool of herself again?

He had stayed still and hadn't run, watching her with those eyes of his. It was her single hope. She could break through his defences. He desired this as much as she did.

'I meant it about the nightmares.' She put her hand to her head. 'The battle. Everything. I rarely sleep except for last night. Last night I slept soundly for the first time in months.'

He laced his fingers in hers. 'You're safe here.'

She kept her fingers curled about his. 'But I want you to stay with me. I know this deep inside me. You are the first man who has tempted me in this way.'

There, she had said it, confessed about her virginity. She waited with bated breath to see what he would do.

He gave a groan. 'There are many reasons why this is wrong.'

'But it is right.' Before he could draw away, she cupped his face with her hands, feeling the rough beginnings of a beard against her palms. She blew on his mouth before she kissed him, making sure their tongues tangled once again.

He gave a low groan and the intensity of his mouth increased. She could feel the power and passion growing within him.

'Aedan?' she breathed in his ear.

'You talk too much.'

His hands roamed over her back, pressing her closer to his hard body. There was no fat on him, simply lean hard muscle.

She slipped her hands under his tunic and felt the rigid muscle under her palms. There were indents and twists in his smooth skin which showed he'd fought and had recovered from several injuries.

He seemed to understand her need to touch him and stripped off. In the dim light, she could make out the network of scars which marred his back. She put her hands against his chest. Her palms brushed his nipples and he gave a sudden intake of breath.

'I believe you require some assistance to disrobe.'

'I am not very good with tight sleeves and you are right, it is a pretty gown. I would have loved it when I was ten. I used to play at being a fine lady.'

'Another confession from the mead?'

'I thought you deserved the truth. I... I've not worn gowns since I was blooded in battle and became a shield maiden. How things work in my world. When shield maidens marry, they put away shields, swords and warfare, returning to gowns, soft words and women's work, but not before then.'

He slowly lifted the gown over her head and threw it on to the straw.

The cool air touched her fevered skin. She quivered in anticipation.

He lowered his mouth and traced a line down to where her breasts were still bound. 'What is this for? Are you injured?'

'It makes it easier for fighting.' Her voice sounded husky to her ears. 'I wear it all the time except at night. You never know when you might have to fight. I didn't take it off yesterday because...'

'You are not going to do battle tonight.' He gave a husky laugh. 'Let me assist you. I have wondered...'

'If it is necessary?'

'Yes.'

He took one end and slowly she twirled until she was free of the binding and could take deep breaths again.

His hand cupped first one breast and then the other, gently kneading and caressing them until her nipples became hardened points. Heat thrummed through her, causing her to gasp. 'They have been in prison for too long.'

'Have they?'

His finger flicked over the nipple points and live jolts shook through her. Before she had time to react he lowered his mouth and took first one and then the other nipple into his mouth. He gently nuzzled them with his tongue, going round and round. A piercing sensation swept through her and her body arched towards the enticing feel of his mouth against her.

He gently lowered her down on to the pile of clothes.

Going on instinct, she let her hands drift lower until she reached his waistband. She feverishly worked on the fastenings.

'If you release me,' he rumbled in her ear, 'this will be over before we have begun. Allow me to feast on you first.'

She gave a slight nod and forced her hands to fall by her sides.

'You see, you can take direction.'

His tongue returned to her breasts and teased them into hardened points once again. When she considered she would expire from sheer pleasure, his mouth moved inexorably lower. He lapped at her belly button before sinking further still.

Stars exploded through her and her body appeared

to have developed a mind of its own. Her hands went back to his trousers, knowing she needed him inside her.

He lifted his body on his elbows and took them off. His rampant erection sprang free.

She reached out a hand to touch it and it quivered, silken.

'I can't wait any longer,' he groaned.

'Please,' she whispered, knowing her body needed much more.

She parted her legs and he entered her carefully. He stilled instantly when he encountered her maidenhead. Fearing that he might stop, she lifted her hips and coaxed him further in, until his entire length filled her, giving her intense pleasure.

She began to rock back and forth, moving faster and faster. To her relief, he began to do the same.

She held on to him and made a wonderful memory. This, this was the perfect way to keep the nightmares at bay.

Aedan slowly came back to earth. One thought kept racing through his brain—Dagmar, the daughter of one of the most ruthless Northern Jaarls, had been a virgin. He had taken her maidenhead and he had no idea how Kolbeinn would react. He had never stopped to consider that the shield maiden was actually a virgin woman warrior, but even her kisses had been artless now that he came to consider them.

He ground his teeth. A primitive anger flashed through him. He wanted to slay her unknown future husband for even daring to look at her, let alone experience what he had shared with her. As an honourable man, he should make an offer to marry her, but he could easily imagine how Kolbeinn would react to such an offer.

He'd be lucky to survive the interview with his limbs intact for daring to raise the subject. Kolbeinn might even use his impertinence as an excuse to attack Kintra. Kolbeinn had made it very clear what he thought about Kintra and its pretences towards freedom and independence. And the people of Kintra would never accept a pagan for their lady. To even think about it showed how unworthy he was to be their King. He was putting his desires above their needs.

Kolbeinn had plans for his only living child, plans which she'd hate and which would probably destroy her spirit. He had no choice but to take her like a lamb to the slaughter if he wanted to save his people and their way of life. After everything that had happened, he knew his first duty had to be to his people.

Her hand came up and stroked his face. 'Did I do something wrong? Did I make a mistake? Speak to me.'

It was one of the things he liked about her—her refreshing directness. She deserved a version of the truth until he could figure out a way around the tangle.

He smoothed her hair from her forehead. 'Why didn't you warn me?'

'Warn you of what?'

'That you were a maiden. That you had never lain with a man before.'

'I did say something,' she retorted indignantly, pulling away from him. 'That you chose to ignore my words is not my problem. Men! I honoured you and now you are angry with me. Perhaps it is you who had too much mead.'

'Your father—how will he react when he discovers what we did?'

'I've no plans to tell him. It is none of his business who I sleep with. He lost that right years ago, if indeed he ever had it.'

He blinked several times. Dagmar's reaction was not what he expected. Tears and cries—pleas, even—that he make it right, coupled with a demand for marriage, certainly, but not this matter-of-fact proclamation that she'd honoured him.

'Will it be a problem, when…?'

He found he could not bring himself to mention when she would arrive at her father's compound that she'd be married.

'I suspect everyone thinks I lost it years ago, but I never found any man worthy of it. I've never met a man who wanted me for me, rather than for what I represented.' Her thin laugh held more than a note of bitterness. 'No, let's be honest. No man until you wanted me.'

A flush of pleasure went through him and he felt his body begin to harden again. If he took her again tonight, he could hurt her. 'Not want you? Are they blind?'

She gave a sigh. 'Flatterer.'

'Hardly that. I have had the pleasure of seeing you without the paint, with your hair loose about your face and your breasts unbound. You are a very desirable woman, Dagmar.'

'Thank you. You make me feel beautiful.'

'I'm honoured that you considered me worthy of being your first lover.'

'Does it matter to you? It is not as though I demanded that I be the first with you.'

'No,' he lied as part of him rejoiced that she had been

a virgin. He also knew his feelings of responsibility had increased towards her. He had to make sure she was safe and any child which might result from their union well looked after. But he also knew that this liaison would end when they reached Colbhasa. Marriage and spending the rest of their lives together was an impossible dream that he could not contemplate. It shocked him that his heart kept whispering what a good idea it was and that he should put the proposition to her. He turned a deaf ear to it. The last time he'd listened to his heart, he had come close to ruining everything.

It was no good pretending that he would not have taken her if she had not begged him to. He had wanted her very badly. He simply wished he had considered the full import of her words beforehand.

'How would you have changed things if you'd realised?'

'I'd have taken more care. With a maidenhead, you should spend more time preparing the woman, making sure she isn't spoiled for the future. This act can be pleasurable for both...in time.'

She stretched slightly and her breasts brushed his naked chest. His body hardened further in response and he knew that once was not enough. He wanted her under him and around him. He wanted to spend days and nights exploring and learning the contours of her body. Except for the wager...

His people waited for him. He tried to picture Mhairi as she had been when they said goodbye—her face turned up towards his as if she was expecting a kiss. She had whispered that she believed in him, that he could save her, if he but tried.

The memory had spurred him on in the early days

when he had searched the length and breadth of Alba for Dagmar, but with Dagmar in his arms, he could only think about a pair of brilliant blue eyes agreeing to help him win his wager, even though she had to know that her life would alter irrevocably afterwards. Suddenly he wanted to find a way to save her from her fate, but he could not think of one that did not harm the people he'd sworn to protect.

'It'll get better,' he said instead. 'Next time, you won't bleed or experience pain.'

She gave a contented sigh. 'It was already beyond describing. I will believe you, though, when you say that it gets even better.'

'Women do not enjoy their first time.'

This time her laugh was far richer. She ran an artless hand down his flank to cup his erection. 'I'm not most women. Are you blind?'

She put her hands on his cheeks and his body began to make its demands known. In another heartbeat he would have her on her back, thrusting mindlessly into her. He rolled away and retrieved his trousers.

She wouldn't be ready for it. Later when she had recovered, he promised his body. Later he would ensure that she experienced true pleasure, rather than merely thinking she had.

'Why have you done that?'

'You need to sleep.'

Her hands tugged at the trousers, inching their way closer to his erection. 'I exist on little.'

He captured her hands and held them above her head. 'I've no wish to hurt you.'

'I'm fine. I told you I enjoyed it.' She twisted first one way and then the other, trying to get free. The movement gave even more encouragement to his member which hardened to the point of pain.

'There is much for you to learn.' He nipped her naked shoulder and she stilled. 'I promise I will teach you when you are ready.'

Her lower lip trembled. 'And in the morning…'

'We need to travel in the morning,' he said, placing a kiss on her bottom lip. 'We should get some rest.'

'I was able to sleep last night in your arms.' Her voice was small and vulnerable as though she expected him to refuse.

Aedan wondered if her tough act was simply a front to hide the very vulnerable woman who called out for help in her bad dreams. A powerful urge to protect her rose within him. He dampened it down and tried to remember that his first duty was to Kintra and the people who dwelt there. But somehow Kintra appeared awfully far away.

'I believe that can be arranged.'

Aedan listened to the soft sound of her breathing. He had betrayed Kolbeinn's trust in a way, but he was not sorry. He could not regret this. He simply had to figure out how he was going to say goodbye to Dagmar when the time came and prevent her from stealing his heart away.

A thin light filled the alcove. Dagmar woke with a thumping head. Her body ached in places that it had never ached before but it was a pleasant ache. She stretched and felt the faint rasp of straw against her naked skin.

A small part of her wanted to believe that it had been a delicious dream that might continue for ever if she was clever. She'd given herself to Aedan after the mead had loosened her tongue, but she'd failed to explain why. He needed to understand that she wasn't one of those women who clung to a man after a night's coupling. She simply desired one night of pleasure to hold in her heart during the dark days which surely must come. The last thing she wanted to do was to jeopardise the *felag* they shared.

She reached out a hand, but encountered empty straw.

She hurriedly pulled on her gown. The rip under her arm split further. She cursed under her breath. Later she'd attend to it. Mor waited at the door and gave her hand a reassuring lick. At least his dog guarded her. She took a deep breath and willed the panic to go. Regardless of his regrets, he still needed her to win his wager and free the hostages.

Aedan and the priest were deep in conversation. He glanced up and gave her a smile which made her stop in her tracks. Her heart leaped. Maybe she'd been wrong about his reason for leaving her to wake up alone. Maybe something had come up. Maybe one of Thorsten's men had appeared.

The sun was too high in the sky. For the first time in her life, she'd overslept. Smoothing down her gown, she hurried over to the pair.

'Your husband has been most generous,' the priest said, beaming from ear to ear.

'Has he?' she said, quite forgetting that she was supposed to be mute.

The priest clapped his hands together. 'The mead has done its fabled work. Your voice has truly returned. I will inform the bishop of the miracle.'

'Worked wonders indeed,' Aedan murmured.

Dagmar shot him an uncertain glance. 'I believe miracles are best not trumpeted. It wouldn't be seemly.'

The priest gave a solemn nod. 'You speak wisdom, lady.'

'It is what I truly believe.'

'Your husband has donated this gold to the church.' The priest held out the gold Aedan had liberated from the robbers. She frowned. She thought Aedan would have wanted it for himself and his people.

'In exchange for your two ponies,' Aedan said. 'A fair price.'

'They are hardly worth this much. They are slow but sturdy. I had wondered how I would get them through the winter. I prayed yesterday for guidance and this happens. I will have enough to purchase the small donkey I've had my eye on for a week.'

Aedan bowed low. 'Nevertheless, it is your payment.'

'Another miracle and the day has barely begun.'

The priest bustled off to say morning prayers for his small flock and Dagmar was left standing with Aedan. Her stomach clenched as her eyes devoured his form. The man looked even better in the pale morning light, standing there with a stupid smile on his face as if he had done something even more wonderful than he had done last night.

'Ponies?' she asked tilting her head to one side. 'You bought ponies with the robbers' gold?'

'To get to your father's quicker. I assume you know how to ride. Time slips through our fingers. If we walk, it will take far too long.'

Dagmar bit her lip. A large part of her had hoped

they would go more slowly now and savour their time together, but she refused to beg. 'How much longer?'

'Eight days to get there with a day to spare, because we have to make sure the tide is right. The passage to Colbhasa can be tricky in the autumn. We may have to wait for the weather to clear. I doubt your father would consider waiting for the weather an acceptable excuse.'

Dagmar pressed her hands together and tried to swallow the sense of disappointment. Less than ten days— more than a week, but not much.

Dagmar drew herself up to her full height. 'I hope you can ride as I mean to go as swiftly as possible. What we shared last night changes nothing. The *felag* remains intact. We will save your people.'

He caught her arm and his hand seemed to burn through the cloth. 'Allow me to finish before you start making pronouncements. Riding the pony will make it easier for you when you get tired.'

'I'm hardly some frail flower. I've campaigned for five seasons!'

'But this was the first time you'd lain with a man.'

Her insides ached a bit, but they failed to compare with injuries she had suffered last warring season. Then she had marched for six days and nights with an injured side to help get Constantine to safety. 'I've always managed after every injury.'

'Even riding with good horses, it would take us several days to reach the coast and then we may have to wait for the tide to be right. The ponies, by their nature, plod at a much slower pace.'

'Last night happened but the once. You do not intend to drink any more mead.' She finished his words for him. Her throat closed. She'd been wrong to press herself on him. What had seemed so right to her was but a tumble in the straw with a warm body for him. He had been under the influence of the mead as well otherwise he would not have touched her. 'I understand completely. Mead can do strange things. We should leave it at that and get on with our fellowship. I regret you were inconvenienced, but you made me feel beautiful for one night, something I thought could never happen.'

Aedan gave her a sharp look as his throat worked up and down.

'I… I…never said that you were an inconvenience. I… I…would never say that. How can you even begin to think it?' he spluttered.

'What then? What did you mean? I know how men can be.' Dagmar stared at his chest rather than meeting his eyes. 'I've lived in close proximity to men. I know how heartless they can be about women. I've heard the sweet prattle before and the disdainful dismissal after.'

Aedan's nostril's flared. 'Don't put me together with the Northern warriors you have known. Ever.'

'Then why? Why leave me to wake up alone?'

He put his hands on her shoulders. The simple touch did much to calm her. 'The ponies are sturdy, but no one could call them fast. It will be more comfortable for you.' He smoothed her hair back from her forehead. 'I would rather have us both fresh for the night's activities…if you understand my meaning.'

Dagmar's heart soared. He intended their joining to continue beyond one night. Despite her earlier fears, he desired her. Maybe he was right and she was beautiful. 'When you weren't there… I woke…and I assumed the worst.'

His face settled into its more familiar harsh planes.

'Try trusting me. We are in a fellowship, working together for a common cause. Without you meeting your father, my life would not be worth living.'

Dagmar swallowed hard. The fellowship would end far sooner than she desired. 'The last man I trusted was my father and we both know how that turned out.'

'Shall we go? Get some miles on the road because in Alba, in the autumn when the sun shines, the rain is sure to follow.'

Dagmar regarded the hamlet. There was something peaceful and calm about this place, as though nothing bad could ever happen here. 'I wish we could linger.'

'I have responsibilities which transcend my desires. You do as well.'

She hugged her arms about her waist, hating that Aedan was right. Remaining here, living in some dream land, was an impossibility.

Dagmar hit her hand against her head. This was why her mother warned her against becoming involved with a man. Her judgement went. Instead of feeling sorry for herself, she needed to think like a warrior again. 'I know all about my responsibilities.'

He caught her hand and raised it to his lips. 'I'm not very good with fancy words. Not in the way my brother was… I want to protect you, Dagmar but…my people must come first. Always.'

'Once our *felag* has finished, my future lies along a very different path to yours,' she said before he had the chance to get the words out. 'I know what is between us will end. My father will never guess it ever existed. Your offer of protection is unnecessary.'

He drew a line along her jaw. 'Even still…'

'Once we get to Colbhasa, I will ensure my father

pays the full measure of his bargain and we will part without a backward glance or a tear.' The words burst forth from far deep in her soul. 'But we will still have this time, whatever our future holds. Please.'

She waited and a tiny piece of her whispered that he'd say that he planned on making an offer for her hand when they arrived at Colbhasa. She hated that she'd be tempted to accept despite everything her mother had instilled in her about men's treachery and how marriage diminished women.

'Then I must be happy with what I have.' He turned his back to her and started to adjust the blankets on the ponies. 'I look forward to exploring your body properly and showing you what pleasure can truly be.'

She released her breath and hoped her heart would be content with that.

Chapter Seven

Aedan guided his plodding pony along the sun-dappled track. The puddles gleamed in the unexpected sunshine. Even the day seemed brighter because Dagmar was in it.

It amazed him that she worried he wouldn't want her after they had coupled once. Not want her? He had trouble remembering when he'd been this hot for any woman, even Brigid in the heady days when he actually thought she cared for him, before he discovered the truth.

It was helpful that Dagmar was being sensible and understood that they had no future together, yet something nagged at him. He'd met the woman who set his senses alight and she could already see an end to it. She saw a future beyond him.

He glanced over to her and his breath stopped in his throat. The sunlight made it seem as though she was wearing a golden crown. She moved slightly, causing the material across her breasts to tighten. His body hardened immediately at the sight of her erect nipples. He slid off his pony and went over to her.

'Why have we stopped here?' Dagmar asked, tilting her head to one side. 'We were making good progress. Shall I change back into my proper clothes? Do you want that demonstration on how to flip a warrior on his backside?'

Her proper clothes and then a remark about her promised sharing of her fighting techniques, a subtle reminder if he needed it that she was a warrior first and a woman second. What he wanted was the woman. He needed to find a way to convince her to remain a woman and not erect her defences until they reached the western shore. He could see them going up by the heartbeat and the priest had failed to give him more mead.

'You will soon discover,' Aedan said, making a decision. A risk, but Dagmar had to come to the conclusion to wear her gown on her own. 'Get down.'

She started to slide off.

'No, not like that, wait until I am there.'

Dagmar made a disgusted noise. 'For Freyja's sake, I know how to get off a horse. I am not some creature made of precious glass.'

'Good things come to those who wait.' He put his hands about her waist and slid her down the length of him. His body needed no encouragement to respond.

Her eyes widened as she encountered his erection.

'We're far from anyone which is excellent,' he said in her ear. 'And I've no wish to share. I didn't have time to properly wake you this morning and I wish to make up for my...lack of manners.'

She displayed no maidenly hesitation, but pressed her body up against his. 'You want me to undress in the daytime?'

'No, I'm about to demonstrate why gowns can be

useful. Why you might consider keeping this one on, not simply as a disguise.'

Claiming her mouth, he backed her up against a tree. With one hand, he rucked her gown up. As he had hoped, she was bare underneath.

His fingers encountered her soft nest of curls, skilfully slipping in and playing amongst the delicate folds. She was instantly wet and sleek for him. He knelt in front of her and tasted the salty sweetness where his fingers had played, moving his tongue round and round. She gave an inarticulate cry and her body convulsed. He slipped a finger inside her and her entire being quivered to a delicious shudder.

Her hands clawed at his shoulders and he glanced up. Her eyes were heavy lidded and her mouth a dusky pink with passion. His body thrummed in anticipation.

'I want you in me.'

'You are—'

She put a finger against his mouth. 'I know what I am and what I want and no one, not even you, gets to make that decision for me. You in me, here. Now.'

He rose and gathered her face between his palms. 'I accept the command with pleasure.'

Her arms tangled about his neck and pulled him closer.

He lifted her bottom and drove into her. She put her legs about his waist, holding him there.

Mewling cries emerged from her throat as he felt her tighten about him.

His body convulsed as her cries reached fever pitch. All around them the birds started singing.

Coming back to earth, Aedan smoothed the hair from her forehead. 'That is why a gown is a good idea.'

She stepped away from him and rearranged her skirts. 'I may have to rethink. Gowns do have their uses, but you are not wearing one and you still managed.'

He smiled. 'I stand corrected.'

'And was this the pleasure you promised me earlier?'

'No, this was merely a taste of what is to come. I have trouble keeping my hands off you in that gown.'

Her cheeks became flame-coloured. 'If it is impeding our progress, then perhaps I should change.'

'Your choice.'

She gave a throaty laugh. 'As I have started in this, I shall wear it for today. However, I will not wear a gown when we arrive at my father's. A point of principle.'

It was on the tip of his tongue to tell her that no matter what she wore or how she acted or even how good a warrior she was, her father would see her married. And the man she married, had children with and shared the simple pleasures of living with, would not be him.

The thought was like a dose of cold water. He couldn't bear to see the light die in her eyes. She'd find out soon enough. He was being a coward, but they had both agreed—they parted at the end and each went to live his or her own life. In her old clothes, she'd be easier to let go.

'I think we might risk sleeping under the stars tonight,' he said instead.

Her eyes sparkled. 'Only if you are sure...'

'I've discovered the perfect way to keep warm.'

'Tell me about Kintra. Tell me about your home.' Dagmar drew her knees to her chest as she sat beside the small fire.

They had stopped for the night by a small dry cave,

easy to defend if they had to, and had finished feasting on the food the priest had thoughtfully provided and some windfall apples Aedan had discovered.

Aedan stirred the fire, sending a series of sparks up into the sky. 'Why do you want to know?'

'Curiosity, mainly,' Dagmar admitted with a sigh. She envied Aedan a home, a place where he belonged, where he was loved and belonged. 'You love the place. That much is clear from your voice whenever you speak of it.'

'Kintra's requirements and the people who live there can drive me wild at times but when I am away from it, I miss it. It becomes a dull ache in my chest. When it gets too great, I return. But this should be the final time I need to be away. The time is right for me to shoulder my responsibilities.'

'But what does it look like? I want to picture it in my mind.'

'Why?'

'Because some day when I am going about my business I may want to think of you. Is that too strange a thought?'

Aedan described the island, the hall and the fields that surrounded it until a clear picture rose in Dagmar's mind. Her heart twisted. Even if there were no lives at stake, Dagmar knew she could not ask him to run away with her and turn his back on this place. The passion he had for it shone out of his face.

'It must be pleasant to have a home like that, somewhere where you truly belong, a place of refuge from the wider world.'

He gave her a troubled look. 'I grew up there. My family has kept a watch over it for many generations. I'm not going to be the person who abandons it to the marauding hordes. What about Colbhasa? Could that be home for you?'

She shook her head. Her heart gave a pang at the lands she'd forfeited through Olafr's treachery. She could have been happy there. 'That will never be my home. I grew up on a small farm on a fjord in Viken. Prosperous enough and my parents would leave each summer to journey to Kaupang and other trading places.'

'Did they take you?'

'If it was to Kaupang, yes, but on the open sea, no. I was left behind with my nurse. Eventually my parents acquired more land and power. My mother had to stay home and rule while my father went off. They used to fight about it, but he would never yield.'

'But he failed to remain there after your mother left.'

'You'd have to ask him why he left. The politics in Viken are complicated. All I know is that my childhood home no longer exists. My mother raged about it for weeks when she learned that. In her final years, she wanted a place to call home and to grow old in. It failed to happen in the way she dreamt.'

Or the way she'd vowed it would when I was a child. Dagmar kept the thought silent.

'Did your mother acquire more land, provide you with a new home?'

Dagmar explained rapidly about the lands Constantine had promised and how they'd farmed them for two seasons in anticipation of being gifted them. 'When my mother died, her funeral pyre shone bright over the loch. But that is all gone because of treachery.'

'Had Olafr's treachery not happened?'

'Then I would have retired from fighting to farm there.' Dagmar watched the flames. They danced like a battle and she could see the faces of those simple farmers who had at first mistrusted them, but had come to realise that they were responsible masters. 'I've seen too many good men die. Dollar was to be my last battle and then I would have concentrated on protecting my interests and being a good steward of the land.' She gave a bitter laugh. 'Old Alf used to say that was what my mother always said at the end of the season, but she was unable to resist the drums of war. But ever since the middle of the last warring season, I've had this longing in my soul to sit and watch sunsets.'

'And now?' There was a catch in his voice.

'My choices are limited—I am an excellent warrior. I can always become a sell-sword if my father refuses to listen to common sense. Eventually I will acquire my own lands where I can sit and watch the sunset without worrying about the next morning's battle. I make you that promise.'

He put his hands behind his head. 'Your father might have other ideas about your future.'

Dagmar rose and raised her fist to the darkening sky. 'My father will understand my need to avenge my men. He'll give me ships. Once he sees my prowess in the art of warfare, he will see sense.'

'And if he doesn't?' Aedan asked into the stillness. At her glance, he stood and came over to her, putting heavy hands on her shoulders. 'I don't want you to get your hopes up, Dagmar. I don't want you to get hurt.'

'I'll find another way.' She brushed his lips with hers. 'You're sweet to worry but I can best my father. I will ensure my future happens how I've envisioned it. I won't be sacrificed on the altar of my father's ambition.'

Aedan's frown increased. 'Kolbeinn is a very determined man. He hates to be thwarted. He possesses the power to enforce his will.'

She put a hand against his face. 'And I am his daughter. My coming battle with my father will wait until you have won your wager. Shall we do some more training? I need to be in perfect condition when I encounter Olafr.'

Aedan ignored her touch. 'Why do I suspect you told Old Alf the same thing about Olafr's intentions? Did you also seek to distract him?'

'Not in this way.'

'It is far too late for training.'

Dagmar hugged her arms about her waist. Why did he hit unerring on the flaw in her plan? 'Without hope, I'm nothing.'

He tilted her chin upwards. 'I'm grateful for what you are doing for my people. If there is any help I can give you without jeopardising them, I will, but I know the size of your father's fleet and my people have suffered enough. My first duty is always to them.'

A conditional promise of help was more than she had expected. She raised up on her toes and put her face next to his. 'I will keep your words in the forefront of my mind when I encounter my father. Right now, I think I need some more help to keep the bad dreams at bay.'

The stars sparkled overhead as Dagmar snuggled deeper into the circle of Aedan's arms a few nights later. For the last three nights, she had tried to pretend that they would never get to the west coast of Alba. The journey had been relatively smooth and each night they had found a place to rest.

Dagmar learned more about coupling than she

thought possible. She had learned that his touch could turn her insides to liquid and that it was pleasant to wake up with him inside her. She learned how to hold his erection and drive him wild. But mostly she had discovered that she fitted with this man and that she enjoyed being a woman.

By concentrating on Aedan and the way he played her body like a harp, she had stopped thinking about her uncertain future. Tonight she found it impossible to sleep. Despite her brave words to Aedan, she had no perfect plan for ensuring her father bowed to her will. She had to hope that her father would be impressed with her skill as a warrior and would see what an asset she was, rather than marrying her off immediately.

On Colbhasa her future would be very different from what she had planned with her mother. Even though her stepmother was dead, it was quite possible that her father had already had discovered some other woman to get his sons on and she'd once again have to fight for her survival.

All the possibilities for dying that her mother used to recite to her came flooding back. All the times when she had wanted to give up and her mother whispered that she needed to be strong in order to fight. She was down, but not defeated. She could fight back. But she had run out of ideas on how to do it. All she knew was that she wasn't going to be a counter in her father's power games. A sigh escaped her throat.

Aedan raised up on his elbow. 'Trouble sleeping? That is unlike you. Lately you have been quite the sound sleeper in the morning.'

'Going over tomorrow in my mind. All the possibilities for the future after we catch the tide.' She made her voice sound steady. 'Once I've shown my father that I am a good and competent warrior, everything should fall into place.'

'How will you do that?'

'I'll fight his chosen champion if I have to.' Silently she prayed that it wouldn't be Aedan. Her father did have a way of twisting things to suit his purpose and he had likely sent Aedan to be slain. 'My mother did that and won. Maybe he will agree to a contest where I can prove my skills. Once I defeat them all, he will have to admit that a daughter is just as good as a son.'

He laughed. 'I believe you can defeat them.'

'Once I do that, I'm sure he will see the wisdom in giving me a ship or two to enact my revenge against Olafr.'

The possibility should have had her brimming with excitement, but it depressed her. There would be so much to do—outfitting the ships, finding the warriors who were willing to serve under her, selecting the target to cause the maximum pain for Olafr and force him to come out of hiding and the men who would die or be maimed because of her decisions.

She was up to the task. One step at a time and not looking too far ahead. She wished she had Old Alf or someone to lean on.

She'd miss being part of a team, though, the way she had been with Aedan and Mor. They did work well together. She could talk to him about anything. Anything except… Dagmar paused. She cared for him. It wasn't supposed to have happened, but when they parted after her father had made good on the wager, he'd take a large part of her heart with him.

She focused on a spot somewhere over Acdan's left

shoulder. What was it that her mother used to say—never regret what you could not have, turn your face to the future and concentrate on what you can achieve. Aedan was wedded to his people and his lands. He wasn't hers, could never be. She only had him for a short and very precious time. She had to be content with that.

'Next summer, I will be leading my own *felag*. You just watch. You can be a part of it, my second in command. You could even choose which king to offer our service to.' She waited with a thumping heart. Aedan of all people had to believe in her dream.

He rolled away from her. Her body protested at the sudden coldness. He rapidly dressed.

'Is there a problem?'

'The sun is starting to rise. We will need to get the boat if we are going to make the tide. We need to get back to our real lives, Dagmar, rather than inventing a future to suit us.'

'Boat? Your currach, you mean.' Dagmar made her voice sound bright, but she could taste the ashes of disappointment in her mouth. When was she going to learn that wanting more only led to heartache? 'A little boat rather than one of the dragon ships the north use. It is supposedly much more adept at manoeuvring which could be an advantage in the right circumstances.'

He tucked her hair behind her ear. 'Very good, you are learning. You begin to think like a Gael.'

'Do you think they will look after the ponies properly? I have grown quite fond of mine,' she said, rather than pathetically leaning into his touch.

'The couple who have looked after my boat are good people. They will be pleased to have the ponies.'

She looped her arms about her knees. 'What will you

do after you take me to my father's, after you win your wager? You have never truly said. Will you marry? Is there someone waiting for your return?'

His hand stilled on her back and she knew that there had to be someone, probably the woman who was the hostage. Her father's gold would make the marriage possible. It must be why he had stopped mentioning her. 'You were never bothered about that before.'

'In the spring, will you find some warlord to pledge your service to?'

She waited with a thumping heart. He had to understand what she was asking. Did he want to spend more time with her once his obligations to his people were sorted? If they both pledged to the same warlord, they could have the summers together. It would be enough— and yet she already knew she was lying to herself. She would hate whomever he married.

He laughed. 'My people will want me to stay. This was to be my final expedition. They have been patient for far too long. I suspect that they will have forgotten my face. And the gold your father gives me will enable much to happen that has been postponed.'

Dagmar concentrated on the horizon which had started to turn a brilliant pink. He had a responsibility to his people. He would have to marry and produce an heir. She had always known it was not going to last. So why did she feel so heartsick? 'This is truly the end then. I'll treasure this time we had together.'

He laced their hands and brought them to his lips. His eyes were inscrutable. 'You'll inform me, if you are with child,' he said.

Dagmar nearly missed a step. With child. Instinctively she put her hand against her flat stomach. It would be good to have a child, a permanent reminder of her time with this Gael. Despite the discomfort of the journey, she'd been happier than she had ever been.

After the divorce, her mother had looked after her. She could do the same for a child, but she would be better. She could see now that her mother had been far from perfect. Any child that she had would never have to fear for his or her life because of a parent's anger. 'Everything will be taken care of.'

'I wanted to let you know that I would be prepared to do my part and provide support if necessary,' he said.

'Child or no, you're going back to your people and I to my new life. What was between us is in the past. I always look to the future and the next battle to be won.'

She put her hand on his cheek. He covered it with his own for a few seconds, but then turned to undo the ponies. Her hand already felt empty. It was probably the last time she'd touch him in that way. She curled her fist up tight to allow the sensation to linger.

'You do not need to come with me to my father's,' she called. 'I can go on my own. I will ensure you get all that is due to you.'

'I must come with you—else how will he know that I have fulfilled my wager? Think.' He smiled, but his eyes were full of silent resolve. 'I will be there, Dagmar. You won't have to face your father alone when you meet him for the first time in more than a decade.'

Dagmar bit her lip. Her plan of escaping to be a sellsword if her father proved obstinate would be more difficult to execute if Aedan remained in the vicinity. She'd just have to wait. She needed to be cautious and not to let her anger get the better of her. 'I hate long goodbyes.'

'As do I. Provided your father behaves as he swore

he would, there should be no need for me to stay. I will be back in Ile before nightfall if the wind is right.'

Dagmar's heart thudded. She hadn't realised that Ile was so close to Colbhasa. It made sense now why her father could threaten Aedan's lands in that way.

'I know not to weep when you go. I rarely weep, only when my mother died,' she said into the silence. 'My father will not guess what passed between us.'

He lifted a brow. 'And if you have a child? You would find it difficult to hide that and your father will be able to count.'

'It remains none of his business.' She pressed her hands together. If it came to it, then she would withstand the pressure.

'When the child wants to meet me, I will be willing.'

'If it comes to pass, then I will consider your offer. No point in crossing bridges until one actually reaches the stream as my nurse used to say.'

She knew the tears would come later, but they would be in private just as she had wept for her mother. This was not about love. It was about mourning the passing of something so special that it had reshaped her world. Not love, she repeated in her mind. It was about a time when she did not have to be strong or striving to be the best and most competent warrior, but a time that she had been able to be her most true self.

Right now, she had to concentrate on ensuring Aedan won the wager and rescued the woman he would eventually marry. She had given her word and she would see it done, even if it was the last thing she wanted to do. Her future did not and never could include Aedan as a life partner.

Chapter Eight

The small tidal island of Orfirisey appeared off the boat's bow while the peaks of the much larger Colbhasa rose behind it. And behind that, the pale-purple haze that were the Paps of Jura shimmered, mountains that anyone in Kintra could see if they faced the right direction. Returning home a free man was very nearly within Aedan's grasp. He would keep Kintra independent, but at the expense of Dagmar's freedom—somehow the prospect was a lot less appealing now than when he'd first started his quest.

Dagmar's white knuckles clutched the side of the boat in a death grip and her face was set hard. She'd changed back into her trousers and once more had become the forbidding shield maiden, instead of the quicksilver woman he had held in his arms and had made love to. Her one concession was not to put her hair into her war plaits, but to wear a single plait going down her back.

Her question about his marriage plans had unnerved him. He had not thought of Mhairi and her plight for days. It was wrong of him, but the prospect of marriage to that woman held even less appeal than it had before she'd volunteered herself as a sacrifice. And yet within a short while, he would have to face the woman and her expectations. He'd always vowed never to marry the way his brother had done, to lie to his wife about his feelings for her.

When Dagmar asked about his future plans, for one wild heartbeat he considered asking her to marry him, but common sense had prevailed and the words died on his lips. What could he offer her? The few windswept acres were enough for him and his people, but it was not what her father would require for his only living child. His people would never accept a pagan warlord as their lady. He could well imagine Dagmar's response if he asked her to not only give up her life as a warrior, but also to give up the gods she held dear.

He had to hope that Kolbeinn would tread lightly on her dreams. And he knew she would always carry a piece of his heart with her, wherever she went.

If she was bearing his child? He tightened his hand about the tiller. He certainly was not going to behave like his brother—attempting to marry off the woman he'd impregnated to a gullible fool like he had been. Neither would he allow Dagmar to raise the child on her own. He'd be involved. Somehow. A problem for another day.

Dagmar shaded her eyes. 'I can make out my father's fleet where they are drawn up on the shore. There are so many of them. He has amassed an army.'

'More than you thought.'

'More than I'd considered, yes.' She flashed a brilliant smile at him. 'Perhaps he will allow me to captain one of the ships without too much trouble. Competent warriors are hard to find.'

'Building dreams again?'

Her bottom lip jutted out. 'Trying to survive. I'll find a way, Aedan, I swear it. My father will not shape my future to suit his purpose.'

'Why does that worry me?'

'I've ceased to be your problem.'

'Until your father pays the wager in full, you and your actions remain my problem,' he said focusing on the boats drawn up on the shore, rather than meeting her expressive eyes. 'I will hold true to the fellowship as will Mor.'

'Cutting it fine, Gael. Tomorrow is All Hallows Eve,' one of Kolbeinn's helmsmen shouted as the currach made its way towards the various longboats which were pulled up on shore.

'The deadline is All Hallows as Kolbeinn knows,' Dagmar shouted from where she sat. At Aedan's request, Dagmar had remained in the boat, rather than getting out to help pull it ashore as was her natural instinct.

'Hush, Dagmar,' Aedan said in an undertone. 'A *felag* can only have one leader, remember.'

'If my father or his followers attempt to back out of his obligations, I will act.' Dagmar tightened her grip on her daggers which were stuck in her belt. 'My father will honour his pledge, one way or another.'

'Keep silent. Please. We come in peace.'

'For now.' She forced her fingers to release the daggers.

She mentally rehearsed her speech to her father

which she had made at least fifteen times on the journey across the sea. He had to understand that she was going to be a shield maiden for the remainder of her days.

She gave a small snort. Hopefully her father would never realise the maiden had stopped being an accurate description of her. She simply had to find a way to demonstrate her skills and make it impossible for him to refuse her suggestion of an alliance to destroy Olafr.

Mor jumped into the water the instant Aedan went ashore.

'Are you bringing what was requested?' the man asked again. His disrespectful tone grated across Dagmar's already stretched nerves. As if she was a thing, instead of a person.

Aedan shaded his eyes. 'Aye.'

She could hear the suppressed laughter and pride in his voice. He was enjoying this—succeeding where all other Northmen had failed. He was going to get his people back when her father must have assumed he'd failed. It felt good that her father was not going to have it all his own way. He must have been counting the gold that he would receive for the hostages and contemplating annexing Kintra into his little empire. How her mother would have clapped her hands and crowed in delight.

'Dagmar, it is time to greet your father.'

Dagmar stepped from the boat and knew she was in an alien place. This place teemed with warriors and ships, rather than being some hard-scrabble farm on a fjord in the north country. She struggled to recognise any of the faces.

Her heart sank. She'd half-hoped that there would be a familiar face, maybe even her nurse waiting on the shore. But she recognised no one, not even her father.

'We thought you dead,' the warrior addressed Aedan companionably, ignoring his announcement completely. 'Or had abandoned your people. The wagers have been coming thick and fast. So many wanted to track you down as a wolf's head that Kolbeinn planned a contest to choose the most worthy.'

Dagmar gritted her teeth and concentrated on breathing slowly. She'd been correct—her father had expected her to slit Aedan's throat.

'I obviously survived.'

'And brought the daughter back. Astonishing.'

'Yes.' Aedan gestured to her. 'Behold Dagmar Kolbeinndottar. I've brought her back where all others failed.'

The man's gaze flickered over her as if she were a piece of meat and totally worthless, lingering on where her breasts swelled under her tunic. She wished she'd bound them more tightly.

Her stomach knotted. This was worse than her nightmares about escaping with her mother. She felt as though she was some prize cow being led to the slaughter. Going to her father's compound did not give his warriors the right to ogle her. They would soon learn that she was not to be mocked or treated like a slave girl.

'Do you think to fool Kolbeinn by offering up some random woman, dressed as a shield maiden?' The warrior gave a derisive snort. 'Better luck next time, Gael, but your arse along with everything else you own is forfeit.'

'What are you saying?' Aedan roared.

The warrior shook his head. 'You have courage, Gael. By Thor, it is a pity you didn't sup longer with

Loki. You have to get up very early to fool Kolbeinn or his men.'

Without waiting to hear Aedan's reply, Dagmar marched forward. 'Are you saying that I'm not Kolbeinn the Blood-Axe's daughter?'

The man gave a chuckle. 'If you are, it'll be news to Kolbeinn.'

Dagmar put her hand on her hip and struggled to control her temper. This cretin of a warrior was not worth paying a single gold piece of blood money. But of all the scenarios she had envisioned, she had never considered that someone might doubt her identity. 'I am Dagmar Kolbeinndottar and daughter of Helga the Red Witch! This Gael, Aedan mac Connall, has brought me here. Escort me to my father immediately or suffer the consequences.'

She waited for the grovelling apology.

The feeble-minded cretin shook his head and turned to Aedan. 'Nice try, Gael, but pathetic.'

'You doubt my word?'

'If you speak true, then Kolbeinn will be undoubtedly pleased to see you.' He gave a crooked smile. 'His Dagmar sports tattoos on her face. Blue-and-black whorls, a new one added for each battle she appeared in. Venomous snakes are intertwined in her plaits and hiss as she walks. Pity you two jokers didn't know that.'

'You can't believe everything you hear,' Dagmar commented. She silently cursed. She'd never thought about painting her face or that her father might believe the rumours. Or that the way she wore her hair would be embellished in such a way. Her mother's subterfuge had worked all too well. 'Only a gullible idiot would believe a person could actually wear poisonous snakes in their hair. What am I supposed to be—a snake charmer as well as a warrior?'

'I knew this Gael's brother afore he died. And he is exactly like him. The mac Connalls will say or do anything to get themselves out of trouble. What did you do, mac Connall, hide yourself for a few weeks before you found some tame young woman to attempt to pass as Dagmar Kolbeinndottar?' He laughed. 'Oh, aye, I will take you to see Kolbeinn, if he is receiving. This should be fun. Can this slip of a thing even lift a sword? Let alone lead men into battle?'

Dagmar darted forward and upended the north warrior. Once the warrior had fallen she pressed the point of her dagger against his neck with one hand and relieved the warrior of his sword with the other. 'Do you still claim I am not Dagmar the Shield Maiden? Do you know how many men's lives I have ended? I added two more to my tally on this journey. Do you wish to be the third?'

He made a spluttering noise. Dagmar pressed the point of the sword into his throat just deep enough to draw a drop of blood. 'Do not tempt me, man whose brains are somewhere other than in his head.'

The colour drained from the man's face.

'Dagmar!' Aedan shouted. 'You're not at war with your father! This man is under his protection. You need someone to take you to his hall. Being imprisoned for murder will only delay things.'

Aedan's voice reached through her anger.

'I should finish you off for your impertinence, but this Gael has reminded me that you may yet have a use.' She lifted the sword slightly from the man's neck. 'Do you?'

The large man blanched and remained on the ground as the crowd which gathered around them laughed. 'Please, lady, I meant no harm. I'll take you to him without delay.'

'Am I who this Gael says I am?'

'I can see the resemblance to your father now.'

'I don't look anything like my father!' Dagmar ground out. 'I take after my grandmother!'

'I never had the pleasure.'

'You're lucky that I've decided to heed Aedan mac Connall's advice. You may live. Be content with that. Now get up and stop grovelling about in the dirt like a worm.'

The man hastily rose and held out his hand for the sword. 'May I have my sword back?'

Dagmar stared at the warrior in disbelief. What did he think—she was an unblooded warrior who had never experienced a battle season? She tucked the sword under her arm. 'I shall give this to my father so that he knows how lax his guards can be. Call yourself a warrior? You gave me no more resistance than a boy with his first wooden sword. Pathetic.' She paused and glared at the man. 'Unless you would prefer to challenge for it. I would warn you that I'm undefeated in such combat. I had an excellent teacher—my mother. I'm sure you have heard the legend of how she won me from my father.'

Sweat poured from the man's face as he gulped twice. 'You...you keep the sword, Shield Maiden. It'd be an honour to escort you to the hall.'

Dagmar stuck the sword in her belt. It had felt good to give vent to her anger, but Aedan was right. She had to be careful. This lumbering oaf would no doubt have friends. She was not at war with her father or his ultimate master, Ketil. All she needed to do was to impress. 'Anyone else wish to challenge my name or parentage? Or shall we permit my father to make good his wager with Aedan mac Connall?'

As suddenly as it had appeared, the crowd melted away. The various warriors and thralls who had stared at her and Aedan with wide eyes appeared to have something very pressing to do.

'I will accompany Dagmar the Shield Maiden to Kolbeinn's hall,' Aedan said as he motioned to Mor to stay and guard the boat. His face had settled into the hard planes that she recalled from the first days of their friendship.

Dagmar nodded, understanding the precaution. If her father refused to recognise her, then they might have to fight their way out.

'I trust there will be no repetition of these accusations or jests,' Aedan roared to the departing people. 'You all saw what Dagmar Kolbeinn is capable of.' His voice quietened. 'I will get the hostages returned and the gold promised rather than Kolbeinn resorting to Northman tricks. No one will be declaring me a wolf's head.'

'Thank you,' Dagmar mouthed, but Aedan did not give an answering smile, instead he appeared grimly resolute.

'If you try anything to jeopardise this situation, Dagmar, you will lose. Do you understand that? This is far too important to me. Without the hostages secured, we remain here battling until our last breath.'

'That would be a very poor option indeed and not my favoured one at all.'

Dagmar made sure her face appeared completely innocent. Inwardly she seethed. They had worked well together in the past, but now it was clearly at an end. As if she'd repay him by behaving badly. Her father was going to try to cheat him. If that warrior had had his way, they would not have seen him until after All Hallows dawned.

This time her father would fail. And it had the bonus that after word spread about her little display, her father would be amenable to her suggestion of commandeering one of his boats. But that would happen after Aedan received his full measure.

Her heart sank as she stared at the gabled hall. Besting that fat warrior had been the easy part. Now she had to confront her father.

The compound teemed with people, but everyone stopped to stare as they processed towards the large hall. Aedan heard the ripples of whispered exclamations and subtle wagering as they passed. While the crowd agreed Dagmar was a shield maiden, opinion was divided about whether she was actually Kolbeinn's daughter, the fabled Dagmar Kolbeinndottar.

The missing tattoos and loosely plaited hair were the problem. Aedan silently cursed. He hadn't even considered that they were Dagmar's most identifiable features. He should have suggested reinstating them, but then she'd have stopped being the woman he'd held in his arms.

The double wooden doors creaked open to reveal a more than spacious hall. Even Sigurd Sigmundson's new hall was not that luxurious. Gold-shot tapestries lined the walls to keep the heat in. Several furs lay scattered on the floor. At the end on a raised dais sat Kolbeinn the Blood-Axe, dressed in his robes and wearing a fierce scowl.

His blond goatee beard was shot with silver and his face lined with wrinkles, but now that Aedan saw father and daughter together, the resemblance shone out. They shared the same stubborn jawline, shape of the face and fierce expression when they wanted to frighten the world, precisely the expression her face currently wore.

Aedan laughed softly to himself. Father and daughter might be more alike than she cared to admit. He suspected Dagmar would hold her own.

'Who goes there?' Kolbeinn's voice boomed out as he shaded his eyes. 'I understand that someone has attacked one of my warriors. Normally I would consider such an act war, but today I'm in an agreeable temper. Explain yourselves and be prepared to accept my punishment.'

'Your warrior was careless, Father,' Dagmar called out. 'Next time he should show more respect when your daughter comes to call. Like you, I take a dim view of such treatment.' She inclined her head. 'And like you, today I am in an agreeable mood. I return your man's sword and will say no more about the insult that he offered me.'

Dagmar stepped forward and slid the warrior's sword toward where her father sat. Only the faintest tremble of her hands betrayed her nerves.

Aedan doubted that anyone else had seen it. They were far too busy staring at the sword which quivered in front of Kolbeinn. Silently he willed Kolbeinn to get out of his chair, walk over to his daughter and enfold her in his embrace. Dagmar deserved a loving father.

The ignorant pig remained seated. If anything his

scowl deepened. Aedan glanced behind him. The ranks of warriors had closed behind them. There was no more room in the hall.

Had Dagmar been correct when she said that her stepmother had poisoned her father's mind against her? That the only reason she lived was because of her mother's precautions? In saving the hostages, had he brought her to her death?

Aedan put his hand on the hilt of his sword and prepared himself for a fight. Dagmar would not have to face this alone.

'What is this? Why do I have need of a sword?' Kolbeinn waved a hand. 'What insult did my man offer you?'

'He denied that I was your daughter. I had to teach him his manners.'

'Why should he have cause to think you were?'

Dagmar stared at her father. She could feel the prick of tears gathering. She never cried and right now she wanted to weep at the injustice of it all. She'd gone over and over the meeting in her mind, but she'd never considered that her father might not believe who she was. She racked her brain for proof.

'Father, it is I, Dagmar, your only daughter.' Her voice trembled far too much. Her mother would have been ashamed of her. Dagmar swallowed hard and tried again. 'Aedan mac Connall has brought me to you as you commanded. He discovered me at the battle of Dollar where I commanded a *felag* in service to Constantine. He has fulfilled his quest. You must release the hostages you held against his return with me. I wait to hear your message. Then I'll act accordingly.'

'That remains to be seen. Come closer. Go into the

light. All I can see is your silhouette and your voice is no longer that of a ten-year-old girl. If you are truly my daughter, then I will know.'

Her father looked smaller, a bit greyer and more care-worn, but he was still her father, the man she had never thought to see alive again. Against all expectations, memories assaulted her—how he'd tossed her in the air when she was small so high that she could touch the roof, how he'd always saved something special from his travels for her, how at her bedtime, he'd come in and tell her story after story about frost giants and great deeds until her nurse declared that she must sleep and how he'd always called her his little warrior, his shield maiden in the making.

Once she'd begged for a doll, but her mother had said that it had to be a wooden sword. He brought both the doll and the sword. She frowned and tried to hold on to the memory of the last time she'd seen him when he'd only had eyes for his pregnant mistress and her promise of sons.

Her father would acknowledge her and her rights. He was not going to cheat her the way he had cheated her mother. And he was not going to cheat Aedan out of what was rightfully his. Not as long as she had breath in her body.

She strode over so that she went nearly nose to nose with her father and stuck her chin in the air. 'Is this better for your weakened eyes? Do you know me now? Or do you, like that slow warrior, need a reminder of what I can do?'

Hard fingers captured her face, twisting her from side to side. She held her breath, willing him to simply know it was her.

Suddenly her father gave a huge sigh and released her. The colour leached from his face. 'How came you by the half-moon scar over your eye?'

She heard the tremor of hope in his voice as if he were afraid to allow himself to believe.

'I was running to see my father when I was about three. I had escaped from my nurse. I fell and caught the edge of his hunting knife. Blood went everywhere, but I kept silent. My father gathered me in his arms and called me his little shield maiden,' Dagmar replied without hesitation. 'It is one of my first memories and the only people who were there were me and my father. It was our secret. He told my mother that I'd fallen on a stone rather than admit his carelessness, but it was his knife that cut me.'

Her father gave a trembling smile. 'I remember how scared I was that something I'd done had torn my daughter's flesh and how your mother yelled at me. Helga never believed me about the stone.'

'My mother was like that.'

Her father got up and enfolded her in his embrace. 'Daughter.'

He smelt of wood smoke and hair oil, just the way she remembered him smelling. Dagmar stood stiffly for as long as she dared, then she relaxed into it. 'Father. It has been over ten years.'

He released her and sat back down. 'Forgive me for my doubts, but I was given to understand that my daughter sported facial tattoos and wore her hair in tight plaits which hissed like snakes when she walked. And this Gael—he would stop at nothing to get his people back. I couldn't risk an imposter.'

'He is like you then, Father. Determined to have his

own way. Far too determined. I'd no choice but to agree
to his wishes or be lost for ever in the mist marshes.'

Her father gave a hearty laugh, but his eyes were
speculative. 'I'd not thought of it in that fashion, but
you are right. He is very like I was as a young warrior.'

Aedan made a disgusted noise, but Dagmar ignored
him. This was about ensuring her father paid out on
the wager. After that, her obligations ended and she
restarted her life and walked the new path she'd chosen. The prospect held even less appeal than last night.

She bit her bottom lip. Once Aedan was truly gone
from her life, war would send out its familiar lure. This
unsettled feeling would vanish in time. He'd made it
clear at the start there was no future for them. It was her
fault that her heart had tried to rewrite the rules and had
asked him to join her. He had refused and there it ended.

'Where have your tattoos gone?' her father asked,
stroking his chin. 'I clearly remember the message arriving saying that your mother had marred your lovely
skin. Ingebord complained about my temper for days.'

'Paint. My mother refused to allow me the tattoos.
She was the one who spread the rumour to make deception easier should the need arise.' Dagmar shrugged. 'I
was going to get it done after this season's campaign,
but events overtook me and here I am. It made travelling to see you easier in a way.'

Silently she vowed that she would not paint her face
in that fashion again. That Dagmar had gone for good.
She would create a new improved version.

Her father slapped his hand against his knee. 'That
sounds like Helga. How she must have chortled. She
knew how to make me angry. Such a simple precaution. I should've made closer enquiries.'

'If you'd done so, you'd have saved your man today.'

Her father's brows drew together. 'I can see Helga in you.'

'I take that as a compliment. I admired my mother greatly. She made me who I am. Her funeral pyre blazed long in the night and there was much lamenting at her passing.'

Her father stroked his beard. 'How fares my old friend Alf? I bade him stay with you on pain of death, to fulfil his life debt to me. He was to keep you safe until I required him. I find it incredible that he allowed you to travel alone with this Gael.'

Dagmar stood straight and kept her chin up. Old Alf was her father's friend. Had her mother guessed at his reasons for accompanying them?

'He feasts with Odin. He gave his life that this Gael might rescue me. My former deputy betrayed me to Thorsten of the Dubh Linn Northmen. Olafr Rolfson deserves to be shunned by all honourable men as he is an oath-breaker.'

Her father made a temple with his fingers. 'And what did you need rescuing from? How was Olafr Rolfson able to betray you, Daughter?'

Dagmar rapidly gave an edited version of Olafr's treachery and how he'd made a secret alliance with Thorsten. A muscle in her father's cheek twitched when she mentioned that Olafr was her mother's lover.

'I know all about Thorsten and his twisted schemes for power,' her father said with a frown. 'He is no friend to Ketil or me, but we did allow him passage to Alba this summer. It made for a quiet life. He will overreach himself. His men are too few to hold Alba for long. Halfdan wants more than Eoforwic. I warned him, but he chose to ignore my advice. In time, he will beg me for help to escape. I plan to exact a high price for my assistance.'

The assembled throng gave a few hoots of laughter and a few called out about the rich pickings in Ireland this past year.

'Halfdan has settled his warriors on lands south of the Tyne,' Dagmar stated. 'He will not seek Alba. He is content to keep Bernicia as a buffer.'

Her father tilted his head to one side. 'You know this how?'

'I'm my mother's daughter. We served Constantine. It was in our interests to know.'

'I had heard rumours, but did not know precisely. Your mother kept you hidden. I wanted to be a good father to you. I wanted to be involved in your upbringing, but Helga refused.'

Dagmar kept back the words that she wasn't exactly hidden. How could she be? She'd served with distinction and there were very few shield maidens. It would serve no purpose. She was not going to stay here long. She would allow him some illusions. And she discovered that piece of her which loved him wanted those illusions as well. She wanted a father who cared. She wanted to go back to that easy time when she had been a child. But that was as foolish as believing Thor's goat of plenty was real.

'Aedan mac Connall brought me back,' she said, gesturing to where Aedan stood, scowling. The scowl had only deepened during her father's recital of his affection for her. 'You made certain promises to him if he returned with me, although I suspect from the reception we were given you did not expect him to.'

'Guessing does you little credit.'

Dagmar gave a deliberate cough and began to tick the points off on her fingers. 'Your warriors talk worse than old women. You failed to inform Aedan mac Connall that you suspected my face was tattooed or that I was a warrior. You sent him to what you confidently expected to be his death. You expected me to slit his throat and spare you any more trouble. How many other wretches have you sent to their deaths in that fashion? I'm not and never have been your executioner, Father.'

Her father nodded. 'You remain upset that I did not recognise you immediately. You women are all alike. I had not seen you since you were ten, what did you expect?'

Dagmar drew a deep steadying breath. Losing her temper would play into his hands. She had to be more cunning. She had to use her brains and prove to him that she was worthy of being one of his warriors. She wanted a sign that he would cherish her as he had when she was little.

'Father, are you going to prove your word is worth more than the spit it takes to say it,' she said, clearing her throat. 'Are you going to uphold your end of the bargain you made with Aedan mac Connall? Or do you intend to dishonour your oath?'

'Any other person would be trembling to even think of casting such a slur.' Her father shook his head. 'Yet you stand here, looking precisely like my mother, and demand it. By Thor, Helga and I made a daughter with guts! Worth the spit it takes to swear!'

Her father's laugh resounded from the rafters. The crowd obediently laughed after him.

'But I'm your daughter and I can remember what

you were like when I was little. All bark and little bite as my nurse used to say.' Dagmar crossed her arms. Easier to concentrate on her father than to think about parting with Aedan. 'It is something you always said to me when you finished your nightly story. *"Make sure, daughter, your word is worth more than the spit it takes to say it."* I have held true to it.' She nodded towards where Aedan glowered. 'However, Aedan mac Connall has not had that benefit. He believes people from the north break their oaths. Prove him wrong.'

She waited and the feeling about needing to be cherished by her father subsided. Focusing on Aedan's needs did the trick. Once he was gone and out of her life, once her obligation had ended, then she could concentrate on more important things like fashioning her new life and trying to figure out a way to wreak revenge on Olafr. She hated that her heart protested at the idea that anything could be more important than the man standing beside her.

'I did indeed promise a few things.' Her father stroked his chin, glancing at Aedan and then back at her. She distrusted that weighing-up look.

He couldn't have guessed about their affair. It was over now and no business of his. She'd been careful not to make any sign of affection towards Aedan.

'And you hold fast to that promise?'

'Of course, my darling daughter who has now returned to me quite grown.' He coughed. 'We will talk of old times later, but now I must attend to my promises. My word holds as firm as it ever did. The Gael should know that!'

'It is good to know that you hold fast to your promises,' Dagmar said. 'Over the years, I'd wondered. My mother's gold...'

Her father made a noise in the back of his throat. 'Remind me, Gael, what is it that you seek?'

Aedan made a low bow and concentrated on Kolbeinn, deliberately ignoring how fragile and utterly alone Dagmar appeared. Any claim to her had slipped from his fingers the instant they'd stepped on Colbhasa's shore.

'I've accomplished my task,' he said, forcing the words from his throat. 'Fulfilled the terms of our wager. Let my people go free, cancel the debt you claimed my brother owed you and provide me with the chest of gold.'

Kolbeinn's eyes turned speculative as he glanced between Dagmar and himself. Aedan frowned. What had the wily old fox seen or guessed?

'I hope this is also the start of a beautiful friendship, one where we both can fish in the same pond,' Kolbeinn said.

Aedan's control on his temper was stretched to breaking point. Friendship with the man? Kolbeinn had thought to have him murdered and harboured designs on his land. He failed to understand men from the north. 'With respect, much can be accomplished as I, too, am a man of my word. I promised you your daughter and I've returned her. We part in friendship.'

'I'm proud to have your friendship, Aedan mac Connall, laird of Kintra, and look forward to working together in the near future.'

Kolbeinn clapped his hands and gave the orders. Very shortly, a woman and two men were led into the hall. The woman gave a small cry and rushed over to

Aedan. She lifted up her face towards him, like a flower seeking the sun. She was one of those small dark-haired women that his brother had preferred and an acclaimed beauty on Ile, but she paled beside Dagmar's golden radiance.

'Mhairi,' Aedan said and ignored the woman's blatant invitation to kiss her lips. Once, maybe, he would have, but not now. The only lips he wanted to touch belonged to the smouldering shield maiden beside him.

Mhairi gave a small pout and placed a slender hand on his arm. 'I missed you dreadfully, but I had faith. I knew you'd return for me. A glorious future awaits us, Aedan.'

'Kintra will have a brighter future.' Aedan gritted his teeth and resisted the temptation to remove the hand talon by talon. Proof if he needed it of Mhairi's marital intentions. Even as a young girl, she had been a scheming witch.

In truth, Dagmar had spoiled him for other women. Maybe in time he would find a woman to take as a wife, but right now the only woman he wanted in his bed was forbidden to him.

'We were certain you were dead,' Mhairi said, dabbing her eyes. 'I couldn't bear it, Aedan. Truly I could not. They were going to sell us in the spring. Possibly as early as Christmas or *Jul* as they call it.'

'Hush now, you're safe.' He put an arm about her. 'Never break down in front of the north. Remember our motto. You've been very brave this far.'

Mhairi laid her head against his chest. 'Yes, I'm safe now with you here.'

Chapter Nine

Dagmar's heart twisted as she watched the reunion between Aedan and the hostages. The dark-haired woman
appeared very familiar towards him. The woman who
had volunteered so that he could attempt to win the
wager. He'd never satisfactorily explained why she had
done that. Worst of all, he said her name with affection and kept an arm about her as he greeted the other
hostages.

She struggled against the unfamiliar urge to scratch
that woman's eyes out. Drawing on all her training, she
forced her face to be impassive. It wasn't her problem
if he cuddled with harpies. They'd finished. After this
ceremony concluded, she'd never see him again, never
contact him again. Yet she knew in her heart she'd cherish every scrap of news she'd glean about him and that
she'd look for him on the battlefield. She placed a hand
on her stomach and wished for a child, his child.

'And the gold?' Aedan asked. 'The chest of gold?'

'Gold?' her father said, fingering his goatee. 'Was
there gold involved? I thought it was merely the debt
cancelling and the hostages. You were gone longer than

I had considered and my memory is hazy. My beloved wife had just perished.'

'I understood gold was mentioned,' Dagmar said, fixing her father with her best furious-warrior gaze. It felt good to give into her anger. 'A chest of it. You bet against his returning with me and lost, Father. Face it or suffer the consequences.'

Her hand went to the dagger she still wore about her waist. If her father continued in this vein, she'd take the tale to Ketil who would have to act. Her father had sworn an oath to the overlord of the Western Isles.

'And you returned because of this wager and no other reason?'

'He gave me little choice and I owed him a life debt,' Dagmar admitted, relaxing her hold on the dagger. 'I stand as one with the Gael in this matter. Our fellowship holds true.'

'You drive a hard bargain, Dagmar.' Her father sighed and spoke quietly to his advisor. A small chest was brought out. 'My dealings with you in this matter, mac Connall, are at an end. Let no man or woman say that I failed to keep my word in this matter.'

Aedan picked up the chest. His face was a perfectly blank mask. 'It has been a pleasure doing business, Kolbeinn the Blood-Axe.'

To prevent herself from trying to catch his eye as he left or looking for one last sign of affection or worse, seeing him put an arm about Mhairi's waist, Dagmar cleared her throat.

'I've done as you requested, Father. I am here. Why did you summon me, rather than sending a messenger? What is so important?'

Her father brushed an imaginary speck from his

cloak. 'My messengers have developed a habit of having only their heads returned. I would have had no idea if the messages had been received or not. Therefore, you must come to me rather than the other way around. How many is it that you and your mother thwarted?'

Dagmar forced a laugh. 'I don't know what you expected, Father. They would insist on trying to kill me. I do reserve the right to strike back when faced with certain death.'

The colour drained from his face, leaving his skin looking like old parchment. Her father was not as young as he used to be, she realised. In her imagination, he'd always strode tall and firm, but like everyone else the years had taken their toll on him. 'Why would they want to do that?'

'To leave the way open for my half-brother, of course.' Dagmar tilted her head to one side. 'Or didn't you know that my stepmother had sworn on all the gods that only her children would inherit? That Helga and her daughter would be wiped from the face of the earth and none would weep?'

'Ingebord lost her temper with Helga. Her words were written on the wind.'

'I see that makes the attempts on my life before I was fourteen all right? Because my stepmother merely lost her temper?'

Her father held up his hands. 'I have never wanted to harm you, Dagmar. It is why I sent my best warrior to look after you when you and your mother left. He knew who came in my name and who came from my enemies. I do have some. It is what Ingebord feared—not content with blackening her name, your mother poisoned your mind against me, too. You're my daughter, why would I wish you harm? Alf and I had a system. Helga was unreasonable.'

Dagmar ground her teeth. Poisoned her mind! Her mother had been more than fair. And she had been ten. The day was etched on her brain for ever. She wanted to storm out now. She could see how this conversation was going to go. Her father did not want to take any responsibility for the trials she had endured.

She'd seen the knives that the assassins carried. She had seen how the poison worked on the puppy who had been unlucky enough to eat her stew before her. After that her mother had forbidden any animals. She'd heard the confessions before her mother had had the men executed. But was there any point? Her stepmother was dead and she lived. It showed the gods had not listened to her. Revenge enough.

'I know of the attempts I survived. They were not figments of my mother's imagination or mine,' she said, taking the time to enunciate each word so there could be no misunderstanding. She refused to allow her father or anyone else to rewrite history. 'I disarmed one man myself when I was fourteen. He confessed everything before my mother had him put to death and sent his head back to you. Or did Old Alf fail to mention it in any of his reports?'

To her satisfaction, her father's cheeks flushed. 'Some men are consumed with ambition and blind to the consequences of overstepping orders. You're my flesh and blood, Dagmar.'

'You would have to ask your late wife what her orders to the messengers were.' Dagmar met her father's gaze head on. 'You did not desire a family reunion before, so why do you want one now? The truth rather than some pap that even an infant would reject.'

'You're a woman after my own heart.'

Dagmar tapped her boot on the ground. 'The reason, Father.'

Her father smiled a wintry smile. 'To marry you off. I need heirs, Dagmar. I need to ensure that my estate which I worked so hard to acquire will be looked after as I reach my twilight years and my eyesight begins to dim. I'm through with wives—one was far too strong-willed for her own good and the other wanted to rule me through her child. I've no wish for a third.'

'Honesty. Good.' Dagmar bit her lip as her mind worked feverishly. It was as she'd feared. Her father cared more about his estates than what happened to her. He intended to marry her off to some warrior who had curried favour with him, but would have little regard for her or her dreams. 'And if marriage to one of your warriors is not what I intend to do with my life? I've not obliged you for over ten years, so why should I start now?'

Her father's mouth became a thin white line and she knew her barb had hit home. Good. 'We all must make sacrifices, Daughter. You're my only living child. I will protect my legacy through strength. You will do as I command.'

Dagmar kept her body still, rather than giving in to her first impulse of smashing his face in. When had he ever earned that right? 'If the warrior I disarmed so easily was one of your best, then I don't think much of them or their ability to keep your estates intact after you are gone. Let me demonstrate my worth as a warrior. Give me ships and men. I will go after Olafr

Rolfson and ensure his punishment for his loathsome betrayal. I will prove I can look after my inheritance by myself.'

Dagmar's heart thudded. He had to accept her offer. She could be his right hand if he'd allow her to be.

'Shortly after you left, your mother sent word that you wished to be a shield maiden and had sworn never to marry. While I had a living son, I accepted Helga's words with reluctance, but the gods decreed otherwise when they took my boy from me.' Her father hit his hand against his knee. 'Time to grow up, Dagmar. Take responsibility. Put away your playthings. There is much for you to learn. You will remain on Colbhasa at my side.'

Dagmar wriggled her toes to remind herself of the gold she carried in her boot. 'Will I?'

'You need a child to occupy your time. I will not have my line perish because you wish to play at being a second-rate warrior.'

Dagmar concentrated on breathing slowly, barely containing her temper.

Her father appeared to think that she was some sort of witless woman. Ordering her to become pregnant because she needed a new pastime? No wonder her mother had left him. The only amazing thing was that she'd married him in the first place. Her mother's choice in men was consistently awful. He was going to learn a valuable lesson—nobody dictated marriage to her. She chose her own future.

For one blinding heartbeat, she wondered if she ran to where Aedan stood, watching the exchange with an implacable expression and begged for his assistance, would he help her escape? Would he accept her sword arm in the service of his people? She half-started towards him and then stopped dead. She depended on no one.

'Who do you intend as my bridegroom?' she said in a falsely sweet voice, the sort of voice which would have had her men running for cover.

Her father, however, gave an indulgent smile. 'That's the daughter I remember—always eager to do her father's bidding. Choose one of the warriors here. I've no particular preference.'

'One of these men in this room?' Dagmar asked, a plan beginning to form in her brain. Aedan remained in the hall, watching her with a perplexed expression. He gave a sudden shake of his head as if he had read her mind, but she paid him no mind. She had to teach her father a lesson and she didn't have time to beg Aedan's permission. All she required was for him to act in the way she knew he would. All she asked was for him to trust her. She would ensure neither he nor his lands came to any harm.

'If he is unmarried, then, yes.' Her father beamed. 'Take your time, Daughter, there is no rush. Tomorrow will be time enough to start. We can run a few contests if you like. See who is truly worthy of you. Yes, that is an excellent idea. We shall have a series of trials. You may judge.'

Her father clapped his hands. The hall roared with approval. An ice-cold calm filled Dagmar. Those warriors would soon be laughing from the other side of their faces.

'Prepare a chamber for my daughter. She is to have the best furs and my second-best bed. You'll have your own household, Dagmar. Your old nurse can help you to make the choice. But you will marry. This hall will soon be filled with the patter of my grandsons' tiny feet.'

'Mor survives?' she stammered out.

'A widow. Her husband perished last winter. She took the name Sif when she married. But she is here and eager to see you. You will have much to discuss. She can give insight into which warrior to choose. You see, I'm not the monster your mother made out. Speak to your nurse—she has sensible counsel to offer you.'

Her father was offering her a distraction. Just as he used to offer a sweetmeat to stop her tears. When she was fighting for her survival, he offered a sop and thought it would suffice. Typical. Her nurse could wait, because right now she would be taking up her father's offer of a bridegroom or rather settling the matter for all time.

'I don't need any more time. I certainly do not need trials of strength or advice from my nurse.'

Her father's eyes turned speculative. 'You've made your choice?'

'Will you abide by it?' Dagmar asked before her nerve failed.

'Yes, provided it is one of the men in this hall and he is unmarried.'

'Swear it. Swear it on the rings you wear on your right hand.'

'I swear it on my rings.' Her father's indulgent smile increased. 'Now will you reveal which of my warriors has captured your heart by merely a look?'

The entire hall erupted into laughter, echoing off the beams. Her father and his men must truly consider her a fool.

Dagmar's heart thumped, like it always did just before she went into battle. She had to win this. Her very future depended on it. She took a deep breath. 'I choose Aedan mac Connall.'

'Aedan mac Connall?'

'He remains in the hall and is unmarried. You swore eternal friendship to him. Therefore, he must be one of the candidates. Or is your word once again worthless?'

The hall went silent in a heartbeat. She turned her back on her father and gestured towards where Aedan stood. 'Aedan mac Connall is my choice. He fulfils your requirements.'

Aedan stood stock still, mouth half-open. The woman standing next to him, clinging to his arm like a demented limpet, burst into noisy sobs. Aedan tightened his arm about her, cradling her, but remained silent.

Dagmar glanced away as a stab of jealous rage shot through her. She went over her scheme in her mind again. Aedan was going to refuse her because he could never have a woman from the north at Kintra. He had to put his people above any feelings he might have for her, a pagan woman. Duty drove him. This part was vital to her hastily thought-out scheme as much as it would break her heart. Aedan would refuse and then the next part of her scheme could begin—the part where she declared that she would never marry then, as no man could possibly match Aedan mac Connall. The words would be far too close to the truth for comfort, but she would be able to tread the only possible path for her currently—the life as a sell-sword. Some day she would have a home and put down roots like she'd vowed. But not today.

'You do what? You choose whom?' her father roared, filling the hall.

'Aedan mac Connall.' She lifted a brow. 'I thought I was perfectly clear the first time, Father. You swore I could have any man in this room. I have made my choice. Deliver my bridegroom to me.'

'You stop this nonsense, Daughter.' Her father shook his fist. 'Aedan mac Connall is not the man I had in mind for you. Allow him to depart in peace with his winnings. Make your choice at your leisure after you have had the opportunity to get to know my warriors. Test their strengths and weaknesses. This is a much better plan. A Northern warrior for a brave woman. What sons you will make!'

Her father's warriors preened themselves, puffing out their chests and giving little swaggers. Choose one of them? Not in this lifetime! And still Aedan remained silent, watching her with an intent expression. He needed to refuse the offer outright. She willed him with her eyes to refuse. He had to know that she would do everything in her power to ensure no ill will followed that refusal.

'Or what will you do? Throw me out?' She turned back to her father. His face had gone a sort of mottled purple. Her mother would have been crowing with pleasure at the sight. 'I can survive by myself, Father. You asked me to make a choice and I have. You agreed to abide by it. You swore it on your rings. Are you an oath-breaker?'

Her father gnashed his teeth. 'Never!'

Still Aedan remained silent.

There was no hope. She could not wait for Aedan to refuse. She had to swear the next part.

'I will marry Aedan mac Connall and no other.' Dagmar kept her back to Aedan, but she could feel his eyes boring into her. 'I must follow how my heart dictates. I swear this on my mother's shade.'

There was the sound of a thump and coins spilling as Aedan must have dropped the chest. Dagmar ignored the sound. A few breaths more and she'd have her father precisely where she wanted him. He would be forced to back down and they could begin the negotiations properly. If only Aedan would shout out his refusal, it would make life much easier.

'Aedan mac Connall is not my man. He is not from the north. I've no control over him. Daughter, be reasonable.'

There was no mistaking the pleading in her father's voice. All bluster and no bite.

'I am merely following your orders.'

Her father ran his hand through his hair. 'By Thor, you remind of your mother and not in a good way!'

'I shall take that as a compliment. My mother would have approved of Aedan mac Connall.'

'Impossible! Come forward, Aedan mac Connall, and explain why it is impossible.'

Aedan's lips turned up into a cynical smile, but he said nothing.

'I will not ask Aedan mac Connall to be your bridegroom.' Her father's lower lip jutted out. 'You can't make me. He is a Gael rather than a Northman. I have never begged favours from a Gael and I do not intend to start.'

'You and Aedan mac Connall have sworn friendship,' Dagmar argued into the silence. 'Are you saying that you lied to me? You refuse to allow me the basic luxury of the choice. Very well, I see no reason why I should give up being a shield maiden and become a peace-weaver to please you. Someone will have me and my sword. Your lands, gold and everything you worked for can crumble to dust when you're gone as I shall not lift a finger to save any of it.'

'You're more stubborn than your mother. May Thor and Odin preserve us—Helga did what she claimed she'd do—she has created a monster who would sooner slit her throat than marry.'

'Your compliments flow today.' Dagmar kept her head high. 'Having heard your answer, I will see my old nurse and then depart. Enjoy the remainder of your life, Father.'

'Wait!' her father shouted. 'I will ask him. Mac Connall, will you marry my daughter? I've no desire to jeopardise our new alliance, but remember the strength of this alliance rests on your answer.'

Dagmar winced as she had not expected the implied threat from her father, but Aedan had to know it was bluster. She kept her head proud and steeled herself for the rejection to come this time. Her father would not carry out any threat. All Aedan had to do was trust her judgement. He had to know she had a scheme to protect him.

A tiny piece of heart whispered—what if...? She silenced it. Aedan would react predictably. He had told her as much last night.

Aedan stepped forward and made a deep bow. His eyes blazed with pure fury. He exchanged a cynical glance with her father. She took a step backwards and belatedly realised that perhaps she should have mentioned this scheme to him earlier.

'I, too, value our new-found friendship, Kolbeinn the Blood-Axe. It is why I held my tongue until you formally asked. Now you have and you deserve my *considered* answer.' He paused and glanced about the room with disdain. Dagmar held her breath. 'Yes, I will marry your daughter, but on one condition and one condition only.'

Dagmar's jaw dropped. He was not doing what he was supposed to. He should have rejected the offer outright because his duty to his people transcended all other obligations. What had she missed?

Her father tilted his head to one side and a broad smile crossed his features. 'And that condition is?'

'That we marry according the rites of my church and Dagmar renounces her former life and swears fealty to me and my people instead.'

'Those are two conditions,' Dagmar retorted.

'One follows from the other.' A muscle jumped in his jaw. 'The only way my people will accept the marriage is conversion to my faith and a swearing of loyalty to Kintra above everything else. If you're willing, then we marry. Otherwise find yourself another husband.'

The words hung in the air before echoing around her brain. Aedan had accepted the offer, but with conditions! Conditions he confidently expected her to refuse, judging from his smug expression.

Dagmar stared at him in disbelief. He should have rejected the offer outright. That tiny part of her heart which had believed he wouldn't rejoiced.

Aedan was agreeing to marry her, but only if she put Kintra first and gave up any hope of wreaking her revenge on Olafr. A true son of Loki!

If she refused, she couldn't claim that he was the one man for her. Her father would argue that if he was the only man for her, she should be prepared to walk over burning coals for him. Therefore she should choose one of his warriors. The result would be the same. She would have to give up being a shield maiden and become a wife, but to a man she neither liked nor respected.

'Well, Daughter of mine, have you grown mute?' Her father gave a triumphant smile as if he'd anticipated and planned for this outcome.

She clenched her fists, longing to smash something very hard. A tiny inkling grew in her. Her father was far too pleased. Was this why he had sent Aedan to get her? Was this something they had dreamt up together before Aedan had even left? Had his seduction been planned all along?

All her insecurities flooded back. Had she been so desperate for a man's touch that she mistook impersonal touches for caresses? When she lay in his arms, had he pretended she was beautiful? Had he thought of the woman who even now prettily sobbed over the loss of him? She had gambled and lost. Badly. Her throat worked up and down, but no sound came out except a strangled cry of rage.

'Will you do as he requires or do you marry the man I pick for you?' her father said, clapping his hands and barely containing his glee. 'Were you attempting to play me false and cause discord between me and this good warrior here? Let's see what you are made of now, Daughter of mine!' He slapped his hand against his knee and chortled. 'Are your words worth the spit it took to say them, Dagmar Kolbeinndottar?'

All of Aedan's nerves tensed to the breaking point. The silence stretched as the entire hall waited for Dagmar's answer. Behind him, Mhairi had begun to weep irritating tears again.

Aedan clung on to his temper by the slenderest of threads. It was typical of Dagmar to take this sort of risk. She never considered the consequences. All she did was react to the provocation from her father. Worse, he could not entirely banish the notion that Kolbeinn had anticipated these events. The man certainly knew how to make Dagmar react.

Dagmar hadn't made the declaration because she wanted to marry him or thought he was indeed the only man for her. If she had wanted marriage, she should have said so earlier when instead she had been busy telling him that their affair was at an end and that she would raise any child on her own without his input.

She had done it because she was certain of his refusal. It irritated him beyond measure that after all they had been through, she considered that he would put his people in jeopardy.

It had been on the tip of his tongue to refuse, but then he caught the eager gleam in Kolbeinn's eye and knew the truth. Kolbeinn wanted an excuse to destroy him. Kolbeinn would use this insult as an excuse to invade and crush Kintra for ever. He could not. He was trapped. He had to make the offer.

Right now he did not know what he wanted. He would not have to deal with the jealousy that made him want to slay any man who might dare look at Dagmar, let alone shared her bed. Marrying her was the best solution for him, but his people would never accept a pagan warlord as the lady of Kintra.

Silently he willed her to accept his offer with its conditions and then abide by her decision. His heart could not stand it if she decided to play him false.

Dagmar stared at him, her blue eyes wide. All colour had faded from her cheeks. 'I am to marry in your church and renounce my gods if I am to be married to you.'

'And give up your old life of warring,' he said slowly as if he was calming a nervous horse. 'My people need someone who will tend to the harvest, who will be gentle and kind and who will be there for them instead of raiding other lands. Are you capable of that?'

She balled her fists. 'Underestimate me at your peril!'

'Then end this ridiculous farce which has put my kingdom in danger.' He inwardly winced. The words were harsher than he intended. But he refused to give Kolbeinn the satisfaction of knowing he was attracted to Dagmar.

Dagmar raised her chin. Fierce, proud and one of the most beautiful women he had ever seen. Her lips turned up into a smile he distrusted. She was plotting another scheme, but neither he nor his people would be punished for it.

'Very well, I accept. We will marry in your church on Ile at which time I will renounce my way of life.'

Aedan wanted to shake her. She continued her games. He knew precisely what Dagmar would do once they were on Ile. She'd vanish in the night before they got married and he'd be left with an enraged father to deal with.

'"According to the rites of his church" were the exact words Aedan mac Connall uttered. I trust he had good reason for using that particular phrasing,' Kolbeinn said before Aedan had a chance to let her know that he was wise to her tricks.

Dagmar waved an airy hand. 'There will not be a priest from his church on Colbhasa. We must go to Ile.' She gave a brilliant smile as if she had suddenly thought of something. 'It will suit me well. I can take proper instruction in his faith as well. I know the process. I have been in the court of Constantine. The priests take a very long time to decide if a candidate is suitable. Aedan is anxious to return to his kingdom without delay. It is best that I go there until such a time as his priest believes I am ready. Once that time arrives, I will renounce everything. You cannot ask fairer than that.'

She held out her hands as if she had nothing to hide. Aedan flexed his fingers and retained a leash on his temper.

'Kolbeinn speaks truly. Those are my conditions. We marry according to the rites of my church, rather than at my church.'

'We do have a priest of his church here. I am waiting for his ransom to arrive,' Kolbeinn said, beckoning to one of his warriors. 'Summon him. Perhaps he will be willing to overlook the need for giving you intense instruction in his faith for a chance of freedom. It is surprising how such things can clarify the mind.'

Dagmar's eyes widened in horror. 'What are you saying, Father?'

Kolbeinn's eyes hardened. 'This marriage alliance will be settled before you leave my compound, Aedan mac Connall. Better than that, it will be settled before owl-light.'

The man allowed him to think that he was the last person he wanted for his daughter and then he secretes away a priest of his faith here! Aedan pressed his lips together. The priest was far too convenient. Kolbeinn had clearly been planning for this eventuality for a long time.

Dagmar's mouth dropped open. 'You mean to see me married today?'

'Why wait?' Aedan said, capturing her hand. Despite his cold fury at her tricks, a warm thrill went up his arm. Dagmar would be his bride. She would be part of his life for ever. 'My people have been without a leader for long enough. I need to return to them. I see no reason to make two trips here.'

Dagmar pulled away and her face became mutinous. He smiled inwardly. He'd guessed her game—stall and hope that something else turned up to prevent their marriage. 'Very well. I accept your offer when it is put like that.'

'Swear it,' Aedan demanded. 'Give your solemn oath on your mother's shade.'

Dagmar went pale and he knew that, despite everything, she truly had other plans than to go through with the wedding. No one played him for a fool, particularly not her. 'Is this truly necessary?'

'You may swear on my sword, Daughter, if you feel your mother's shade would be ashamed of her daughter contracting such an alliance.' Kolbeinn's smile increased. 'Make a binding oath. You required it of me.'

'I will swear on both. My mother would never be ashamed of such alliance.'

The gleaming sword was brought. Dagmar placed her slender hand on its hilt and swore by all the gods. Her face was grimly resolute. Aedan had never seen anyone who looked less like a blushing bride than Dagmar did.

Dagmar bowed towards her father. 'We are done. May I go and get some air while you find the priest and put your proposition to him? I wish to find my old nurse and renew my acquaintance with her.'

Her father nodded and waved a hand of dismissal. 'Sif will be delighted to see you. She often speaks of you with affection.'

Aedan narrowed his eyes. Dagmar would wriggle against every possible restriction. It was one of the things he admired about her.

Kolbeinn rubbed his hands together. He appeared altogether too pleased with this turn of events. 'I will not have my new ally marrying some strange half-man. He marries my daughter, a woman. Insult my house at your peril, Dagmar. Wear one of your stepmother's old gowns. She had plenty and has no use for them now.'

Dagmar lowered her brows. For an instant, she appeared about to refuse, but then she glanced between them and gave a smile which Aedan instinctively distrusted.

'My stepmother's gowns may remain mouldering for ever. I already have the required gown,' she said and turned on her heel.

As Dagmar swept past them with her head held high, Mhairi grabbed Dagmar's arm.

'Why did you have to ruin everything?' Mhairi said in a low furious voice. 'I shall remember this day for ever.'

'Mhairi!' Aedan said in a low voice. The last thing he required was Mhairi acting up. She, of all people, should understand how important this alliance was for Kintra. She'd offered her life for it.

'I only speak the truth.'

Dagmar removed Mhairi's hand from her sleeve. Her eyes blazed with a fury like Aedan had never seen before. 'I suspect it will be a day that we will all struggle to forget.'

Chapter Ten

The now silent throng of warriors parted and Dagmar reached the outside and gulped mouthfuls of life-giving air. How she made it through that crowded hall without collapsing in a heap, she'd never know.

Her mind reeled as she struggled to control her temper. She'd gone into that hall thinking that she'd be a shield maiden for ever and she'd come out betrothed to Aedan, not only betrothed but about to give up everything her mother had instilled in her as being necessary for life. After today, she'd never be able to be the sort of independent woman her mother envisioned. She'd given her oath.

Her heart thrummed. She was going to marry Aedan. If he cared even the littlest particle about her, if their time together had meant anything at all to him, he would have understood what she was trying to accomplish and would have given her the time to allow tempers to cool. Why had Aedan done it? Why had he not acted how she had anticipated he would?

She kicked a pebble and sent it scurrying away. Or had he already had an alternative scheme? The look her father had given Aedan seemed to indicate there was more there.

She clenched her fists as fresh fury swept through her. She had been so naive, so ready to believe that one gorgeous man found her attractive, that one man could not keep his hands off her. Aedan had cynically seduced her and she had laid her heart at his feet. She had given him her virginity. How he must have laughed. All he had to do was to couple with a freak. Was it any wonder that he'd insisted on her wearing a dress when they were travelling so he could imagine another woman beneath him?

The various wooden houses leading to the harbour wavered in front of her eyes and she blinked rapidly, trying to restore some measure of calm. She had never even considered that her father might send a potential husband to get her after what had happened to his messengers, particularly not a Gael.

The door opened with a bang and Aedan emerged with a face that could have been carved from granite. When he saw her, his expression appeared to relax for a heartbeat before hardening again.

'Did you plan this with my father? Before you left on your quest?' she asked before he had a chance to utter a word. Half of her wanted him to take her into his arms and kiss her roughly. And the other half, the more sensible half, needed to know how deeply he was involved in this plot.

She wanted the time they had shared to be something more than a means to an end. She wanted to think their affair had been between two people, rather than Aedan using her to save his people. She wanted to believe in dreams again. But she feared deep down that she already knew the truth. He'd been open about it, if she'd cared to listen. But she'd spun her own reality, just as she had done when she was a girl and had believed the skalds about her parents' undying love.

'You are here. That is a surprise. I expected you to be already running towards the harbour and my currach.'

His cold tones made her cringe. She looked in vain for the gentle man who had held her this morning until the sun rose. All she could see was the furious warrior.

Her stomach roiled. If he'd planned this, would he be this angry? Possibly. She had only thought she knew him.

She attempted a nonchalant shrug. 'Why would I do that?'

'Steal my boat? Depart to places unknown? Leave me to face your father's wrath alone? Leave me to watch helpless as my lands are destroyed and my people enslaved?'

She stared at him, shocked. They had travelled together. They had been intimate but he didn't *know* her. 'I gave my oath. I will abide by it. I always do that to the best of my ability.'

He crossed his arms. 'Is that so?'

'A warrior is nothing without her word.'

'But you are more than a warrior, you are a very stubborn woman who insists on getting her own way. And your way has been thwarted.'

'Until I formally renounce my old life, I remain a shield maiden. Even renouncing that life will not change how I value my honour and how I strive to keep it.'

'Why were you ready to destroy my life?'

'My father would have married me off to some preening oaf with more muscles than brains. You should have trusted my instincts. I had everything under control.' She put her hand on her hip and glared back at him. 'You haven't answered my question. Instead you seek to distract me with nonsense about me running away. The only time I left a battlefield before the battle was over was when you carried me away. Answer my question—did you and my father scheme together before you departed to make this marriage happen? Is that why you came after me? Was there more, much more to that blasted wager of yours? Get my daughter back and you can have her? Was there even a wager? Was that the gold he paid you to seduce me?'

'Why would I do that?'

She ticked the points off on her fingers. 'You knew my father wanted me married. You knew my half-brother was dead. You knew that I will inherit a fortune on my father's death and that an alliance would safeguard your people.'

His mouth took on a bitter twist. 'One would have to be a simpleton not to know that. I considered your father would never see me as a potential son-in-law. As far as I knew, he loathed my guts and everything I stood for. Equally, I'd no reason to acquire a pagan bride. Fortunes have a way of turning to dust if one strives too hard for them.'

'You will now have one of the most powerful Northmen on your side in any dispute. You and your people will no longer suffer.'

His eyes blazed. 'To keep my country free is why I agreed to this! Kolbeinn has the habit of using the slightest insult as an excuse to invade. And refusing to marry his only daughter ranks above slight insult to my mind.'

'I would never have allowed that to happen.'

'Just like Olafr would never resort to treachery.'

'You should have trusted me. You trusted me back on our travels.'

'That was different. I only had my life to consider, not the fate of my people.'

'Did you seduce me to ensure it would happen? To give yourself that added edge if it came to trials? Everyone else in that hall appeared to be expecting trials of strength. Get Kolbeinn's ugly daughter all inflamed for you and she'd choose you no matter what her father did? The stupid cow.'

The words were out of her mouth before she could stop them. They seemed to hang in mid-air.

His harsh laugh rang out. 'I appear to remember that night somewhat differently.'

Dagmar's cheeks grew warm as she remembered how she had begged him to sleep with her. But he had been the one to keep her goblet full, hadn't he? He had been the one to hold her the night before. It was only because the gang appeared that he had let her go. He would have seduced her then. 'My memory remains hazy. Too much mead,' she bit out.

'What do you take me for? Why call yourself ugly or stupid when you are blatantly neither!'

'Men have mocked me for years for my lack of looks,' Dagmar answered truthfully.

'When was the last time any man saw you without the paint and plaits in your hair?'

'When I was fifteen, but even before that they used to jeer at me.'

'Jealous fools. Why do you trust their opinion and not mine?'

Dagmar hated that a tiny hope built in her breast and that she wanted to believe him. Maybe Aedan had not completely lied to her. He had made her feel beautiful and it was her feelings which mattered. 'Maybe for the same reason you do not trust me.'

'Any hope of trust between us has ended.' Aedan made a cutting motion with his hand. 'You could have asked me about the possibility of marriage last night. You didn't. You blundered in and assumed. You never thought about my duty. You only considered your dream of being a sell-sword and wreaking vengeance against Olafr. Now it is going to be just that—a dream. You are going to be a king's lady and I hope you make a better job of it than your mother did.'

Dagmar's throat closed. She examined the ground, hating that Aedan was right. 'I know,' she whispered. 'I reacted to my father's smugness. He planned to marry me to someone who would despise me. I could feel it in my bones. But if you had let me, I would have made it right.'

'Do you plan on leaving? Or are you staying to see out what you started?'

Indignation filled her, blocking out the other emotions. 'I gave my solemn oath. I will do as you command and renounce my former life totally and completely, but...'

His lips turned up into a humourless smile. 'There is always a but with you. Where my people are concerned there are no buts. You must pledge your heart and soul to protect them and that will be your overriding concern, not how many warriors you want to kill or vows of vengeance you may have taken.'

Dagmar hugged her arms about her waist. Each of

Aedan's words felt a hammer blow to her heart. Her mother's warnings resonated—she was fundamentally unsuited to marriage. A small piece of her heart screamed that she was wrong, but Dagmar ignored it. 'Until you forced me to swear it, I could have found a way out of it.'

'Both our options appeared limited to me, once you declared that you would marry only me. It is why I had to make the offer. My people need this alliance. We need to be able to fish in these waters without fear of attack. We need to know that our women will be safe from being stolen. Our marriage will give me this. Will you deny my people their right to live in peace?'

Dagmar concentrated on the ground. No words of love or caring in his speech, instead it was only about duty to his people. Always. If there had been anything between them, she had killed it. 'Once on Ile, my father would have had no control over me or you. I could have pledged my sword to you…there were other ways besides marriage.'

'Try thinking about someone other than yourself for a change. I couldn't take the risk.'

She ground her teeth. That he was right did not make it any easier. She had singularly failed to understand what precisely his duty entailed. She was the one who had blundered and now they were left with this mess—a marriage neither wanted, a marriage doomed to failure like her parents' had been.

'My father insisted on a gown,' she wailed. 'I had sworn that I would not willingly wear a gown in front of my father. And now this.'

'I did warn you that if you tried anything, you would end up the loser.'

Dagmar gave an unhappy nod. He had warned her and she had not listened. 'I thought we were a team. We worked well as a team.'

'That team finished before we arrived here. You wanted nothing to do with me. You were not even going to tell me if you bore my child!'

Her heart quietly broke. She had wounded him with her words when all she'd wanted to do was protect that child and his future wife. 'Look on the bright side, there is no need for us to couple until we know if I carry our child.'

He caught her arm and his face contorted. 'No. It will be a real marriage, Dagmar. I want sons. My people need to feel secure.'

'Men always want sons,' Dagmar said bleakly. 'Sometimes they get daughters.'

'I would welcome any child of yours.'

His eyes slightly softened and for a fleeting heartbeat she glimpsed the man who had held her in his arms, the man who had listened to her dreams. Aedan was wrong. Her heart leapt. She had not killed everything. Damaged, yes, but there could be a way back to the friendship they had shared on the road. However, she refused to be fooled again.

'My lady, you have returned!' An elderly woman rushed up and interrupted them.

Dagmar's heart expanded. Maybe not all was dreadful. Her nurse was here. She'd recognise her anywhere. 'Mor? Are you truly here?'

'It is Sif Gilbreathdottar now,' her nurse informed her. 'I've not been Mor for many years.'

'Sif, then.' Dagmar held out her arms and was enfolded in her nurse's warm embrace. 'Whatever they call you, you remain mine.'

Her nurse was shorter than she remembered and a fair bit wider. But there was something pleasingly familiar about her as she enfolded Dagmar in her arms and hugged her tightly. As though everything would be all right if she simply held her nerve, as though everything would be fine because her nurse loved her. Dagmar took a deep breath.

She had to do as Old Alf suggested when he discovered her sobbing her eyes out after the berserker attack, wishing for her nurse—she had to examine the situation for the positives, including that she lived, breathed and was able to fight another day. Aedan remained and he was marrying her. He continued to say that he thought her beautiful even if she wasn't sure she believed him any more. She had a chance to put down roots the way she had always dreamt of doing. Surely that had to be better than being forced to marry one of her father's warriors or ending with a blade in her back from Olafr?

'What happened to you?' she asked her nurse.

'Ingebord did not want to have me looking after her son. She called me a dirty Gael and boxed my ears. But your father insisted. If I was good enough for his daughter, I was good enough for his son. She then had me change my name. Your father chose it because I had red-gold hair when I was young.'

'It is just as well my stepmother is dead. I would have cut her heart out if I had heard her unkind words to you.'

'You were always a fierce child when someone threatened your loved ones,' Sif said complacently. 'But in the end, it worked out. Ingebord might have treated me like dirt under her nails, but others came to my aid.'

Her nurse then gave a brief account of her life—how she'd married a warrior, but they had never had any children and he had died the winter before. She'd returned to the household after Ingebord died at Kolbe-inn's specific command. There was a note of expectation in her voice and two bright spots appeared on her cheeks. Dagmar had a horrible inkling that her nurse and her father might be… Her mind skittered away from just the thought of it.

'This is your old nurse? The one who taught you Gaelic?' Aedan asked, breaking into the recital before Dagmar could ask if her suspicion was correct.

'This is Mor as she was. She has taken the name of Sif,' Dagmar replied, linking her arm with Sif. 'I'd like to take her with me when I go to Kintra. I shall make a comfortable home for you and you can live out your life in peace, Sif.'

Aedan inclined his head. 'I am sure that can be arranged.'

Dagmar quietly added that to her list of positives. Her nurse would be living with her. She would not be completely on her own. She could lean on her and learn how to run a Gaelic estate properly.

Sif went red and then white. 'It is very kind of you, Dagmar, but…'

'But?' Dagmar looked at her in dismay.

The bright spots on Sif's cheeks deepened. 'I'm happy here with your father.'

'You and my father?' Dagmar winced. Her suspicions were correct!

'We have grown close in the last few months.' Sif

gave a shrug. 'I've adored your father since he rescued me from the slavers, Dagmar, even when he only had eyes for your mother. I understand his moods better than your mother or Ingebord did. What I have, I hold.'

Dagmar sighed. The reason for her needing to marry so rapidly and give him grandchildren made sense now, as did her father's cryptic remark about producing no more children from his loins. His love for her old nurse dictated his actions. 'I suspect he means to keep you as well.'

Sif's face became wreathed in smiles. 'In any case, I will be seeing you a great deal in the future when you visit your father. He has missed you, whatever your mother told you. We'll only be a short boat trip away.'

Dagmar grabbed Sif's hand. 'Know the offer is there. You are a slave no longer. You can leave whenever you wish…should you change your mind.'

'I've not been a slave for years, my dear. I'm a free woman and far freer than I ever was with my pig of a drunken father who beat me,' Sif answered. 'Now I had best see about the food and drink before I make sure you are suitably arrayed. These warriors have prodigious appetites.'

She bustled off with her hips swaying as she issued orders.

'I'll never understand women. She was offered freedom and she chose to stay,' Aedan murmured.

Dagmar's heart squeezed. She never thought to hear that sort of tone from him again. 'There is no discerning the ways of the heart.'

'Stop stalling. Go and change.' Aedan shaded his eyes and stared off into the far horizon where a mist rose from the sea. 'I want to go before the tide turns. If the ceremony is short, we might make it.'

'But the wedding feast M—Sif is having prepared?'

'Your father must yield. I agreed to a marriage, not dining with him.'

'But did you know what my father had planned for me?' Dagmar caught his sleeve before he turned to go. 'I deserve the truth.'

His eyes turned cold. 'I thought it might be a possibility, but a slim one, one I completely discounted. It has happened now and there is nothing either one of us can do except make the best of it. My people's safety will always come first, Dagmar. Remember that and we will get on.'

'Here you are, Gael. You're a hard man to track down. I thought you might still be bathing,' Kolbeinn said, coming up to him with a huge smile after Aedan had finished bathing in the lake.

Aedan had washed the dirt from his body, but he had refused the offer of fresh robes. He refused to become one of those men who was beholden to his wife's family.

Kolbeinn dug his elbow into Aedan's side. 'You're a sly one. I do not know how you did it, but you did.'

'Did what?'

'Got Dagmar to agree to wear a gown. What else? I know what her mother tried to twist her into. It shows despite everything Dagmar remains my daughter who used to beg for pretty clothes instead of for the swords her mother thought she should desire.' The man gave a huge smile. 'I want grandchildren, Gael. I am not getting any younger. Give me some. Between you and Dagmar, you should be able to create sons to rule the seas.'

'If you want grandchildren, you will need to do something about Olafr Rolfson. Your daughter has sworn to destroy him.'

Kolbeinn's gaze darted everywhere but on Aedan's face. 'He is aligned with Thorsten. Beyond my control. I'd like to help, but…'

'You control the passage back to Dubh Linn,' Aedan bit out. 'Do it. He insulted you by trying to have your daughter killed. If you want her to settle down instead of plotting how to achieve it, find a way to dispose of him. You owe it to your old friend who perished.'

Kolbeinn gave a huge sigh. 'You speak the truth. I cannot afford to allow the insult to go unpunished. I will dispatch my best crew on the next tide. I give you my word.'

Aedan closed his eyes. Dagmar would be safe and have one less reason to be a shield maiden. 'Are you willing to accept me even though I am a Gael and intend to keep my lands free from Northern interference?'

'Needs must.' Kolbeinn shrugged. 'You remind me of me when I was your age. You took the challenge and you returned with her in the allotted time. None of my warriors has been able to do that. Why wouldn't I want you as a son-in-law? It is why I gave you my fourth-best sword. Where is it?'

'It broke and I took another one from the battlefield. Old Alf did recognise it, though. Said you would not have sent it unless your wife was dead.'

'That was Sif's doing. She recalled the code Alf and I had agreed if ever Ingebord died. She begged me as she had a soft spot for the way you demanded a chance. For me, I won either way.'

Aedan ground his teeth. He had been played by a master. He'd sworn to Dagmar that he'd had nothing to do with it, but Kolbeinn's crowing showed he or rather Dagmar's nurse had hoped he'd develop feelings for her. 'You think you have won.'

'I know I have.' Kolbeinn gave a hearty laugh. 'By the gods, Dagmar reminds me of Helga in her prime. She was the most beautiful woman to sail the seas. I was mad for her. Her blasted temper drove us apart. Always had to have her own way. She had no interest in having more children after Dagmar and refused my bed. I needed sons. I offered to have Ingebord as a second wife, but Helga made me choose. I had to go with the woman who promised me sons.'

The pleading note was clear in Kolbeinn's voice. As if he knew he'd wronged Dagmar and sought to justify it. Aedan struggled to keep his temper. The man had ducked his responsibilities. And it was not up to him to give him absolution; that was a matter for Dagmar.

'Whatever happened between you and Helga is in the past,' he murmured. 'Dagmar and I will create our own marriage.'

Kolbeinn tapped his fingers together. 'Just as long as I have grandsons.'

'You will have whatever Dagmar gives you and nothing else.'

Dagmar hesitated at the hall's door. She'd taken as long as she dared changing. Sif had found some autumn berries to twist in her hair after Dagmar refused to wear the golden bridal crown her stepmother had worn. Much to her surprise, her mended blue gown brought her some comfort. Aedan had considered her beautiful in it. His eyes had shone the first time she put it on. More than anything she wanted to see the shining of his eyes again. She wanted to feel that he wanted her as a woman.

The Christian priest stood next to Aedan. The priest appeared absolutely terrified as her father loomed over the proceedings with an axe. Aedan gave a small grunt of approval when he saw her.

'You took your time, Daughter,' her father said pointedly.

'The purification ceremony took a little time to complete.' Dagmar bobbed a perfunctory curtsy. 'Sif insisted on it being done properly.'

'I've discovered that Sif speaks much sense,' her father said. 'Our rites as well as yours.'

'Quite,' Aedan answered, glaring at her father. 'I would hardly like for anyone to say that I failed to marry your daughter thoroughly and completely.'

Her father gave a deep chuckle. 'A man after my own heart. You will do, Gael, you will do.'

Dagmar ground her teeth. Her father seemed to be twisting the truth to suit himself. He was behaving as if he had never sent Aedan to his death but had instead engineered the match right from the start.

Her father nodded towards the soothsayer who read the runes and mumbled the words of the north marriage rite.

'You are now married according to our custom,' her father said. 'It is the turn of your priest, Gael.'

Aedan lifted a brow. 'My priest?'

'I make a present of him to you. Do what you like with him as long as he says the words making you one with my daughter.'

'I'm honoured, my lord,' the priest said with a nervous bow.

'He will do that,' Aedan assured her father. 'I doubt he wants to be here one heartbeat longer than absolutely necessary.' He nodded to the priest. 'Begin.'

The priest's throat worked up and down, but no sound emerged. Several of the assembled throng made catcalls while others yelled ribald encouragement. Dagmar ground her teeth and willed him to get on with it.

'Do you know what is required of you?' he blurted out in a high squeak. 'Do you come here with a free heart?'

'I've witnessed such things before,' Dagmar said. 'I was at Constantine's court. My mother felt it best that we attend various services. I understand the enormity of what I undertake and do so willingly.'

She held her tongue and did not say that she had considered the services at court pathetic mumbling and overly stylised, not like the simple prayers the priest in the hamlet had said. That man had clearly been a holy man. Certain things were best kept private.

The priest visibly relaxed. 'You're ready to accept our saviour into your heart and soul?'

Dagmar glanced about her. There was no going back. If she stayed here, she'd be married off in a fashion she did not care for. Her gods had not answered her prayers—not today or any time before. There was no escape and what she hated was that her heart kept whispering that she did want this, she wanted to be Aedan's wife and share her life with his. She ignored it. It was listening to her heart that had led to this trouble in the first place. 'Yes.'

The cold water hit her face as he intoned the words

of baptism. Several of her father's warriors laughed, but her father held up his hand, silencing them.

'This is my daughter's choice. I respect it. It is how my grandsons will be brought up. All my men will respect this faith as well.'

Dagmar was proud that her only outward sign of annoyance was a tapping foot. If she had anything to do with it, he'd only have granddaughters.

However, after her father's intervention, the hall was wreathed in respectful silence.

The priest took out a cord and wrapped it about their hands. At her father's questioning frown, the priest hurriedly explained. 'This is called a bann and it is the custom among my people to ensure the couple are bound together.'

Aedan confirmed the custom and her father gave a half-nod. 'I will have my daughter married correctly. Proceed.'

The rest of the marriage ceremony passed in a blur as she heard Aedan's firm answers and her own as if she was watching from a great way away.

'You may kiss the bride,' the priest said.

She lifted her mouth, expecting a passionate kiss, but Aedan merely brushed her lips. A cool and impersonal kiss, unlike the ones they had shared on the journey.

She fingered her mouth. Had she killed everything between them? Was there a way forward for them? Had there ever been a possibility of a way? Or did he think of her as other men had done—someone to be ridiculed and pitied? Had it truly all been a sham? Her knees trembled and she put a hand on Aedan's arm to keep her balance.

'Shall we go? There is no need to stay for the bridal feast.'

Dagmar stared at the fur rugs which dotted the floor. His voice held no warmth. She had hoped he might return to the man who had held her for so long last night, just listening to their breathing which rose and fell in unison.

'Yes, if we stay, they will put us to bed,' Dagmar said to the floor as the priest began to intone his final blessing. 'I'm in no mood for my father and his jokes. He appears far too pleased with this.'

Aedan put a hand against the middle of her back. 'The wind is in the right direction. It will serve as an excuse.'

The priest finished the blessing and stepped back behind her father.

Her father cleared his throat. 'Now to the feasting and then the bedding. I've dealt with the problem as we discussed, Aedan.'

'What problem?' Dagmar asked, glancing between the two men.

'I've sent word to Thorsten. Your quest for vengeance is now mine. No one attacks my daughter and lives long,' her father said, spreading his hands like the priest had done. 'Think of it as a wedding gift. You can get down to the important business of giving me a grandson.'

'Aedan needs to return to his lands,' Dagmar said, fixing her father with her gaze. Aedan had convinced her father to deal with Olafr? Part of her rejoiced, but the other part knew it was because he feared for his people, rather than because he understood her need to punish the man. 'He has been away from them for too long. The wind is in the right direction. I must think of such things now.'

Her father shook his head. 'I know these Christian marriages. The woman must be properly bedded or she can claim that the marriage is not valid. It is precisely the sort of trick Helga would play. You remind me too much of her and her sly ways, Dagmar.'

'We've agreed it is valid…' Dagmar began.

'No, your father is correct, Dagmar,' Aedan said with a grim mouth. 'A wise precaution. We stay here for the feast and we will be properly bedded tonight. Then none can question. We will have satisfied both cultures. After all he has given you a wedding present.'

'Only because he requires me to breed.'

Aedan's hard fingers gripped her elbow. 'I required a helpmeet.'

'Say the words, renouncing your former occupation,' her father commanded.

'I pledge that I will be a peace-weaver, a woman and a wife instead of a warrior from now on,' Dagmar said the words quickly, so they tripped out one after the other. She hated how her insides churned as if she had betrayed her mother and everything her mother had worked so hard to achieve. And yet she knew deep down she wanted more than endless battles and war. She wished there was a way to have both, but…

'This isn't an execution, Dagmar. It is the start of a new life.' Aedan put his face close to hers. 'It can be a wonderful life.'

Dagmar turned her face away. 'That is easy for you to say. It feels like my life has just ended.'

Chapter Eleven

The room where Dagmar had to spend her wedding night, her stepmother's former chamber, was hung with gold-shot tapestries of people coupling and the bed piled high with furs. A light repast of bread, cold meat and mead along with two goblets stood on an intricately carved chest. The overall effect made Dagmar's stomach roil.

Bad enough that she would have to endure this night, a night which would make a mockery of the previous nights she had spent in Aedan's arms, but to spend it in her step-mother's former living quarters heaped insult on injury.

Her nurse took great delight in informing her that her father was giving her the tapestries as part of her dowry and that every year on the anniversary of her name day, at her stepmother's insistence, he had placed a length of expensive cloth in an iron-bound trunk for when Dagmar married.

Dagmar made a scoffing noise. Her stepmother had probably calculated that the gift would fail to reach her and would fall by default to her son and whichever woman he married.

'I am as ready as I will ever be,' she declared.

All the women, including Mhairi, crowded around her. The Gaelic woman still wore the accusatory look as though Dagmar had ruined her life deliberately. Dagmar winced. Proof if she required it that marrying Aedan and making her home amongst the Gaels carried its own set of problems.

She was going to go into a different sort of battle for the rest of her life and she needed to work out how to win allies because the prize was a home where she and her children could grow up in safety. Her children would never have to run in fear for their lives, she vowed. And she wasn't asking for Aedan to love her, simply to respect her. Her heart called her a liar, but she refused to listen.

'Mhairi,' she said, forcing her voice to seem light and unconcerned. 'Is there anything I should know about your customs with bedding?'

The woman put her nose in the air. 'What would I know about such things? I'm unmarried. I might as well become a nun now. No respectable man will make me an offer after this.'

She had gambled everything on marrying Aedan after her stint as a hostage, Dagmar realised. She felt vaguely sorry for her, but she should have realised that she played a high-stakes game. 'I find much depends on the dowry.'

Mhairi sniffed. 'And you know so much about our customs.'

'Surely you have seen wedding nights in the past. Is there anything special I should know?'

Mhairi gave a reluctant nod. 'I have. The first time was when Aedan's brother married his lady. She was white-faced and petrified as she stood there in her shift with her hair all about her shoulders just like you are now. Brandon, Aedan's brother, threw open the door and she practically fainted at his nakedness. How it went I couldn't say, but they displayed the bloodied sheet the next day even though everyone knew he left her bed in the middle of the night to go to his mistress. Everyone knew he never graced his wife's bed after that. Once is all it took. They had twins.'

Once. Dagmar put her hand on her flat stomach. She was not going think about having a child, but hope sprang in her breast. She'd not used any of the simple precautions her mother took to prevent pregnancy. In a hostile world, a child to hold was a good thing. A child would help bind Aedan and her together, but she could understand how it might have the potential to divide them, too. Her birth had certainly caused things to change between her parents.

'Aedan explained to me about his brother's boat and how his children died.'

The woman blinked in surprise. Dagmar took some small satisfaction from that. 'Did he? Everyone loved Brandon. He was the bravest king we could ever hope for. Aedan is...'

'The King who saved Kintra from the Northmen.' Dagmar forced a smile. 'Aedan spoke of his brother on the journey here.'

'Did he say how deluded Liddy had been about Brandon? She actually thought he wanted to marry her, that he was hot for her, her with the birthmark on her face. They married and *pfft*...'

'What happened?'

Mhairi gave a malicious smile. 'She discovered the

truth. He had only married her for her dowry, for what she could bring to Kintra. He was a tomcat, prowling amongst women. They say that he would lie with any woman with a pulse except his wife. Did Aedan also confide about Brigid, my cousin, his fiancée who died and the reason he stayed unmarried against the wishes of his people?' Her gaze raked Dagmar and seemed to highlight every flaw. 'Interesting that he chose you after so long. Everyone knows how alike the brothers were. Two peas in a pod.'

Mhairi's words thudded through her. Brandon lay with every woman except his wife. Then Aedan refusing to marry until now. A small piece of her protested that Aedan was not like that. Simply because his brother had behaved in that fashion, it did not mean he would do so, too. 'I knew she had died.'

'Aedan was consumed with grief at her loss and left to be a sell-sword under Ketil's command. Some doubted that he would ever marry. They said he buried his heart with her body.'

'Enough gossiping. There are more important considerations.' Her nurse pulled at her sleeve and made a fuss of plucking a remaining red berry from her hair.

'What is it, Sif?' Dagmar asked, pulling away. 'My hair was fine as it was.'

'Don't you believe everything that one tells you,' she murmured. 'She has an axe to grind. She kept telling anyone who would listen that she was going to be the next lady of Kintra while Aedan was gone and now you are. People's hearts can hold more than one person. I saw how he looked at you when you appeared in your bridal finery. Lance the boil of suspicion before it festers in your mind and poisons your marriage.'

'Do you think…?'

'I suspect, despite that woman's words, she is no virgin and that she is breeding.' Her nurse made a little clicking noise of disapproval in the back of her throat. 'If I'm right, Aedan mac Connall will have had nothing to do with the making of that bairn. I saw how they parted when he left to find you. I wouldn't have given him your father's sword, if I thought… Anyway, there will be more to her story. I can feel it in my bones.' Sif patted her backside. 'And my bones rarely steer me wrong, even if they are more padded these days than they used to be.'

Dagmar squeezed her nurse's hand. Her nurse obviously had attempted to matchmake between them and keep Aedan alive. 'You've a soft spot for him. Who does he remind you of? Your brother? The one who died before you were kidnapped?'

'You will always be my little girl. You're far more striking than Helga ever was.' Her nurse examined her handiwork. 'Tonight, you glow. He won't be able to keep his hands off you. I know men, my dear, and your warrior is definitely a man.'

The door banged opened and Aedan was pushed in with plenty of ribald comments about the need for rest, huge appetites and lying comfortably. Even though Dagmar had heard the jokes before, they'd never been about her.

Before the door closed completely, his dog slipped in.

'You can't bring that dog in here. You risk extreme bad luck.' Mhairi made a shooing motion with her hands.

Mor gave a low rumble in the back of her throat and Mhairi retreated.

Dagmar clicked her fingers and the dog came over to her, licking her fingers. The tight knot in her stomach relaxed. Aedan would never have married that woman despite her earlier claims. Mor disliked her and Aedan listened to his dog.

'Mor can stay. Where else would she sleep on a night like this?' Dagmar fondled Mor's ears. 'She has only ever brought me good luck.'

Mhairi rolled her eyes. 'Dirty beasts, dogs.'

She flounced from the room. The rest of the women slipped from the room until they were standing alone. Outside the air rang with drums and shields being beaten to ward off bad luck.

'You are sure that you don't mind having Mor in with us?' Aedan asked.

She occupied herself with pouring some mead so that she wouldn't stare at his chest. 'Mind? Why would I mind? Mor is my travelling companion.'

'Some people would.' He took the goblet from her fingers.

'I'm me. I've reason to be grateful to her.'

'Eat. You barely touched anything at the feast. Your father keeps an excellent table.'

Dagmar obediently took a piece of bread from the plate. Part of her had hoped that he would simply hold her, but he made no move to do so. If he had done what Mhairi suggested and had deliberately seduced her, then she refused to make it easy for him.

'Why did my father send a crew out to take vengeance against Olafr?'

'Because I asked him to.'

She pressed her lips together. 'He certainly dismissed me when I tried to speak to him about such things.'

'I put it in terms he understood.' He shrugged. 'You and your father are more alike than you might care to admit.'

'My father values your opinion more.' Dagmar fought against the urge to throw something. 'You're a man and now his son-in-law. It is the way of the world, even if I wish it was different.'

'I merely made the point that if he wanted grandsons, taking over your vow would be one way of ensuring it would happen. Only you can give him what he desires.' He looked at her over the rim of his goblet. 'You don't have to face Olafr alone. You don't have to be the one to administer the final blow. You just need to know it was done.'

'Logically you are right, it doesn't have to be me. Knowing it is done will be enough.' She forced a light note into to her voice, but she knew she'd convinced no one. What Aedan said had merit, but it still felt a failure. 'But why did you convince him?'

'Because I want to keep Kintra safe,' he said too smoothly. 'Far better to have your father risk his men than have one hair from the head of my people harmed.'

'If they don't find Olafr?'

'Then Thorsten learns Kolbeinn the Blood-Axe is my ally and he raids me at his peril. Either way, my people are safe.'

Dagmar gave an unhappy nod as his words extinguished any slim hope she had that he'd done it to help her. This was all about protecting Kintra. It always had been. She'd been naive in the extreme to think he had feelings for her. She'd been played by a master, the poor pathetic fool that she was. She wrapped her pride about the wound and stood up straight. Her mother had taught her to keep such considerations hidden from those who would exploit the weakness.

'What happens next?' she asked after she had nibbled at the food and sipped at the mead and had regained some semblance of balance.

'We go to bed, to sleep. You look half-dead.' He took the goblet of mead from her nerveless fingers. So much for her nurse's confident prediction of her glowing beauty making Aedan's blood rise to a boil. His was an impersonal touch and perfunctory.

'That is because I spent most of last night awake.' She forced what she hoped was a husky laugh. One last try, something to remind Aedan that they had shared something special.

She waited with bated breath to see what he'd do. Outside the noise increased with catcalls telling him to get on with it and other coarse comments about what they should be doing.

'My father is giving us some encouragement. He is trying to be helpful.'

A muscle jumped in his cheek and his lips became a thin white line. 'I'll be damned if I allow that man to dictate when or where I perform!'

'He will be expecting to see a bloody sheet.'

He stilled. 'Why? You swore such things were unimportant in your culture.'

'He knows I was a shield maiden. Shield maidens are supposed to be virgins. Sif knows your customs and he is determined that no one will have cause to say anything against this marriage.'

Aedan swore softly. Dagmar was going to be humiliated when the linen sheet had nothing on it. She'd have been a virgin, but he'd already taken her maidenhead.

She was far too keyed up to enjoy it and he wanted their first married joining to be special, something to be remembered, not endured with ribald joking outside the door. Until her father's interference, he had planned on taking her to the hut he'd occupied when his brother was alive, his refuge from the mess he'd made. Before Brigid's betrayal he'd planned it for his bride. He hoped Dagmar would be different from Brigid and would appreciate it. He consigned her father to the furthest corner of Hell.

'Something needs to be done or otherwise your father won't be satisfied.'

'My thoughts exactly.' Dagmar's brows wore a worried pucker. 'Do you think if he does not see the blood that he will demand to actually see us couple instead? With weddings in the north country, sometimes the couple would perform in public to placate the gods and ensure the bride's fertility.'

'That is definitely not going to happen.' Aedan threw the covers off the bed, revealing a pristine white linen sheet.

'What are you going to do?'

'Cheat.' Aedan took the small eating knife from the chest. 'No one will be able to tell whose blood is on this sheet.'

He prepared to cut his thigh, cursing Kolbeinn as he did it.

Dagmar put her hand over his wrist, stopping the motion. 'Wait! I'll do it. My blood.'

'Are we going to argue about that as well?'

She gave one of her smiles. His heart twisted and he realised that he needed them in his life. He was taking out his annoyance at Kolbeinn on Dagmar who looked beyond beautiful, but exhausted. 'My parents used to argue. Then they stopped and the awfulness started.'

'I led a quiet life before you happened along,' he said to the sheet.

'Did he, Mor?'

Mor the traitor gave a slight shake of her head.

'Up on the bed then.'

Her body bore a network of scars where she'd obviously received wounds. He hated to mar her skin again. Silently he renewed the vow that he'd secretly made during the wedding—that she would not have to fight again. If Kolbeinn's crew failed to punish Olafr, he'd do it himself, but Dagmar would not lift a sword again. She'd suffered enough.

'It is going to have to be deeper,' she said with a frown. 'That is no worse than a pinprick. The point of the exercise is that I bleed on that sheet.'

'I don't want to hurt you.'

She removed the knife from his fingers. 'Five summers campaigning means pain holds little fear for me.'

He winced slightly as the knife sliced through her flesh.

She grasped her thigh and forced the blood out, gasping slightly as she did it. Aedan's stomach twisted. Less than a day into the marriage and she bore a fresh wound. He was worse than his brother for breaking promises.

'That should do it,' she said briskly and rubbed the blood on to the sheet. 'Where did you learn this trick?'

'I'll get a cloth.' He turned his back on her and forced the bile back down his throat. He'd never been sick at the sight of blood before, but seeing Dagmar's white thigh gleaming red, he struggled. She'd probably laugh at him, tell him that it was barely a trickle. He schooled his features and turned back towards her. 'The cut is noticeable.'

'I can tend to it.' She got off the bed and dipped the cloth in the mead before dabbing it on the cut. 'Do you want the floor? Or the bed? Your choice.'

Aedan frowned. The ease between them had vanished and it caused a hollow to open in his chest. He had destroyed her dream, but he had to think about his people. 'I'll sleep on the floor and you take the bed.'

Dagmar curled herself into a tight ball. She could hear the steady sound of Aedan's breath intermingled with Mor's.

She had tried and tried, but sleep refused to come.

She could understand him not performing as he called it, but did he have to sleep so far away? He had barely looked at her after she cut her thigh. Despite her brave words earlier, she knew Mhairi had spoken truthfully. Like her father, Aedan knew kings needed sons and he'd remained unmarried until now, until he was left with no option.

She firmed her mouth. Begging was not going to happen, but the first time he looked at another woman, she would be sharpening her knives. She was not going to be made into some cowed wife who allowed her husband freedom while accepting none for herself.

'Are you awake, Dagmar? I need the sheets. I see the Gael performed as your father and I hoped.' Her nurse's whisper penetrated through Dagmar's confused dream.

Dagmar blinked awake. Her nurse stood by the bed. Most of the furs had fallen on the ground and even in the dim light, the stain on the sheet was clearly visible. 'Where is Aedan?'

'He has taken your trousers and tunic. Your father ordered me to burn them, but Aedan said that he would deal with them.'

'Probably wants the pleasure of burning them himself.' Dagmar's mouth went dry. She leapt out of bed and started searching on the floor. 'Where are my boots?'

Her nurse wrinkled her nose. 'They are there. I am not to touch them. I had brought a pair of fur-lined slippers which had belonged to Ingebord, but your husband insisted you'd prefer your old boots.'

The tension eased from her shoulders. Her boots were here. She still had the gold, in case everything went wrong. And the sketch she'd made of the house she'd build for her mother when the vow was fulfilled. That piece of parchment had travelled with her for the last nine years. 'My husband spoke true.'

'I have brought a selection of gowns.' Her nurse clapped her hands and a number of gowns were carried in—all in deep green and silver. Her stepmother's colours.

'I will wear my own gown, rather than one of my stepmother's.'

Her former nurse gave one of her hard stares, the sort which used to command instant obedience from Dagmar. 'The blue gown you wore for the wedding looked to be fraying at the seams. You will need new gowns sooner rather than later. Even your mother when she was married wore gowns.'

'I will deal with my clothes when I get to Kintra, but until then I wear the blue gown. The style they wear is sure to be different. I am the Lady of Kintra, not a Northern lady now.'

'I really think you should look at everything in the trunk your father saved for you.'

Dagmar remembered the tone of voice from when she was little and had done something wrong. This time, however, it was about pleasing her father. 'There won't be time. Aedan will want to leave as soon as possible. Making silly noises over unwanted gowns makes me want to gag.'

'When you were little, you used to love going through your mother's trunks, trying on her jewellery and finery.'

'When I was little, many things were different. I believed my father actually cared about me, instead of seeing me as a tool to further his own ambitions.'

Her nurse gave a long-suffering sigh. 'Every time your name day arrived while you were gone, your father would take himself away and get blindly drunk. He has missed you.'

'He can keep his kindness. I haven't required it for over ten years.'

'You need to stop thinking like a child.'

'I've experienced five years of the blood and stink of war. I've earned the right to be called an adult.'

'You still see your mother and father with a child's eyes,' her nurse scolded. 'Your mother was far from blameless, whatever she claimed. Your mother was quite vocal about only ever having one child. Your father wanted many children. Your mother was always threatening to leave him if she did not get her own way. He did not think she meant it until she went. She'd humiliated him in front of everyone. He lost his temper.'

'I know my mother's side.'

'What you might not know is that your father loves you and has always loved you. He rescued me because he worried that his wife, your mother, was neglecting you. Once Alf found you playing in the embers of a fire. Your mother was too busy with her sword practice to be bothered with what you did.'

Dagmar pressed her hands against her eyes. She could dimly remember Old Alf telling her the same sort of tale about the time he'd found her playing in the fire. Her mother had laughed and said that his memory was going. It was entirely possible that her mother had become distracted. She often forgot the time or to eat if she became too involved in practising her skills. 'How do you know this?'

'Alf brought you and your burnt forearm to me. Tears streamed down your face. It was the first time we met. Your father forbade me to go with you both when you left because he thought your mother would return, once she calmed down, as she needed help in looking after you.'

'He misjudged her.'

'Yes, he did and he misjudged Ingebord's determination as well.' Her nurse continued in a softer voice. 'Over the years, he did often speak of you to me. It is why he kept me with him when Ingebord would have seen me gone. He always hoped you'd return.'

'I won't wear my stepmother's things.'

'But you will take the trunk. Look at it with an open mind when you do?'

'As you will give me no peace until I do, yes.'

'I've packed another trunk full of tapestries which used to hang in the hall back when you were small.'

'My mother's tapestries? The ones which had belonged to her mother?'

Her nurse tilted her head to one side. 'They may be. What you do with them should be your choice. Just as it was your mother's.'

'Sif, my mother didn't have a choice.'

'We always have a choice. She chose her path, but I remember her well enough to know she'd have wanted you to be happy and content. Have you been?'

Dagmar traced one of the motifs on the chest. Her mother had warned her to never marry because she would be unhappy. However, Dagmar knew she'd be unhappier away from Aedan than with him. 'My mother's memory will not be disgraced.'

Her nurse caught her hand. 'I know, but remember your parents' marriage is not yours. Aedan mac Connall is a good man and he cares about you.'

Dagmar blinked hard. 'You will be telling me next that you believe in people living happily ever after.'

'Why not? Your father and I—that is what we are doing.' Sif put her hand over Dagmar's. 'In the darkest times you have to believe, Dagmar, and I for one believe in you and your ability to make this marriage work.'

Chapter Twelve

Kintra with its gabled roof shone out over the water. To the right Aedan could make out the gleaming stone cross which honoured his dead nephew and niece, the one he had put up once he discovered how his brother had sought to conceal the truth about why the boat had capsized by blaming Liddy, and how his brother had failed his people through insisting vast amounts of gold be spent on a fleet of unseaworthy ships. Like every other time when he spotted the cross, the weight on his chest increased and he renewed his vow to keep Kintra safe. He would not fail it like his brother had.

Aedan concentrated on Kintra bay and the purple Paps of Jura rising behind. He'd rescued his people. His brother's legacy of debt and extravagance no longer cast a shadow over Kintra, but would they see it that way? Before he left, there had been grumbling about how he always managed to put Kintra into more danger. He would have to convince them that Dagmar represented safety, rather than servitude to the Northmen, or the grumbles from a few could swell to an angry chorus.

Despite her nurse's confident prediction that Dag-

mar would wear a new gown for the journey, Dagmar
had appeared at the waterfront wearing her blue gown
and her boots. Part of him wanted to cheer her independence, but another part of him worried she'd find
her new role impossible. In saving Kintra, would he
destroy this woman's spirit?

'I take it, from Mhairi's delighted screams about the
crowds of people thronging to the shore, we are looking at Kintra,' Dagmar said, wearing one of her fiercest expressions.

Aedan reached over and touched her hand. She
flinched and turned her face away. He hated that she
had retreated into her shell again. He'd had no time
to speak to her this morning and reassure her that all
would be well before her nurse had bustled in. He at
least had managed to secrete her old clothes away before the old biddy could dispose of them. They were far
too much a part of Dagmar to destroy.

'That is indeed Kintra, your new home. Try to look
as though it is something more than a dung heap when
you greet people.'

Her scowl deepened. 'You put words in my mouth.
I know nothing about your home. I can barely see the
shore.'

He sighed and piloted the boat to the jetty.

As Mhairi had predicted, everyone who lived close
to the bay was on the shore and more kept arriving with
every heartbeat until the wharf area teemed with his people, laughing and cheering as each person came ashore
until only Dagmar remained thunder-faced on the boat.

Aedan held up his hand and the throng fell silent. He
extended his hand and Dagmar's cold fingers curled
about his. He led her on to the jetty.

'Who is this woman?' one of the farmers called out. 'Another woman you rescued from that butcher?'

'Dagmar Kolbeinndottar, now my wife and your new lady. You are to welcome her with Kintra's customary warmth.'

Dagmar stood on the rickety jetty. A faint breeze whipped her hair into her mouth. With impatient fingers, she pushed it out. She hated that everyone was staring at her like a prized cow. When she had worn her paint and had fastened her hair in plaits, at least she had been able to hide behind them. Out here she felt naked and vulnerable.

At Aedan's announcement, the crowd of people stopped cheering and instead regarded her with hostile eyes.

'You married a Northwoman?' someone called out. 'Why? Aren't our women good enough for you? Mhairi became a hostage for you!'

Several others uttered a few choice phrases in Gaelic, making unflattering comparisons. More proof if she needed it about her physical assets, but her heart kept whispering that she needed to give Aedan another chance. He had made her feel beautiful. Dagmar kept her back straight. *Never, ever allow them to see your hurt*—the advice from her mother proved as worthwhile now as it had done on the practice field.

'Because I value peace above all things,' Aedan declared in a ringing tone. 'Kolbeinn has cause to keep his promises. He favours us with his daughter, his only living child, as Kintra's lady.'

Dagmar's heart thudded. This was far worse than being at Constantine's court. There they had accepted her because she was part of Constantine's army. When she first went to her mother's lands, Old Alf had been there before she and her mother arrived and had eased the way.

Here they would judge her on her ability to keep an estate, not on how well she fought or who her mother was. On any great estate like Kintra, the lady had much to do, from ensuring a good harvest to making sure all were clothed and tending to those who were ill, a thousand and one mundane tasks.

Her mother had left such things to Old Alf's woman rather than bothering with them. When she died, Dagmar silently vowed she'd be different. She'd had plans to learn after she gained her lands, but the battle and Olafr had happened. She had striven to be the best warrior and now she'd strive to be the best lady, and that included defending the land against any raiders.

'I look forward to getting to know you,' she said in Gaelic. Her voice sounded high and frail to her. 'I'm sure I will soon feel at home here. From what I can see of Kintra and its sheltered bay, it has great potential.'

'The Northwoman knows Gaelic!' rippled through the crowd.

Aedan held out his hand to help her down, but she ignored it. She wasn't like that Mhairi, leaning on men. She stood on her own feet. She fought her battles herself. Those men had mocked her, but they would guard their tongues from now on.

Dagmar bit her lip and concentrated.

Face the future and the next battle, instead of trying to win the last one again.

Practical considerations instead of dream-spinning about a future with Aedan that could never be. They were not going to go off adventuring. They would be staying in this place. The gabled hall loomed over the bay. 'I should like to see where we will live.'

'We wait for the priest's blessing. It is customary.' Aedan gestured towards the assembled throng. 'Where is Father Cathan? He may have arrived a few weeks before I departed, but I do expect my priest to adhere to certain standards which include greeting the laird when he returns.'

A man with a narrow face and a sallow look strode forward. The sneer on his face increased the closer he came to Dagmar. Dagmar concentrated on a point behind his left shoulder, rather than flinching.

'You wish to have a blessing on this pagan marriage? Why did you not consult me first before contracting such an unwise alliance, Lord? You've wilfully imperilled your immortal soul and that of all the souls in Kintra.'

'Far from a pagan marriage—' Aedan's face became hard '—Kolbeinn the Blood-Axe ensured the marriage was done according to the rites of our church. My wife has renounced her old gods. She understands the requirements of being Kintra's lady.'

Not trusting her voice to adequately explain the enormity of it, Dagmar gave a vigorous nod. It was only standing on this jetty that it truly hit her. She had sworn to end her entire life and had been reborn, but she'd given up everything for a man whose people despised her.

The priest's eyes widened. 'She has become a true daughter of Christ?'

Aedan held out his hands. 'Why would I of all people risk my immortal soul? Why would I forget my sacred oath to serve my people?'

'I can speak for myself,' Dagmar said, clenching her fists. 'The priest who travels with us can confirm it. I recognise the gods of my childhood as being false.'

The priest seemed to shrink under Father Cathan's gaze. 'You were forced to convert this woman?'

'I… I had no choice. Those pagans…you've no idea what they can do to a man. She served in King Constantine's household before…and I thought…'

'May St Michael and all the angels preserve us.' Father Cathan gave a humourless smile. 'The marriage is void. It was done under duress. The priest can barely speak for fear.'

Dagmar's heart thumped. Maybe her prayers had been answered after all. She glanced out at the sea of ordinary faces, many of whom had gone white at the priest's words. They were not her people, but they were Aedan's. He had risked everything for them.

Her father would destroy Kintra if she left. Or if he could not bring himself to do it, he'd open the shipping lanes to pirates and raiders. And the next warrior he'd send after her would treat her roughly. There was no choice. She was staying. She might not be happy about the way Aedan had tricked her, but she had given her oath.

'No!' Aedan shouted before she could explain. 'The marriage is not void, Father. You are mistaken in your interpretation. The marriage stands!'

The priest blinked in surprise.

'I'm merely concerned for this woman's immortal soul. Such decisions should not be taken lightly. Nor should marriages be conducted at the point of a sword.'

'One wonders if you have ever lived in the real world, Father Cathan,' Aedan said drily.

The priest had the grace to flush.

'I knew what I was doing,' Dagmar said as loudly as she could. 'I've studied Latin and can read the script. My mother ensured it.'

'Impressive, but did you repent in your heart? Many Northmen in my experience mouth the words, but never understand their meaning.'

Dagmar glanced at Aedan. His eyes held a vague plea. She gave a nod, knowing what she had to do. The wind whipped her hair from her face, but she kept her gaze focused on the middle distance.

'The marriage is valid.' She looked over the gathered throng and added in Latin. 'Do you wish to insult my father, Father Cathan? Now that the hostages have returned safely and are not languishing in some slave market? Do you think you can withstand being a slave better than the good father who stands beside me did?'

She glanced back at Aedan who gave her a slight nod. The hard knot in her stomach eased. She silently blessed the fact that her mother had been determined that her daughter would be able to understand what the priests were saying or writing.

'My Lady?' The priest who had married them pulled at her sleeve.

'Yes, Father…'

'Alcuin. Can I say that you have a pleasant smile? Your people might appreciate seeing it.'

Mor gave a soft woof as if she agreed with Father Alcuin. Something warm grew in Dagmar's heart. That stratagem had worked with the priest she and Aedan had encountered the day after the mist. She wanted these people to like her, not be afraid of her. She could show Aedan that she was capable of learning. She returned the priest's smile. 'Father Alcuin, you give excellent advice.'

She turned back towards the gathered throng and picked out a matronly-looking woman. She concentrated on giving her a smile. The woman blinked twice and returned the smile.

'Who will give this rescued priest a home? He has been through much,' she said loudly.

Aedan's priest blanched. 'The good father can reside with me. He will be upset after his trauma.'

'Then you will bless the marriage,' Dagmar said. 'So that the people here know that everything was done properly.'

His eyes grew colder and she knew that he would be waiting for her to make a mistake, but this time she had won. 'Aye, I will do that. Tomorrow, on the proper day for marriages, but first I need to minster to the returned hostages.'

'No!' Aedan roared. 'You will bless this marriage here and now.'

The priest went white. 'Marriages are traditionally celebrated on the Feast of All Saints.'

'Would you gainsay your lord? Do it now!'

The priest gave a huge sigh and mumbled the words. Dagmar risked a glance at Aedan. His face was set on harsh lines.

'There will be no more talk of void marriages,' Aedan declared.

Father Cathan gave him a filthy look and nodded towards the stone cross which dominated the skyline. 'I must attend to my duties. Come, Father, we must get you settled. It will be good to have some intelligent conversation.'

A steady drizzle started as the mist rolled in, obscuring the Paps of Jura. Despite the wetness, the population stayed out to welcome their King and his new lady back. Dagmar noticed that the atmosphere improved once Kintra's priest had departed.

Dagmar forced her shoulders to relax and practised smiling at everyone she passed. Frequently, they returned her smile. As she walked along, she kept noticing how the defences were lax. They could never have withstood a long siege from her father or anyone else. Dagmar missed her footing. Olafr. He had not attacked them yet, nor had he been at her father's. There would be a reason for that. Olafr was not one to give up easily. He would ensure she was dead and he would seek to punish the man who had saved her.

Aedan put his hand under her elbow. Her traitorous body quivered with awareness of him. 'Be aware, people often throw oatcakes at newlyweds. It is to bring prosperity to the marriage rather than a sign of displeasure.'

'And you think I might react badly to the custom?'

'Your brows have drawn together and your scowl has returned. If you are not worried about the crowd's behaviour, what are you worried about?'

Dagmar forced her brows to relax. If she confessed her fears about Olafr, Aedan would tell her it was no longer her problem. It was her father's. Except when did her father ever do what she wanted him to?

'It is probably nothing.'

'Except you can't help thinking about the ground. Relax, Kintra is well defended.'

'How did you know I was thinking about that?'

He gave a little laugh. 'It is what you do when you are nervous. Remember, you told me?'

She stared at him. 'You remember that?'

'Why would I ever want to forget?'

Her heart did a little flip and she discovered that she wanted to believe Mhairi had spoken falsely, that this marriage was more than a cynical exercise in self-preservation by Aedan. Maybe there was a way in which she could explain her fears. 'There are some things I noticed that we should discuss...'

'We can talk after we negotiate the oatcakes and the broom.'

'Broom?'

'I have to carry you over it. Then we will be alone and we can talk.' He lowered his voice. 'And do other things...'

Dagmar hated that the hard knot in her stomach eased. Maybe there was a chance for them if she could prevent Olafr from snatching it away.

Dagmar struggled in Aedan's arms at they crossed the threshold. He set her down rapidly. She plucked several oatcake crumbs out of her hair. 'What did you want to talk to me about?'

'You seemed unconvinced about Kintra's defences.'

'I am.' Dagmar rapidly listed the problems she had seen, including how large the harbour was, and her suspicion that the women would know little about self-defence. 'Kintra needs to be prepared in case of a raid.'

'My new alliance, including my marriage to you, is supposed to prevent that.'

Dagmar clasped her hands together and knew there was little hope for it. She'd have to confess her fears. It would be worse if these kind people suffered because of her. 'What happens if Olafr's ship slips through my father's net? He could come from the south, rather than the north. It would be something my mother would do. He knows your name, Aedan. He knows you took me.'

'You are worrying about nothing. He has his new alliance with Thorsten to think of.'

'I suppose I won't fully relax until I know his head has been forcibly removed from his shoulders.'

'He doesn't know you are at Kintra.'

'He knows your name. He knows you spirited me away. He didn't make for my father's. He might come straight here instead.'

The colour drained from Aedan's face. 'Why only say this now?'

'Because I had other things on my mind.' She lifted her chin. 'Changing my clothes fails to change how I view the world. And I made an error in not considering the possibility before now. It would have been worse if I'd kept it a secret. If he comes here, he will lay waste to this place and enslave all those who live here.'

Aedan stared at Dagmar as the full import of her words hit him. Olafr knew who he was and where he came from. Unless Kolbeinn's men intercepted him, Olafr would be coming here. He should have considered the possibility earlier. 'If he knows my name, he would have come here whether you were here or not. You should have warned me earlier.'

She bowed her head and drew a line in the dust with her toe. 'An uncharacteristic mistake. I apologise.'

'Apology accepted. I should have considered it as well.'

Dagmar's face lit up. 'We were both thinking of other things.'

'But you think there are things which can be done quickly, things which will give my people a chance? I will not be the one who surrenders to a Northman. I will not lose these lands for anyone or anything.'

Dagmar's throat worked up and down. 'Yes. Most can be done in a matter of a few days.'

He placed his hand on her shoulder and silently bade goodbye to his plans of bedding her straight away. 'I have to call a meeting of the elders. There are things which need to be done immediately.'

'Will you tell them about Olafr?'

He shook his head. 'It would cause panic.'

'Doing nothing is not an option.' Dagmar looped a tendril about her ear and leant forward. 'Maybe you could explain that, based on your experiences this summer, you want to increase the defences. We don't have much time if my gut is correct. Once Olafr can get a crew together, he will sail for Kintra. You could explain at the wedding feast.'

Aedan put an arm about her shoulders, but she stood stiffly away from him. He swore softly under his breath. Dagmar had retreated into her shell again. 'I wasn't planning on holding a feast.'

The light vanished from her eyes and he regretted teasing her even slightly. 'I see.'

'You don't. I planned on spending the entire night enjoying you without roving gangs singing ribald songs and banging drums outside the door, but...'

'Spending the entire night with me?'

He froze. He had forgotten how fragile her confidence about being a woman was. She might appear tough, but she had little faith in her own beauty. He lifted her chin so she was forced to look into his eyes. Her generous mouth trembled. He ran a thumb over it.

'Where else would I want to spend it? I objected to your father and his methods, not you in my bed. Never to that.'

Her eyes dropped. 'I'd not considered it.'

'Liar.' He dropped a kiss on her forehead. 'You should. Will you allow me to speak to the elders on my own? You can keep the bed warm.'

Her eyes blazed. 'I am not frightened of them.'

'But they may be frightened of you. They have cause to hate change, Dagmar, of any sort.' He thought about the cross which dominated the headland and his part in the debacle. If he hadn't been so wrapped up in Brigid's betrayal, he'd have taken steps, but he had failed them and there were those who distrusted him for it. 'They have cause to. It needs to come from me.'

Her face fell slightly. 'Is that what I am consigned to? Being your bed partner so my father can get his grandsons?'

'Your father has nothing to do with why I want you in my bed.' He ran a hand down her flank. She trembled and his body responded instantly, but he knew if he gave in, he would not be able to speak to the elders and Father Cathan would have a chance to spread his poison. 'Have you forgotten what we were like together? Will I have to remind you?'

His lips captured hers and drank from them. She gave into the pressure and opened. In that meeting of mouths, he knew she gave him strength.

With the last vestige of self-control, he put her away

from him. 'If we keep this up, there will be no defence against Olafr and I'm not ready to lose you to him.'

'That would never happen. I could best him any day.'

'I am hoping it will not come to it.'

The light which had been missing returned to her eyes and she gave a playful push against his chest. 'Go. This once I will yield, but not for ever.'

'Did the meeting go well?' Dagmar asked from where she sat beside the hearth. Mor had stayed with her, keeping her company. It had been hard to let Aedan go, but she was trying to take it slowly. Her mind kept returning to the kiss they had shared. He desired her.

Aedan appeared weary as if he had argued long and hard. She stood and held out her arms. He walked straight into them, enfolding her in his embrace. They remained like that for a long time.

'How did it go?'

'They have agreed to most of your suggestions except for the sinking of the ships to narrow the harbour and training the women in self-defence,' he said against her hair. 'I am not sure if a number of the older farmers were convinced about my explanation.'

'They are making a mistake. The entrance to the harbour is too wide.'

'My cousin believes it would interfere with the fishing nets. He reminded me that I have been away having adventures rather than fishing.'

'And the reason for not instructing the women?'

'Father Cathan spoke against it. Apparently when he was administering to Mhairi, she told him about your past as a warrior. He believes the Good Lord will protect Kintra's women rather than unnatural women.'

'Just as in the past? Your aunt… How many more women must be taken before he relents?'

He held up his hand. 'I know, but going against Father Cathan directly will be difficult. He is already trying to say that I've made a mistake in bringing a woman from the north here as my wife. I look after the earthly needs, but Father Cathan is concerned about their souls. He could preach against them, against you. It will make life more difficult. For now, I will allow him his victory.'

Dagmar firmed her mouth and silently vowed she'd find a way. 'Something needs to be done about protecting the women.'

He tilted her chin upwards. 'All the time Father Cathan was pontificating, I was thinking about this.'

His mouth came down on hers and claimed it. Dark and hot, calling to the banked fire within her. Dagmar gave into the passion in the kiss. She looped her arms about his neck and pressed her body close. His arms instantly tightened about her as his lips moved down her neck.

She knew it was to distract her, but her heart couldn't help thrilling. He did want her. He made her feel desirable and she loved that feeling. It didn't matter what others thought. It mattered what Aedan thought and, while she knew it wasn't deep abiding love, she would take it.

'Shall we begin our marriage properly?' he growled in her ear.

Her fingers pressed against the hard muscle of his chest, circling his nipples. 'I thought you'd never ask.'

'How little you know me!'

'That can be remedied.' His mouth reclaimed hers and there was no time for talking let alone thinking.

* * *

Later as she watched him sleep, Dagmar realised that he'd failed to tell her what had actually happened at the meeting, the little decisions which could make a difference to Kintra's ability to withstand Olafr's onslaught when it came.

He'd used their passion against her, but it also meant that he had not actually forbidden her from doing anything. He might wish not to antagonise Kintra's priest, but she refused to have women be left vulnerable.

She would find a way to demonstrate to everyone that Aedan had not made a mistake in marrying her.

Dagmar stared at the tangle of threads which marked her fourth attempt at threading the loom several days later. She needed to acquire cloth to make a gown and she needed to find a way so that she could teach the women self-defence. Normally to puzzle out her problem she would have resorted to sparring with a partner, but she doubted that Aedan would allow it.

'I shall have to figure out another way,' she said to Mor, who lay at her feet with her head buried in her paws.

'My lady?' A matronly woman bustled in, carrying a bundle of cloth.

Dagmar realised with a start that it was the woman she'd smiled at on the quayside. She hastily stood up and tried to smooth out the creases of her gown. 'May I help you?'

'I've brought you a wedding gift.' The woman shoved the bundle towards her. 'You smiled so sweetly the other day and Father Cathan was so unwelcoming, even when he blessed your marriage. It made me want to cry. Not that a body should go against a priest, but he lacks something…'

Dagmar gave a small shrug. 'I have learned that it is sometimes best to simply smile and go about one's business.'

'I brought you a gown.' The woman's cheeks became bright red. 'Not that there is anything wrong with the one you are wearing but it seems far too fine for every day. And Mhairi said that you normally wore trousers.'

Dagmar stared at the simple wool gown in disbelief. It was a deep blue, but made of serviceable wool. 'This is for me?'

'It belonged to my daughter Annis, but she is gone now and unlikely to return.'

'What do you mean gone?'

A shadow of intense sorrow passed over the woman's face. 'She is one of the disappeared. She vanished over a year ago. Right before Lord Aedan returned with the stone cross. Hopefully now he is married, Lord Aedan will stay here. When he is around, the Northmen leave us alone. We begged him the last time to stay but…he wanted to rescue the hostages. Other men could have done that. He should have trusted them and now there are rumours that we are about to be attacked, but I don't believe it.'

Dagmar fingered the material. The opportunity she'd hoped for was right in front of her. She had to get the words right, but if she did, the woman might become an ally. 'I'm sorry for your loss. It will be an honour and a privilege to wear such a gown. I will ask Aedan to search for your daughter.'

'Oh, no, my lady. He has already done that, more than a body should. When he is here, he is a far better lord than his brother, no matter what the others say. She simply vanished. I fear for my other daughters.'

Dagmar pressed her hands together. An opening. 'I think I may have a solution. I could teach your daughters to protect themselves. I know how to fight.'

Two bright spots appeared on the woman's cheeks. 'I heard the gossip. From Mhairi…you normally wear trousers so you can fight in battles. The Lady of Kintra can't…wear such things, you understand? Whatever would Father Cathan say? He does preach powerful sermons.'

Or do such things?

Dagmar kept the words back with difficulty. She had known what she was giving up when she agreed to the marriage. She had to think that she could do this. That she could do whatever she set her mind to. 'I'm not advocating your daughters wear trousers. I want to teach them how to defend themselves in case of a raid.'

'I hate to think what Father Cathan would say about that! It is unnatural, ain't it?'

'Personally, I would rather have Father Cathan bleating in disapproval and my daughters safe at my side than listening to his consoling sermons after they've gone missing.' Dagmar pressed her hands together and willed the woman to understand.

'And if my girls knew how to defend themselves…'

'They wouldn't be as vulnerable. No one would have to know except for the surprised raider who encountered more than he bargained for.'

The woman gave a decisive nod. 'I like your way of thinking. I think you will be good for Kintra.'

Dagmar fingered the cloth with its intricate pattern.

It hadn't been as hard as she'd feared. 'Did you weave this?'

'Aye, my lady. That I did.' The woman cocked her head to one side. 'Are you having trouble with that loom? It's a right pain in the arse, if you will excuse my bluntness. Should have been burnt years ago. Lord Aedan's mother used to supervise the weaving, but she never actually did any herself. And Lord Brandon's wife brought her own.'

Dagmar struggled to keep her face straight. 'That is good to know.'

The woman nodded. 'I will send my eldest girl, Keita, along. She is an excellent weaver. And if anyone can get that loom working, she can.'

Dagmar laughed. 'Maybe that is something she can teach me.'

'Aye, if a few hints fall from your lips about this here avoiding capture, I'd be right grateful.'

Dagmar laughed. 'Now it is my turn to like your way of thinking.'

Chapter Thirteen

'A new gown?' Aedan asked when he returned. 'I preferred the blue one.'

'This one is more serviceable. The blue one is far too fine for everyday work and it needs to be repaired again.

'Where did you get this one? From your father's trunk?'

'A wedding gift from one of the women here. Apparently Mhairi has been gossiping about my lack of appropriate clothes and my pretensions of being a warrior and several women saw an opportunity.' Dagmar pressed her hands against her eyes. Her back ached slightly from bending over the loom. With Keita's help, she had managed to get started. Keita had proved eager to learn about defending herself and they had agreed to meet tomorrow morning.

Aedan gave a soft laugh. 'Pretensions, really? I wish all my warriors had those sorts of pretensions.'

'I'm pleased you find it amusing.' Dagmar concentrated on her small piece of weaving. 'Mhairi is going to be trouble.'

'Give her time. Mhairi has suffered greatly.'

'She expected to marry you.'

'Hardly her fault, but I married someone else.' His jaw jutted out. 'Before she volunteered to be a hostage, I would never have considered her. She can be judgemental, but she does want what is best for Kintra. Give her time. Give everyone time. They will realise how lucky they are to have you as their Lady.'

Dagmar nodded, believing him about his relationship with Mhairi, but she also knew in her heart that Mhairi had to have had a strong reason for volunteering in the first place. It had to be more than thinking Aedan would marry her. 'She is going to make my task of winning over the women more difficult.'

'Not everyone approves of her. Concentrate on them first.'

'Like Annis and Keita's mother. She gave me the gown and sent Keita to help thread the loom. It was a kind thing to do.'

Aedan's face became grave. 'I searched for Annis, but there was no sign of her. Since Sigurd became the Jaarl of Ile, the raids have mostly ceased.'

Dagmar concentrated on the loom. She should confess about teaching Keita, but Aedan might forbid it. There was a raid coming, she could feel it.

'How are the defence preparations going?'

'Slowly.' Aedan ran a hand through his hair. 'My people distrust anything new, something it would appear Father Cathan has encouraged. There are a thousand other disputes they want sorted first.'

'And yet Father Cathan's stance is new because he has only recently arrived.'

He gave her a sharp look. 'You offer a unique perspective.'

She inclined her head and made a decision. There was little point in adding to Aedan's troubles. After she had demonstrated that Keita could learn, then she'd confess. 'I try.'

He reached for her. 'And I know what I would like to do. What I was thinking about all during my cousin's dreary lament about the state of the fishing nets.'

'Maybe it was the same thing I was thinking about.'

She gave her mouth up to his because it was easier than explaining about her scheme and risking rejection. If only he could see it in operation, then he'd understand why she felt so strongly about it. Begging forgiveness rather than asking permission was by far the better option in the circumstances.

One more day, then she'd confess to Aedan about her training some of the young girls in self-defence. Keita had a natural flair for it. Once she could demonstrate that it could be done, then she was certain that most everyone else on Kintra would want to follow. Keeping the women and children safe was one of the most important parts of running an estate.

'Are you certain that this is the best way to escape from a raider?' one of Kieta's friends who was watching the lesson asked. Dagmar had been quietly pleased that the other girls had come to watch.

'Swords are heavy and you may not have one to hand should you be attacked. However, most people carry a knife and if you know how to get your attacker off balance, you can use those precious few heartbeats to run.'

'But please can we try the sticks? I heard you used to be a warrior.'

'I am your lady now.'

The girl instantly went quiet. 'No offence, my lady. We have never met a real warrior woman before.'

'Mhairi said that you weren't a real warrior, that you just liked pretending to be one,' Keita said. 'And my second cousin said that all this extra work is not about providing a defence, but because Lord Aedan had given our fishing rights to your father.'

Dagmar attempted to control her temper. Of all the wrong-headed gossip! In the end all she could do was laugh. 'Well, your second cousin would be wrong.'

'But you are not really a warrior,' the girl persisted.

Dagmar glanced over and saw Mhairi standing in the shadows, watching the exchange with a smug smile on her face. Anger flowed through her veins. She gestured towards Mhairi. 'Come here. Join in. Do not just lurk in the shadows, sending your deputies into battle. Let us speak honestly with each other.'

Mhairi reluctantly came out of the shadows. Her face appeared tinged with green. 'I always speak the truth, even when it pains me.'

'Do you know how to defend yourself should the Northmen come calling?'

'Me?' Mhairi said, straightening. 'Don't be ridiculous. Of course I do. I am an excellent fighter. I just don't feel the need to swagger about. In any case, your father will protect us. It is why Aedan married you and not me.'

Dagmar reached down and picked up two sticks. 'Let me see. After all, what can be the harm, since I don't really know how to fight?'

The woman grasped the stick awkwardly and Dagmar immediately knew that Mhairi had lied, that she had never been properly taught.

'Right, you fight back. Land a blow on me.'

Mhairi made a few half-hearted attempts. 'This is nonsense.'

'This nonsense can mean the difference between life and death. Or being captured. Or being forced against your will.' Dagmar landed a gentle blow on Mhairi's shoulder. 'Come on, you are making this too easy for me.'

Fury sprang from Mhairi's eyes. 'You don't belong here. You don't belong anywhere. You never will. You are a freak. You should go. Nobody wants you here, least of all Aedan.'

'How do you know?'

'He told me that he had to marry you!'

Dagmar lowered her shoulder and flipped Mhairi on her back. She put the wooden stick against the point of Mhairi's neck. 'No, I am good at what I do and I don't need to depend on a man to do it or to get me out of trouble. And whatever the circumstances, Aedan married me and I am now the Lady of Kintra, not you.'

Mhairi let out a bloodcurdling scream.

'What is going on here?' Father Cathan came running, his cassock flapped behind him. 'This is an outrage! Let this poor innocent woman up at once!'

Dagmar lifted the sword from Mhairi's neck. An odd calmness settled over her. 'An outrage? I am merely demonstrating what happens when unwelcome visitors come to call. Women who cannot defend themselves perish or get taken as slaves. Or would you rather give sermons to empty pews?'

The priest stood in front of Mhairi, spreading his arms wide. 'Our Saviour will provide protection. Strike me and you will see.'

'You should ask Father Alcuin if the raiders spared him!'

'The noise could be heard down in the practice yard,' Aedan thundered as he came running. 'What is going on?'

Father Cathan went red with fury. 'Blasphemy is what is happening here. This dear child has been cruelly and unjustly attacked. If I had not intervened, she would be dead. See how she lays on the ground, injured.'

Aedan's gaze flickered between Dagmar and where Mhairi lay groaning on the ground. Dagmar clenched her jaw. There was no way she had hurt her.

'It is true, Aedan,' Mhairi called out from where she lay. 'Your wife attacked me. Unprovoked. You have married a mad woman. You must put her aside…for all our sakes. Immediately.'

'That's right. That's what I saw,' Father Cathan proclaimed. 'She attacked poor Mhairi without cause. She is wild. For the good of everyone, you must put your wife aside.'

Dagmar clenched her fists. 'If I had wanted Mhairi dead or injured, she would be. I used a blunt wooden stick to demonstrate how easy it is to disarm someone and why *every* woman must learn the art of self-defence. Despite what Father Cathan believes, it is needed. I would have told you, but the girls are not ready. They needed to feel confident, rather than humiliated.'

Aedan's brow furrowed. 'We'd best discuss this inside, Dagmar.'

'I am doing what is needed.' Dagmar stalked off.

Mhairi gave a smirk. 'I always knew Dagmar would revert to the savage she is.'

Aedan struggled to keep his temper. It was quite clear what he had witnessed and that Mhairi was in the wrong. 'Get up. You deliberately provoked my wife! You challenged her to a fight. If she had wanted to, she could have hurt you. I believe Dagmar showed remarkable restraint.'

'The poor woman is injured,' Father Cathan bleated.

'I doubt it.'

Mhairi rolled about on the ground. 'I am going to lose the baby and it is all her fault.'

'Whose baby do you carry because it certainly is not mine,' Aedan roared.

Mhairi glanced at Father Cathan, who went bright red again, this time in embarrassment. Aedan suddenly realised what had happened and that Mhairi's volunteering might have had an added dimension. 'I would rather not say.'

Aedan fixed the priest with a hard stare. 'It is just as well that Father Cathan is not a tonsured monk then.'

'I... I have ambitions,' the priest bleated. 'The bishop...'

'Not with my people,' Aedan retorted. 'No one uses and abuses my people. I suggest you consider doing the honourable thing, Father.'

Without looking back, Aedan walked into the hall, but his footsteps echoed. The hall was empty and cold. 'Dagmar?'

There was no answering sound, not even a knife whistling past his ear or her boots hitting the door as she took aim at his arrogant head. He'd have deserved that. He should have trusted her. He should have listened to her reasons before acting. She'd tried to tell him about Mhairi's designs and he'd refused to listen.

Aedan stood still. She could not have simply left him! Not before he'd attempted to make things right.

'Mor? Where are you? We need to find Dagmar.'

There was no answering bark. He should have realised that something was wrong. Over the past few days, Mor had chosen to stay with Dagmar, rather than shadowing him, behaving precisely like Liddy's dog had done when Brandon had been alive. Mor knew he had been an arse. He'd been too blind and wrapped up in his own self-importance to see it.

At the shore a variety of coracles and currachs were drawn up on the shore, waiting for the tide to come in. Even his currach stood in the exposed mud. Dagmar could not have departed that way. But she was perfectly capable of marching away, abandoning him, and she'd take his heart with her if she did so.

In the space of a few breaths, the world had become an empty and desolate place. How could he have worried about this land and these people when she had become his entire world? Without her in it, his life would cease to have any meaning.

He rapidly retraced his steps and went up another path towards the cemetery. Of course, Mor had led her there. The dog was doing what he should have done in the first place—taking Dagmar to his hut, to the place he'd built as a refuge.

He rounded a bend and there on a grassy knoll with a frown that made his heart sink sat Dagmar with her head bent, examining the sole of her boot.

'Dagmar,' he called softly.

She scrambled up. The look of despondency was instantly replaced with a scowl. 'That priest was making trouble.'

'I know. He admitted to being the father of Mhairi's unborn child.'

'He did? What is going to happen?'

'I have sorted it. If he has any sense he will marry the woman.'

'If she has any sense she will refuse him.'

He went over to her and gathered her hands within his. They were ice-cold. Proof if he required it that she was upset. He could have taken her fury, but not this quiet sadness.

She gave a half-hearted attempt to pull away, but he tightened his grip.

'We need to talk,' he said.

'Talk?' Her eyes blazed, but he could see the pain they tried to mask. 'Or maybe you will kiss me again so that I forget to ask questions. I am not sorry about trying to protect your people, Aedan.'

She pulled away and started off down the path with Mor following at her heels.

'Dagmar! Wait!'

Dagmar picked up her pace and ignored Aedan's cries to stop and listen. That Mhairi had confessed about how she had tried to undermine Dagmar. Her brain kept humming—her mother was right after all—she was unsuited to marriage. She had allowed her temper to get the better of her and she might have hurt Mhairi.

Sex with Aedan had been indescribable, but what she really missed was that feeling of belonging and comradeship they had shared on their travels and she had no idea how to get it back.

Dagmar stumbled over a root. She fell sprawling and the sole of her boot came off. Several gold coins spilled out. She gave a loud curse. She had not fastened it properly earlier.

'Are you hurt?' Aedan asked, reaching her before she had time to replace the gold and repair the boot.

'Only my pride. I was going too quickly.' She dusted the dirt off the trousers and hoped he'd wouldn't notice the soft gold pieces gleaming. A fight about that was now inevitable and she would not give them up. Not now, not when there was every possibility that she might have to flee.

'What is that?' He bent down and picked up a coin and her scrap of parchment.

'My emergency fund,' Dagmar answered. She scooped up the coins. 'I must have knocked the sole of the boot when I tripped. Normally I am much more sure-footed.'

'You keep gold in your boots?'

'My mother had to leave our home with very little warning. A simple precaution.' Dagmar replaced the coins and clicked the heel into place. 'I obviously did not fasten it properly.'

'Were you going to tell me about the gold?'

'It never came up.' Dagmar gave a half-shrug. Her mother would have vanished into the night, but Dagmar couldn't. She'd learnt the lesson about not giving up on anything too well.

'Never came up?' Aedan lifted a brow. 'And this drawing?'

'When I was eleven I made a sketch of my dream

home, so that I'd know what I was fighting for. It is important to remember a life exists beyond war.'

'Your house on the fjord.'

'That is gone now. This would have been my own. I would have built it if I had won the battle at Dollar.' She concentrated on making sure the sole was stuck on firmly this time. Putting into words what those boots represented to her was impossible. They were the last thing she possessed of her mother's. They represented freedom and the ability to fight back. She doubted if Aedan would understand. 'I don't notice the extra weight. Better to be safe than have regrets.'

'Marriage should have two people in it, not an entire kingdom.' His mouth became a thin white line but it was the expression in his eyes that made her heart squeeze. 'What I want you to know is that I suspected you were teaching the girls to fight back and approved. How could I not? Each one who has been taken has been engraved on my heart. You were doing something I couldn't.'

Dagmar concentrated on her boot. She should have trusted him. 'Like you were with the knife, you were waiting for me to say something?'

His eyes sparkled. 'Exactly, but this way, I didn't have to confront Father Cathan.'

'He may be a priest, but he is a pompous oaf.'

'There I agree with you. I should have confronted him earlier. Now will you come with me?' He gave a soft laugh. 'It is where I think Mor was leading you, where I should have taken you first.'

'She has more sense than her master.'

'She does indeed.' He held out a hand. 'Come with me. Please.'

Dagmar kept her hand curled about Aedan's. There was comfort in the way he held her hand. She might be able to salvage something from this. She'd made a mistake earlier and allowed herself to be manipulated, but the truth had been uncovered. *Face forward and keep the past behind you like your arse* was one of her mother's favourite mottos.

As they reached the top, the sun sparkled on the bay like a series of diamonds. This had to be the spot which Aedan had described when he'd explained why his life held more than war. In a stand of trees stood a small stone hut, far better built than the ageing hall which dominated Kintra's shore. She immediately fell in love with it.

'Who does this belong to?' she asked before her nerve failed her. 'Who lives here?'

'Come inside and discover.'

Inside, a bed piled high with furs occupied the far wall. A trunk stood next to it. Against the right wall a table stood with a bench in front of it.

'Why are you being so mysterious about it?' Dagmar's stomach clenched as she struggled to breathe.

Aedan placed several dishes on the table while Mor gave a satisfied bark and settled beside the front door.

'It belongs to you now if you will have it. My morning gift to you.' Aedan gestured about him. 'Your private place…for when the people of Kintra become too much. A place which belongs only to you. A place you can truly call home which no one can take away from you.'

Dagmar's heart expanded. A home of her own. Her gaze narrowed.

'Why are you giving me this now? Why not when I first arrived? Why keep it hidden?'

He put his hands on her shoulders. 'This place was my refuge when my brother was alive. It can be your refuge now if you require it.'

'But why?'

'This hut is all my design,' he said, running a hand along the table. 'I built it after the mess with Brigid. I couldn't bear to live in the hall with my brother.'

'You wanted to leave.' Her heart thumped. 'Is it the same reason you keep leaving Kintra?'

Aedan's mouth twisted down. 'You need to know the whole story. I should have shared it with you before we married so that you could see the sort of man I really am.'

Dagmar went over to him. 'What happened?'

Aedan put a finger to her mouth. 'My brother and I were close when we were young. Then he discovered women. And all the women seemed to love him, but one day, I found a woman, Brigid, who took my breath away. She appeared to be interested in me, not my brother.'

'Did you build this for her?'

Aedan's eyes became bleak. 'We were to be married. I was ambitious and spent the time fighting the Northmen. I left her alone too much.'

'One day, I returned early and went looking for her. Her mother had no idea where she was.'

'Had she been taken?'

'I discovered them together, her and my brother, intertwined on the grass, clearly having made love. My brother swore it had only happened the once because I had left her alone.'

'I would have beaten him to a pulp and broken the engagement, ensuring everyone knew the truth.' Dagmar clenched her fists. 'The woman obviously had no taste and fewer morals. There are things you don't do to a brother.'

She listened as Aedan described how they had fought, but the woman intervened to save Brandon. Aedan found he could not hit a woman, but he had ended the engagement. Brandon promised that he would deal with the problem and Aedan left, returning on his brother's wedding day.

When he returned, he discovered Brigid, pregnant and footsore. She had escaped from the convent where Brandon had placed her and was about to give birth. She begged for his help and forgiveness as she had made a mistake. Like a fool he'd forgiven her. However, the birth was bad and she'd screamed out Brandon's name and he'd known the truth. He'd gone to fetch Brandon from his marriage bed, but Brigid and the baby died. Brandon declared Aedan had deliberately attempted to ruin his marriage and they fought again. This time Aedan had beat him to a bloody pulp. Brandon however had kept quiet about who had caused the injuries.

'What did you do then?'

'I left to make my fortune elsewhere and I built this hut to be away from Brandon. Everyone thought my isolation was because I grieved over Brigid, but I didn't. I simply wanted to be away from him and his lies. The worst part was that when I was away and in battle, I felt relief, as though my life might count for more than being my brother's cat's paw. I swore that I would never again be manipulated by anyone.'

Dagmar's heart thudded. 'I am sorry Brigid and your brother behaved so badly. But you weren't to blame for her death. Women often die in childbirth.'

'I allowed Brandon to manipulate me again. I believed him when he proclaimed my sister-in-law had deliberately taken chances with her children's lives because she and Brandon had had a fight, instead of questioning Brandon about his fantastic design for his new boat. Right before his death, he tried to force Liddy into a convent, claiming that because she had wilfully caused the death of their children, he should have the right to marry a far more suitable woman. He even forbade her to put any memorial to them. To my shame I never questioned him until the new fleet capsized, killing many good men shortly after his death.'

'The stone cross for your niece and nephew is part of your penance,' Dagmar said with sudden insight.

'The flawed boat design was responsible for their death, not my sister-in-law whom I had treated as an outcast. I put that woman through Hell because of my brother and his self-serving lies. The cross is there to remind me of my folly. It is also there because my brother should have taken responsibility. There are times that I wonder if he chose to die in battle rather than face what he had done. And when your father arrived demanding gold, I knew my brother had borrowed the gold, rather than being showered with it because he had saved a Northern warlord from certain death as he had claimed. Once again I would have to clean up his mess or my people would suffer.'

'You wanted to protect your people,' Dagmar finished for him. 'I knew Father Cathan disliked me and would object to teaching the women self-defence. I remained determined, however.'

'I trusted you to be so. I should have explained that

I approved of you doing it, but I wanted to be able to deny it. I am becoming like my brother.'

Dagmar drew a deep breath. 'No, you are not. You are a man who takes his responsibilities seriously. You want what is right for your people. Mhairi and Father Cathan knew that. They sought to drive a wedge between us. That is never going to happen.'

'I won't allow that to happen either. You must trust me on this.' He put his hands on her shoulders. 'It is why you should have this place, in case everyone gets too much. They try my temper at the best of times, but I have to remain here for them. I can't abandon them again. It can be your refuge where you can sit and watch the sunset, rather than giving in to their petty slights.'

Her heart soared. He was offering her his inner sanctum. He did have feelings for her and he understood how difficult it was for her to adjust. 'Always. We are a team.'

'Shall we seal it with a kiss?' he asked, reaching for her.

She smiled. 'I believe we have time.'

Dagmar glanced towards the sea, more out of habit than anything. She swore long and loud. Aedan's hands fell to his side.

'Problem?'

'My mother's sail. Olafr is coming this way from the south and the oath-breaker has the gall to use my mother's sail as if the *felag* belongs to him!'

'We need to get back.'

'I'm sorry, Aedan.'

'For what? There is no way the news of our marriage could have reached him. You were right to insist on the defences. He decided to come after me and my lands because he thinks we are an easier proposition than your father. The Devil take his soul. This has nothing to do with you, Dagmar.'

Dagmar gave a tight smile. Aedan's words were designed to make it easier for her, but she knew he was wrong. Olafr had come for her. And she knew Aedan would put the safety of his people in front of hers. He had to. 'Thank you for that. You are the King of Kintra and I await your orders.'

'Do you want to get the women to safety or do you wish to stand on the shore and greet him with me?'

'My trousers have been burnt.'

'No, I hid them until you had need of them. It is why I took charge of them instead of your nurse. I should have told you, but...'

'You were frightened I might I leave if I had them to wear,' she finished for him, understanding now what drove this man of hers. 'Trust me now.'

He gave a half-smile. 'As if the clothes you wear on your back could make a difference to the person you are inside.'

Dagmar concentrated on the ship which was sweeping ever closer. There were a thousand things she wished she had done with Aedan. 'I would like to stand next to you, but dressed as I am now. There is every chance Olafr will not recognise me and we may be able to use it to our advantage.'

'Dagmar, don't take any chances.'

She brushed her mouth against his. 'I won't if you don't.'

Chapter Fourteen

Aedan stood on the shore with Dagmar standing beside him, her head held proud. Despite his offer of warrior's garb, she remained in her gown. She wore her hair in several plaits. Her only weapon was his old dagger which she had stuck in her belt, insisting she needed nothing else.

His men were ranged behind him. They carried a motley collection of shields, ancient swords and pitchforks. But the women and children along with both priests had made their way to the newly built shelter.

The ship had come in peacefully with shields hung on its sides, rather than the shields being in the warriors' hands, ready for battle. He agreed with Dagmar that it was a ruse. Olafr had arrived with intent to cause mischief, rather than coming in friendship.

His guts tightened like they had not done since he faced his first battle. Finally, he had something which really mattered to him to fight for. He was not going to give Dagmar up without a fight.

'We meet again, Gael,' Olafr said as he strode on to the shore. The Northman had a sleek confidence about him.

'To what do I owe the pleasure, Olafr Rolfson?' Aedan asked, keeping his hand on his sword. 'You are a long way from Dollar.'

Olafr smiled at him menacingly. 'You took something which belongs to me. That was wrong.'

'Did I indeed?'

Olaf's gaze flickered over Dagmar, not appearing to recognise her. 'Yes, perhaps your lady wife would be interested to know how you stole a Northwoman. Such things cannot be allowed to happen.'

To her credit, Dagmar remained stony-faced and silent, but her hand closed about the dagger. Aedan silently willed her to trust him to take care of her.

'Indeed. Why do you require this?'

Olafr planted his sword in the sand. 'I require Dagmar Helgadottar or I shall lay waste to your lands. I will take your women and I will enslave them. Your men are no match for mine.'

Behind him, the Northmen beat their swords against their shields. Aedan knew his men would be no match for such a band, but he had little idea of what else he could do.

'And if I give you Dagmar?' he asked, keeping his voice carefully neutral.

'I will leave as I came—in peace. Your little kingdom will be safe.' Olafr's sneer increased. 'You have until owl-light to produce her.'

'I don't need until then. You will never have her. Your promises are worth nothing as you are an oathbreaker. And even if they were worth the spit it takes you to say them, I still would refuse.' Aedan beat his sword against his own shield. 'What say you, men? Will we give up Dagmar? Will we give up Kintra's lady to the Northmen?'

'Never!' his men roared back.

'Do we show this piece of scum what the men of Kintra are made of?'

His men roared their approval.

Olafr blinked twice. 'You have ensured your lands will be laid waste. Prepare to die!'

'Dagmar means more to me than this land ever could. But it will be your death, not mine, which happens today.'

Olafr raised his hand and Aedan balanced on the balls of his feet, preparing to run towards the arrogant Northman. He knew he could reach Olafr before the fighting properly began. He tried to recall what Dagmar had said to him the first day—something about Olafr always exposing his left side when under pressure.

'No! I refuse!' Dagmar shouted above the noise. 'This will not happen! Olafr the Oath-breaker, you usurped my command. I demand the right to fight you for the leadership.'

Olafr's eyes bulged and his hand dropped to his side. 'Dagmar? You are here. I failed to recognise you... without your tattoos.'

Dagmar stepped away from Aedan. Her heart soared. Aedan had put her before his men, before Kintra. He had showed her that she mattered to him more than everything. Right now, she had to hope that he trusted her and her instincts. He had to allow her to do this. She was the only one who could save Kintra and, to do that, she would have to fight Olafr.

'I am here and I am ready to protect my people. More than that, I am ready to reclaim my *felag*.'

'Dagmar? Is it really you?'

'You were always blind, Olafr.'

Olafr's mouth turned down like a petulant child's. 'This is not your *felag*. It is mine.'

'You fly my mother's sail. My mother gave me this *felag* on her deathbed.' With each word she spoke, Dagmar's confidence grew. In a fair fight, it was not a contest—she would win. 'All the men acclaimed me its leader while her funeral pyre burned. None, not even you, challenged me for that right to lead. And none have done so since.'

Behind him, Olafr's men began muttering. Dagmar's heart leapt. Maybe some were actually still loyal to her. She still might be able to end this without too much bloodshed.

'Dagmar?' Aedan said in an undertone. 'You don't have to do this. My men and I can fight. We can take this scum. He means to trick you.'

'I'm the only one who can do this,' she replied without hesitation. 'I am the only who has the right to lead this *felag*.' She smiled at him. 'Trust me.'

He put his sword to his chest. 'With my life. With Kintra. If you can do this, then do it.'

Dagmar turned back to Olafr. 'What say you, Usurper? How came you to lead this *felag*?'

'You left,' Olafr said with a shrug. 'The *felag* was leaderless. I did what I had to do. Your mother would have expected it. The men acclaimed me. It is my *felag* now, Dagmar, not yours.'

She held out her hands to the Northmen. 'Do I belong to the *felag*?'

'That you do, Dagmar! Dagmar Helgadottar is one of us for ever!' one of the Northmen called out. The rest, several with less enthusiasm than the rest, beat their swords against their shields, signalling their agreement. Dagmar made note of the reluctant ones as a problem for later.

'The *felag* has spoken with an overwhelming majority. I belong. Therefore, I have the right to fight for the leadership. It is a privilege granted to every member when they feel the leadership is lacking. And, Olafr, I believe the leadership is lacking with you in charge. Will you fight me for it or will you return it as you were never intended to have it in the first place?'

Sweat dripped down her back. Olafr would agree to the fight. If he backed down, he would be proclaimed weak and the men would desert him. He had to know if she retook the *felag* without a fight, she would name him a wolf's head. He would have to fight and she'd finally be able to avenge Old Alf.

'Fight! Fight!' screamed her former men.

Olafr blew on his nails. 'Very well, if you insist on challenging, I will fight you. I've never thought your skills up to much. Shall I give you time to change?'

Dagmar set her jaw. Olafr would find a way to use it to his advantage and she refused to risk Aedan or any of his men. And it would give her the opportunity to demonstrate that clothes did not make a difference; skills were what counted. 'No need. I can fight one such as you in these clothes.'

'Always the impetuous one, Dagmar. I look forward to helping you on your journey to Valhall.'

She turned back to Aedan. 'Aedan, may I borrow your shield and sword?'

'Of course.' He handed her his weapons. 'You can do this, Dagmar. I have faith. It doesn't matter what he says. I know what your fighting skills are. I've seen them in action. I might wish you didn't have to fight him, but there is no one I trust more with the defence of Kintra.'

Dagmar stared up at the clouds and blinked rapidly. His words of encouragement gave her heart. He understood why she was doing this.

'I love you, Aedan. I wanted to say it aloud, if just once.'

Something in his eyes flared. 'I look forward to you saying it more than once. Are you sure you don't want to change?'

She shook her head. 'He will attack Kintra if I do. I don't trust him.'

'We can hold him.'

'I refuse to take that risk.' She met his eyes. 'Trust my judgement. I will demonstrate to the women and men of Kintra that it is actions, not clothes, which make a warrior.' She hesitated. 'Should I fall…'

'Should you fall, I will finish him off, but life would not be worth living for me without you. You will succeed. You will avenge Old Alf and save my kingdom.'

She took several practice swipes with the sword. She had to admit the sword was well balanced. She would have preferred a slightly smaller shield, but she could adjust.

'Shall we begin, Olafr?'

Olafr made a mocking bow. 'You think you are so good, Dagmar, but you are nothing. Your mother used to despair of you.'

'My mother had terrible judgement about certain things.' She beat the sword against the shield. 'Begin!'

He charged. Dagmar raised her shield and easily

blocked the blow. Round and round they went, Olafr probing and Dagmar blocking and testing, waiting until he made a mistake. She had to admit that he could fight.

Olafr began to swagger a bit, adding little flourishes to his moves, and she knew she had him. When she judged the moment right, she struck a blow towards his left. But he brought his shield down on her arm, causing her to drop the sword. Her feet tangled with her skirt and she stumbled backwards as he kicked the sword from her reach. She swore under her breath at her own stupidity.

'Bad luck, Shield Maiden!' Olafr circled his sword above his head. 'Prepare to die!'

She gave a look at Aedan. He nodded and she knew what she had to do. Her hand went to her dagger and she counted.

Olafr gave a mocking smile. 'I always knew you weren't that good.'

'No, I am better.' Dagmar launched herself from the ground, throwing her dagger at the same instant, and connected with his throat.

Olafr gave a gurgle and fell to the ground. Dagmar picked up his sword and finished him off.

Led by Aedan, the people of Kintra began to chant her name. Dagmar raised the sword above her head.

'I claim the *felag* as mine to do what I will with. To go where I say.'

Her erstwhile men knelt down, accepting her leadership. Several called out that they had not realised the depth of Olafr's treachery until today and they would follow her to the ends of the earth.

Her body began to tremble. She had done it. She had regained her *felag*. Dagmar saw her mother's sail flapping in the faint breeze and knew she had finally proved herself worthy. And she also knew that she never wanted to fight again. There were no new worlds she wanted to conquer. She wanted to make lives better. She wanted to have children. She wanted to sit and watch sunsets with the man she loved beside her.

'Dagmar,' Aedan said, coming to stand beside her. 'What are you going to do?'

'Give me three of your most trusted men.'

Aedan called them forward.

'Take Olafr's body to my father in one of your currachs. Tell him that I did what his men failed to do. Ask him to send his best captain. There is a ship he can add to his fleet. In the meantime, put these men under guard. Those who prove loyal to me may stay here if they choose, but my father will deal the others.'

Aedan stiffened beside her.

'A problem?'

'With your orders, no. If some have been loyal, we will find a place for them and their families somewhere on Ile, but Father Cathan approaches and I could really do without his pomposity.'

Father Cathan was hurrying forward with a broad smile. Dagmar felt her elation seep from her. Aedan caught her hand.

'Stay with me whatever happens, Dagmar. It is your turn to trust me,' Aedan said in an undertone.

Dagmar forced her feet to still. 'I will stay.'

Father Cathan stopped and his smile became a disdainful look. 'Lord Aedan, your wife. She has blood on her gown.'

'Father Cathan, it appears we are to have a double celebration.'

The priest stopped and tugged at his collar. 'A double celebration?'

'My wife has saved this land from the threat of a Northern raid. You should be on your knees thanking her.'

'I intend to have a service of thanksgiving.' The priest gave a superior smile. 'I felt certain my prayers assisted in some small measure. But why two celebrations?'

'I assume you did the decent thing and asked Mhairi to be your bride. She is the mother of your unborn child, is she not?'

Father Cathan turned bright red. 'For the sake of my career, she refused me. I have suggested she join a convent. She has promised that she will think about it.'

'Who suggested she volunteer as a hostage?' Aedan asked grimly.

His eyes settled anywhere but on Aedan's face. 'It was her idea.'

'A pity for you. I regret it, but I cannot allow someone who would behave in that manner to preach to my people. The bishop will be informed.' Aedan put his arm about Dagmar's waist and pulled her close. 'Father Alcuin will take the service of thanksgiving.'

'But the bishop...'

'A good bishop requires his priests to set an example,' Dagmar declared. 'He will take a dim view of such things, particularly when a king like my husband makes the full circumstances known. He will also commend Father Alcuin on the number of souls he has managed to convert.'

Father Cathan went white. 'I shall pack my bags immediately. I can tell where I am not wanted. There is an abbey in Ireland which will take me.'

'Mhairi may remain here until she decides what she wishes to do with her life,' Dagmar continued. 'Regardless of her motives, volunteering to be a hostage was a very brave thing to do. It may be that one of my men finds favour with her.'

Aedan inclined his head. 'My wife gives excellent counsel. I suggest you take it. If it was up to me, I would send you to preach in the north lands. Thankfully for you, my wife is of a gentler nature.'

The priest gulped and scurried off.

'I believe that problem is solved,' Dagmar said with a laugh. 'I had not guessed that the priest was her lover.'

'It was the only thing which made sense.' He put a hand under her elbow and her body thrilled to his touch. 'But there are other more pressing problems. Will you wear trousers and tunic to the service or something else? Your gown has seen better times.'

Dagmar smiled back at him. Her inclination was to wear the trousers and she nearly said so, but there was a devilment in his eyes. He expected her to.

'I'll check the trunk my father supposedly kept for me before I make up my mind.' She lifted her chin. 'It may be that my former nurse chose well. It is wrong for me to waste time hating cloth. It is the person who wears the clothes who matters. My stepmother is dead along with her prophetic dreams. That should be enough.'

'You haven't been tempted to look before now?'

'I thought such things were best left in the past.'

'Sometimes, you have to confront your past in order

to grab hold of your future. I learned that lesson today.' His eyes sparkled with hidden lights before sobering. 'I am here with you, Dagmar, whatever you find, whatever you decide to wear because you are my beloved and nothing will change that.'

Not allowing herself second thoughts, Dagmar opened the lid of the trunk. It was completely full of cloth. She doubted if her former nurse could have packed it any tighter. First were several lengths of richly embroidered cloth—one for each name day her father had missed. She carefully laid them to one side.

Underneath a dark-green apron dress shot with silver embroidery lurked the sort of dress that a lady might wear to a great feast, but it was clear from the motifs and the colours that it had been woven with her stepmother's dark beauty in mind.

'A pretty enough dress,' Aedan said. 'What do you think?'

Dagmar gave a tight smile. 'I'd rather go naked. It is a colour my stepmother favoured. Her assassins used to wear such a device.'

'Clothes do not kill,' Aedan said, laying a hand on her shoulder. 'You survived and her dreams are dust.'

'But I still have the memories. Perhaps it can be given to Mhairi as a thank you.'

His eyes bulged. 'Why would you do that?'

'I can afford to be generous and it will irritate her no end.' Dagmar gave a soft laugh. 'Had she not goaded me earlier, our marriage would have continued to disintegrate. I feel as though I have our fellowship back.'

He captured a hand and raised it to his lips. 'This is one fellowship which will not break.'

'I hate proving you right. It may have to be the trousers and tunic after all.'

He gave a husky laugh. 'Next time we shall have to wager on it and you can pay a forfeit. In private.'

Dagmar concentrated on the trunk. The words telling him how much she loved him threatened to spill out. He made her feel as though she belonged. 'That might make losing more palatable.'

'Is there anything else? Anything that might work or is it all your stepmother?'

She gingerly moved the dress and gasped. 'I thought this had been destroyed!'

She carefully lifted up a crimson gown with its heavy gold embroidery on the hem. A faint lavender scent intermingled with something which reminded her of her childhood rose. Her body began to tremble. 'I can't do this.'

Aedan took the gown from her. 'Did this belong to your mother? You have tears in your eyes.'

Dagmar blinked rapidly. 'She was wearing it the day my father brought my stepmother home. The faintest whiff of my mother's scent lingers. Impossible after all this time, I know.'

'Stranger things have happened.'

'I thought I had lost everything except the clothes I stood up in and then to find this.'

'I know.' Aedan gave the gown back to her. 'I know how you treasured your mother.'

Dagmar fingered the material as the memories assaulted her, taking her back to that fateful time when her only thoughts had been to escape from doing sword practice. 'I can remember her doing the embroidery. I had forgotten she could sew with such a fine hand.

She'd promised me that she'd wear it for my name day.' She paused, remembering. 'Underneath it, she wore her shield-maiden clothes. I remember when she first tried it on. She'd made her decision before he returned. Or maybe she always wore them, just waiting for her chance to leave.'

Aedan took the dress from her nerveless fingers. 'Whatever happened it wasn't your fault. You were their child. You were the innocent bystander in their marriage which became a war.'

Dagmar gave a sigh and peered further into the trunk. 'Her brooches are there as well, the ones which had belonged to her mother. She always claimed he'd destroyed them in front of her.'

'She kept you safe in her own way.'

Another memory assaulted her. Before her father had left on that fateful voyage, she had heard her parents quarrelling, something that had become commonplace. His father accused her mother of not wanting any more children, a charge she denied, but they had slept in separate chambers after that.

'Yes, she kept me safe. She was a good mother in her way. She wanted to prepare me for a hostile world.'

'Why did she become a shield maiden in the first place?'

Dagmar rocked back on her heels. 'Her stepmother wanted the estate for her half-brother after her father died. She was made to fetch and carry like a slave before she rebelled. She took the inheritance she thought she was due and made her own way.'

'She had reason to fear the same for you. It sounds as though your parents made their decision and there was nothing you could do to stop it. The only people who can save a marriage are the people in that marriage.'

Dagmar buried her nose in the gown and it was like having her mother's warm embrace wrap around her. 'She once caught me looking at my scrap of parchment and laughed at me for desiring such a house. She was a restless spirit. Every time we amassed enough gold, she found a reason why we couldn't settle, why we had to fight one more season. She loved the drums of war in a way I could never understand. I loved her, but I want something different from my life. You've shown me that my life has many possible pathways, not just one narrow one.'

Aedan put a hand on her shoulder. She covered it with her hand. 'Are there any more hidden treasures?'

'I think that is all.' She hit the bottom board, but it tilted slightly. 'Wait, there is a false bottom.'

She removed the board and discovered a deerskin-wrapped bundle. She rapidly undid the knots and the tanned hide fell away.

Inside was a dark-blue gown with a set of ribbons and a pair of matching slippers—all the right size for a ten-year-old girl along with a pouch filled with gold coins. Dagmar felt the tears well in her eyes. A single drop escaped and stained the cloth before she could wipe it away.

'He brought me a blue dress for my name day, not just a woman to teach me to be a lady. He did remember.'

'What are you talking about?'

'The day my parents divorced was my tenth name day. I had asked for a proper gown so I could become a lady. I had some notion about being allowed to stay up late at feasts so I could hear the skald sing properly rather than straining my ears. He brought my stepmother instead to teach me to be the lady I had wanted to be. I thought it might be all my fault that he fell in love with her. If I hadn't asked for the dress...'

Dagmar put her hand to her head as her mind reeled. Her nurse was right. She had been looking at things with the eyes of a child. 'Maybe he intended to send the chests. Maybe my mother never asked for them. She always said that she was not going to look back, that she wanted to face the future. The truth might be complicated.'

'What are you going to do with it?'

'Save it until we have a little girl. My father is not perfect, but he remains my father and I hope he loves me.' Her voice trembled on the last words.

Aedan gathered her hands between his. 'Whether your father loves you or not matters little because you are loved. Your mother loved you. Mor loves you and most importantly I love you.'

Dagmar stilled. 'You do? How could you possibly?'

Aedan nodded and his eyes grew warm. 'One of the biggest regrets of my life is that I did not ask you to marry me—properly before your father forced my hand.'

Dagmar stared at him. 'You wanted to marry me? You weren't doing it out of duty?'

'After I learned the truth about my brother and how selfish he truly was, I became like one of the dead walking. You brought me back to the land of the living. I told you that you had to think of other things beyond a life dedicated to war, but you made me think of a life beyond duty. You gave meaning back to my life.'

'Is that why you lingered in my father's hall when he was asking me to choose a husband?'

'I was silently offering up prayers to whoever might listen that somehow everything would fall in my favour, that I wouldn't have to say goodbye to you.' He pulled her tight against his chest. 'I cannot offer you my heart because you already have it. You've had it since your face lit up when I returned with the fish.'

'You were very tardy in giving me your heart. You had mine when you took me through the marsh.'

'It is why we need to stay together. I cannot live without my heart by my side. Should you wish it, we can go adventuring together.'

Dagmar's heart soared and she knew she was busy making dreams in clouds, but they were good dreams and dreams she'd work hard to make come true. 'I spoke from my heart when I told my father you are the only man for me, the only man I have ever wanted as husband. You make me feel beautiful in a way that no one else has ever done. You made me realise that there is a life beyond war and fighting and that I want to live that life. I want to have your children and watch them grow without fear for the future. I want to spend time watching the flowers grow, but I want to do it with you by my side. I want to put down roots and that means staying at Kintra and keeping these people safe.'

He drew her into the circle of his arms. 'My being married to you has little to do with your father becoming my ally and everything to do with you. This afternoon when the sword slipped from your hand and you were at Olafr's mercy, I felt as though my life had ended. Without you in my world, it is utterly meaningless. We go wherever you want to, Dagmar.'

'Right now, I want to go to the service of thanks-giving in my mother's gown. Later, after the feast, we can retire to bed and you can demonstrate precisely how much you cherish me and my invaluable counsel.'

'I could not have put it better myself!'

Epilogue

One year later—Kintra, Ile

'Almost there.'

'Is the blindfold truly necessary, Aedan?' Dagmar asked. 'It is fairly easy to work out that you are leading me up to the hut. It will be good to be back. I only hope there is not too much to do as it has been a while.'

'Feast your eyes on this.' Aedan whipped the cloth from her eyes and revealed a brand-new hall standing where the stone hut had been. Its wood gleamed golden in the afternoon sunshine.

Dagmar stood for a moment astonished. It was the sort of hall she had often dreamed about having when she was being a sell-sword with her mother—spacious and welcoming. She spied the raven gables and knew Aedan had used the design from the sketch in her boot. He had recreated her dream house. 'When was this done? It is absolute perfection.'

'I thought we needed something larger now that we have twin boys. The wind whistles through the hall far too fiercely for little babies to thrive.' He gave a crooked smile. 'I needed to do something while you were in confinement. Your father lent me some craftsmen so that the gables were like your childhood home.'

'My father was in on the surprise?' Dagmar tapped her finger against her mouth. 'I thought he seemed entirely too pleased when he was here to meet the twins. I thought it was because he had finally achieved his dream of having grandsons.'

'The raven gables were a more appropriate present than the bodies of the men who had betrayed you.'

Dagmar gave a small shudder as she recalled what happened last November. 'When that happened, I knew I had to be pregnant. It was the only explanation for my shameful behaviour when I discovered what he had done to those men who had conspired with Olafr to bring about my downfall.'

'How like my wife to still be embarrassed about fainting. It merely gave me the excuse I wanted to cosset you.' Aedan gave a laugh which warmed her. He had done more than that, demanding the heads be removed immediately from the spikes. But he had allowed her to continue teaching the women various self-defence moves as long as she was careful.

'I take it that everyone knew about the hall. It was why people kept asking me daft questions about the colours I'd like to have in the new tapestries during my confinement. Here I thought they considered me a bit simple.'

'Hardly that.' He laced his fingers with hers. 'But you need to give me your verdict. Do you approve of your surprise?'

She flung her arms about his neck. 'I love it. When can we move in?'

Aedan lifted her up and carried her over the threshold. 'Now.'

Dagmar looked about her. The reason for the long and circuitous route became clear. He had had their trunks moved from the old hall. Tapestries did hang from the walls. And in two cradles lay their baby boys. Mor gave a sharp bark and the young girl who had been watching over them made a small curtsy before vanishing. Suddenly she was left alone with her family in her house.

Dagmar's heart expanded. She knew some day she and Aedan might go raiding again, but for now, they had their family to raise. She had finally discovered the one place in the world where she truly belonged and she meant to stay there for as long as possible. Some people like her mother thrived on change, but she had discovered how much she valued putting roots down and watching the seasons slowly roll around.

She raised herself up on her tiptoes and brushed her lips against Aedan's. 'My luck certainly changed the day you kidnapped me.'

He raised a brow. 'Kidnapped? I saved your life, but you restored mine. I know who bears the greater debt, my love, and I plan to spend the rest of my life showing you my gratitude and undying devotion.'

* * * * *

If you enjoyed this story you won't want to miss these other Viking novels by Michelle Styles

Sold to the Viking Warrior
Summer of the Viking
Taming His Viking Woman
Saved by the Viking Warrior

Author Note

Traditionally the battle of Dollar in 875 is held to be between Constantine of the Picts and Halfdan, King of the York-based Vikings, in which Halfdan won a great victory, beating Constantine and taking control of the entire north of Scotland. The only trouble with this view is that, according to the *Anglo-Saxon Chronicle*, in 876 Halfdan had settled his warriors on land south of the Tyne. Between him and the north of Scotland lay the client kingdom of Bernicia. It does make much more sense, as some accounts have it, that the Vikings from Dublin came over and won. In 877, legend has it that Constantine was beheaded by a Viking on a Fife beach.

Evidence exists of the High King of Ireland, who happened to be married to Constantine's sister, burning longships' enclosures which belonged to the Irish-based Vikings in the years before the battle of Dollar. This could explain why the Irish-based Vikings decided to attack Pict-controlled Alba.

We also know that during this period the Western Isles were controlled from Manx by Ketil, who is mentioned in the *Laxdaela Saga*. While they raided Ireland, they do not seem to have been as aggressive towards Alba as they were in charge of the sea roads with the Western fleet based mainly on Colbhasa or—to give its modern English name—Colonsay, a word which means Kolbeinn's Island in Old Norse. Islay was known as Ile or Il in the writings from the time.

There is some evidence that shield maidens were real. According to the sagas, once a shield maiden married she put away her male clothes and settled down to the business of bearing children. In a saga or two, a former shield maiden does divorce her husband and take up her weapons again. Unlike in the Christian world, divorce was possible in the pagan Viking world. Indeed, a number of sagas including *Njall's Saga* use divorce as a turning point in the story.

My primary sources for Scotland in this period are the *Anglo-Saxon Chronicle*, the *Chronicle of the Kings of Alba* as well as some Irish annals. However, actual evidence is very scanty and in some cases nothing was written down until hundreds of years after the events.

It is doubtful that anyone can ever know the full truth, but it is fun to speculate.

If you are interested in learning more about the Vikings in Scotland, Ireland or even shield maidens—these books might prove useful:

Ferguson, Robert *The Hammer and the Cross: A New History of the Vikings* (2010 Penguin Books)

Jesch, Judith *Women in the Viking Age* (2005 Boydell & Brewer)

Magnusson, Magnus KBE *The Vikings* (2003 The History Press)

Marsden, John *Somerled and the Emergence of Gaelic Scotland* (2008 Tuckwell Press)

Oliver, Neil *Vikings, a History* (2012 Orion Books)

Parker, Philip *The Northmen's Fury, A History of the Viking World* (2014 Jonathan Cape)

Roesdahl, Else *The Vikings: revised edition* translated by Susan M. Margeson and Kirsten Williams (1998 Penguin Books)

Williams, Gareth ed. *Vikings: Life and Legend* (2014 British Museum Press)

*Laura Lee is devastated when Jesse Creed claims her
new house doesn't belong to her, but to him! Until he
can prove it, Laura Lee isn't moving. But living with the
alluring rancher is surprisingly tempting…*

Read on for a sneak preview of
A Ranch to Call Home
by Carol Arens

"I will not allow you to steal my ranch," Laura Lee said.

"It isn't yours for me to steal."

"Oh, no? Look around. What here belongs to you?"

"The walls, the floors, the windows." Rain pummeled
overhead. The hiss of two people breathing heavily
wound Laura Lee's nerves tight. Any second now she
was going to snap like the string on an overtaut violin.
"The roof."

"No one lived here when I moved in. And all of a
sudden, you claim it's yours?"

Glancing down, Jesse looked surprised to see that he
was touching her. He let go, straightening his fingers
slowly, one by one.

"Whose chair did you put that ruffled pillow on?
Whose hay was in the hayloft?" He dipped his head, his
nose within inches of hers while those green, dark-lashed
eyes stared at her unblinking. "Whose bed were you
sleeping in?"

Not his, certainly! If that were the case, it would mean that Johnny had betrayed her. And Johnny would never! How foolish and disloyal would she be to believe the word of this stranger over the word of her one true love?

"Everything I found here was left behind by the previous owner."

"Whose name was?"

"Corum Peterson."

That made him back up a step. Judging by his startled gaze, his arrogance took a tumble.

"Show me your deed, Miss Quinn."

"Show me yours. Assuming it exists."

The storm had nothing on Mr. Jesse Creed as he pounded up the staircase to the attic. If she didn't know better, she'd think it was thunder pounding the treads.

There hadn't been time to go through everything up there yet, but she'd bet her happy future with Johnny on the fact that there was not a legitimate deed stashed in a dark corner.

Listening to boot steps thumping the floor overhead, she went to her bedroom, easily located her deed, then came back into the parlor, where she sat down on the only chair.

Let him prove his point standing up while she confidently reclined. No doubt he would stand before her shifting from foot to foot in shame, given that she had a deed and he did not.

Sitting back, she smiled. Partly because she wanted to cover how nervous she was with this situation, but also because Mr. Jesse Creed was going to leave her home like a dog with his tail tucked between his legs.

Imagine having the gall to besmirch Johnny's with such a whopping lie!